RED ROVER

Michelle LeFort

DEDICATION

This book is dedicated to my girls. May they have the strength and determination to achieve everything they desire in this life and genuinely reflect back to the universe their kindness, decency and grace. No one deserves to suffer abuse and true survivors are strong and determined. I dedicate this work to the children who suffer and live with scars that dictate their fate. To transcend violence/abuse and to come out the other side is a sign of integrity that no one understands-no one but another victim.

Contents

You WILL be disturbed!

ACKNOWLEDGMENTS

If you are a grammar natzi, this is probably not the book for you. I wrote it and did not hire an editor for this one, because I wanted to blur the lines of reality and confusion. This book is intended to disturb you on multiple levels, confuse you and make you think about the fact that you cheer on the serial killer. We sometimes find we are not the person we think we are. I wanted to give this book to you raw and confirmed, in an attempt to value the integrity of the work.

German heritage provides a wealth of information on body-type and mental ingenuity, per my mother. However, my zest for life had to come from my father's side of the family, French. The combination is uncanny, in ways that one finds uncomfortable. Luckily, I looked like my father's side of the family and inherited his mother's fine facial features. It was no surprise that I was pretty ... and for that, I was truly grateful. My childhood downfall, beauty, as an adult made my job easier. People have a thing for pretty. You can get whatever you want with 'pretty' and I did.

The conversation at the dinner table turned to politics for only a moment before Evan Gerard must have seen the dull sheen glass over our eyes. Julie Gerard, his wife of seventeen years even yawned. I held up quite well, but then again, I was trained.

The chandelier shook a tiny bit as the breeze blew in from the open glass patio door, a reminder that I might close the curtain. Privacy was everything this evening. Julie and I had planned it that way. "May I?" I asked before I rose and closed the blinds fully. Julie nodded.

"Six of one and ten of another … you know the saying." Evan was winding up his political rant.

She was a beautiful woman. Why the two of them had no intimacy was a foreign concept for me. I found her quite attractive. Julie had a great mind, great social skills, was from a wealthy family and had the most beautiful eyes a person could wish for. Brown with light brown lashes that were unencumbered by thick mascara; she wore a more natural look. It suited her. Getting lost looking at her startled me. This was business, not pleasure and keeping that thought in the forefront was all that mattered. I cushioned myself by turning back to Evan's uneventful banter.

That afternoon Julie and I had played a round of golf. Every moment we could parlay conversation, we spoke of the plan for the evening. A few months ago, she had let me in on the fact that her husband did not find her attractive and the fact that they had not had sex for over four years seemed to rattle me more than it did her. How could that happen in a marriage? It was a get out of jail free card, milk and cream and butter in one place and yet, he had no interest in her? That's the part I could never figure out. Why would he not find one of the most beautiful women I had seen attractive?

Julie thought it was her job. As the associate dean of students at Mirabelle Preparatory School, she spent a lot of time working. Perhaps he just found the alpha-female unappealing? Was she too smart? Did she belittle him? Did she make him feel unimportant? Perhaps he took for granted what he had? Perhaps his deviant mind felt he was above the gift he had … and elsewhere seemed greener? I knew his mind better than he did and knew that his little mind landed him in a predicament. He was classic, A-typical in his methodology and I was here to solve that situation. Whatever the case, we had put the plan in motion. Our occult seduction would be her last attempt and my final statement. It hurt I that she was so pretty and that I liked her, but this was business for me.

5

We had played the course beautifully, aced holes that men were finding difficult and yet paid little attention to the game. She was lithe and agile, quite attractive. Her willingness to please her husband almost left me with a fondness, almost.

Julie rose with her plate, "let me just get the dishes cleared. Charlie, can I get you some coffee, or would you like a brandy? More wine?"

I thought it over and felt the coffee would do me more justice. "I'll have coffee please. Cream and sugar?"

"Of course," She gracefully moved around the deep mahogany table, gathering the dishes. She had taken great care in dressing for the evening and it showed. As she neared me I could smell the faint perfume. It was quite attractive, citrus and spice.

"Here. Let me help." I started to rise.

"Don't be silly. You're our guest. Evan, can you show Charlie to the den please?"

"No, I insist. I can help." I rose and grabbed the rest of the dishes and followed Julie into the kitchen as we talked about our golf game in the short time it took to clean up and wipe down everything. I made sure it was all wiped down to my liking; even the table and chairs, quickly wiped clean.

Julie came in just as I finished up and Evan wandered back in the room from wherever he might have been.

Julie wiped her hands on a towel and laid it on the table. "Evan, can you show Charlie to the den? I'll bring in drinks."

"Certainly. This way, please." He left his chair and expected me to follow suit down the hall to the left. What an arrogant ass.

The room was again, deep and rich. Mahogany shelving and hardwood floors gleamed in the light as he hit the switch. A small library with rich leather chairs and an executive desk against the windows were immediately seen as the room's finer points.

"Do you read? I know you're into art and all, but reading isn't for everyone." Evan lit a cigar and poured himself a brandy.

"I do, actually."

"We collect rare volumes of the classics, but they are hard to find."

He moved to the sofa and I followed.

Julie entered with my coffee and a glass of wine; her third of the evening and it was early. Nerves must have gotten the best of her.

I wanted to ask if she were nervous, but there wasn't time. The key was to get in, get out and head in another direction. My hands started to tremble with excitement. The thrill of the game always got me revved.

Julie sat next to me, between Evan and me on the couch. Her white blouse could not cover the hard nipples, the taught breasts and her ivory skin beneath. In choosing an outfit, we were both careful to examine our finer points. She chose a black skirt that hit just above the knee and I chose black, tight slacks with a light flare that fit over my heels. My jade V-neck tee below a sheer cream lace sweater was enough to grind the motor of any man. Who could resist the two women in front of him? The question was, of course, could Evan resist us? What man could resist two women at one time?

Julie seemed to settle down and glancing my way to receive the 'go' nod, she began her plight.

Julie's voice softened, her mood changed into sexy, seductive, abstract. "Evan, I've been talking to Charlie about our lack of intimacy in this marriage."

He moved in his seat, becoming uncomfortable.

"It's not like that. Charlie and I thought that maybe it would help if we … you know, had help."

"What do you mean?" Evan's interest was careening out of control. His arousal peaked. He put out the cigar. "Go on …"

"Well, we were thinking that you might enjoy the two of us …"

"Are you kidding me?" Evan perched on the edge of the couch.

"No. I thought it might help you to see a softer side of me. I know that it bothers you that I work so much and that I take such risks in my work and not in our life. That's about to change."

Little did she even know how much that statement would ring true?

"Exactly how might this work?" He asked.

Julie and I had spoken of the tactic we would use, and to my amazement, she progressed quite nicely. She turned to me and locked eyes with mine. The game had begun.

Julie knew my rules of no kissing, so she had made use of her lips on my collarbone to arouse her husband. We had practiced all afternoon after our golf session. It was amazing. Too bad she had to be punished. She was an amazing lover. He was a fool. She kissed on my neck, up to my earlobe. Roving, her hands began to slide under my shirt, touching my belly, taught, almost rigid with muscle. I watched him.

His breathing became erratic and I knew we had him. I reached over and grabbed his hand, my breathing as ragged as his. Placing it on Julie's back, I popped her bra in one swift movement and guided his hand under her blouse and to her breast.

She moaned and I saw his excitement. It was easy to lead them to the bedroom. Once there, I dropped them off on the bed.

"I need one moment. Where's your restroom?" I cooed.

Julie pointed to the master bath, my destination.

Inside the restroom, I looked myself over in the mirror. Perfection. Making sure my hands and feet were in place, I reached inside the back of the toilet, where I had visited earlier in the afternoon and pulled out my tool. Choosing this tool had been easy. It was sitting in the pawnshop waiting for me. In Ohio, all you need to do if you want to carry a concealed handgun is to get a CCW license. I took the twelve-hour training course, took my certification of competency to the sheriff's office and submitted my fingerprints and a color picture ID and a week later, I was the proud owner of a Sig Sauer P239. A semiautomatic, mechanically locked, recoil operated, double and single-action triggered piece of art. The eight-round capability worked perfectly for me, and a reload was impossible. I had to make eight work.

In my hand, I felt safe. All that tonight came down to was now only a moment away. Hearing them from the master bath made it all easier. She was working masterfully, an artist. I could hear her begin to moan. Why in hell this bastard could be fucking her daughter was under my evolution of understanding and just thinking about it made the last look in the mirror. A glance at my own childhood was an easy determination for my strength. I undressed and put my clothing in a plastic bag that I had found under the cabinet that afternoon. No need to put body fluids of any kind on them. The Guafenisen that I took for three days prior nearly dehydrated me to the point of pain, but it was necessary to dry up any fluids I might leak in my fond moment. Stark naked except for my hands and feet, I was about to enter hell. SHOWTIME!

In the bedroom, again, they were both naked, waiting for me. He was looking for me when I walked in, a clue that he had no intention of making love to his wife, but was hell-bent on another person he should not have, me. At first, he didn't notice the gun in my hand, but it became evident when I raised it, about fourteen inches from his face, and pointed it at his head.

"What the fuck?" He was trying to move out from under Julie.

I wrinkled up my nose. "Surprise."

He backed as far to the headboard as he could, but I was near enough to gauge his movement. It's all in the plan.

"Julie ..." She didn't hear me at first. Poor thing. She was so intent upon having sex with her husband scumbag. "JULIE!" I cut through the room. Evan was silenced with the gun pointed at him.

She turned and the focus she gave me when she saw the gun was amazing. Such a rush … "Baby, we have some work to do here … might wanna pay attention for a minute."

She was lost. I felt for her, but knew the outcome would help her out. Each would get what they deserved. In the next hour, I made them have sex. At first I thought he had lost his erection, but come to find out not only did it stay, but he couldn't get rid of it. That made my job hard, because it was taking too long. He was awkward, a horrible man. How did he ever think he could please anyone? I was so bored. Finally, I derailed him.

"Look, asshole … you need me to go get your daughter again?" I was getting very angry.

"What are you talking about?" He whined, sweat pouring off his body even though I had turned the A/C so low it was cold. I never left DNA.

"Baby, it's why I'm here." I said.

"What?" Julie finally asked for what she didn't want to hear, so we took a break. She slid off him.

Evan started to realize that his comfort with the gun-game was untrue and that he had made himself believe his little sexual fantasy was coming true. Wrong!

I sidled up to the bed again, never having moved. I had shaved my entire body, head included as usual, but the goose bumps lit my flesh as I started to help them understand. "I am surprised at the time it takes to let me fill you in, but you two win the prize. An hour later? I would have asked a lot more questions when I didn't pull the trigger in the beginning. Sorry to say, no sex game."

Julie trusted me too much. "What are you talking about, Charlie? What's going on?"

"Here it is. Evan has been having sex with Amanda for almost four years." I waited for her to catch her breath.

"Yes." I continued. "He has been fucking your daughter. That's why you don't get what you need and you know it. I know you know it. Admit it to me. You knew, didn't you? Had a little inkling that you pushed to the back of your brain?"

She looked him dead center.

He started to gravel. I moved the gun closer, daring him to lie. "I didn't … she came to me, baby. You must believe me. I know I'm sick. I know. I'll get help. I'm so sorry." He started bawling, as if on cue. Sometimes I wondered what the genetic makeup of a prick like this took on.

"Tell her." I said.

"She's right." He sobbed and then stopped as quickly as he started, and then he got some balls. "How did you know? Did Amanda tell you?"

"Oh, please. Spare me the wiggle room. Nice acting, but no. I read all about it. You see, poor daddy-baby-fuckers never realize that we tell somehow, someway, or we don't survive. She blogged it, fuck face."

His sheer terror then registered.

The gun became my communication tool. And, to Julie, my night began.

"Julie, do as I say and your life will be spared. HE is going to die. I promise you, you won't remember. I slipped some Triazolam in your wine this afternoon, so that will help you. You won't remember any of this, baby." I drew in a long breath. "I am so sorry, but you deserve this just as much as he does. Amanda deserves retribution and she will be better off. However, you will still make her suffer so much pain … there is no clear answer. This is for Amanda."

Her eyes pleaded for me to stop, but I couldn't. She was to blame as well. The wives never thought they were to blame, but they were. Just as much as the husbands, but her, she seemed to understand all too well. "Do as I say and you will live. Understand?"

She nodded. She had grown to trust me as her friend. My job, my manner of speech, my dress, it was all per plan. She trusted that I did my job at The Museum of Natural History, as the curator, very well and that I could be trusted with million dollar pieces. She had said it before. She trusted me.

I began the demands. "Reach into the nightstand and grab the glass vial sitting in the corner. Stick out your tongue and pour it on." Reaching into her nightstand, she took out the vial of medication that would make her forget. She complied and I poured the powder on the tip of her tongue. "Swallow."

She did.

"That's a good girl ..." I pushed the cold gun to Evan's forehead. He didn't know if he should look at me--or the gun. It made his eyes cross occasionally. "Blow him ... I don't want to see his penis erect any longer."

She swallowed hard, flipped her hair over her shoulder, holding it with one hand, but she did it. She sucked him off expertly and it finally came to an end less than two minutes later.

I was in control. "There is a knife in the drawer of your nightstand. Take it out."

She fumbled but managed to take the filet knife out of the drawer.

"Cut off his penis." I watched his eyes. Huge. Bulging now.

She hesitated so I put the first bullet in him. Lowering the gun, I shot him in the chest, right in the middle, far enough from his heart that we had a few moments.

"It's easy, baby. Just hold it up and cut it off." She was horrified. The sound of the gun put her in motion however. He, on the other hand, was gone. Alive, but his eyes were trying to rid himself of the horror. She cut his penis off and laid it on the bed.

"That's my girl. I promise, the next time you find someone fucking a child, YOUR child, maybe you'll think twice about doing something about it." I shot him in the head, right between the eyes and she didn't even scream.

Right on time, she passed out from the drug. Less than twenty minutes … I placed the gun in her hand after wiping my prints off, squeezed a little so that her prints were on it and then fired two more rounds into his motionless body.

Success!

The plane was full. Boarding should be spelled "Bored-ing" but it went off without a hitch. I had already talked to three people at the airport about how I had waited over two hours, I loved being annoying, and asked if the plane was delayed to have them all inform me I just arrived too early. I had only arrived fifteen minutes early, but they would remember what I wanted them to. Suckers. They would be questioned possibly and all they would remember out of their busy night and the timing was that I had been early, even though I would never appear before I got to the airport on camera. My only demise, sometimes a detective might ask for the video even though everyone remembered me. I made sure of it.

Exchanging flights in Dallas, again, was uneventful and no one would catch that I changed clothes and wigs and caught a different plane even though I had tickets in the name Charlie McCant and had boarded that plane, only to make myself throw up in the aisle, for effect, and leave the plane with the help of a flight attendant--due to my illness. They would remember I was checking into a hotel until the flu passed. In actuality, my new identity was assumed and I flew out of Dallas on a different airline. They would all remember that I was in a hotel, sick and had missed my flight.

Once I landed in Seattle, I rented a car under the name Sherry Conrad, the same I flew with, and, of course, donned another wig and outfit and drove back the way I came. It was always challenging finding my next victim, but I had. He was in Topeka, KS.

I had no intention of arriving in Topeka so soon, but rather, Denver. My plan had intermittent necessity and Denver would be my home for a couple of months. Kansas, a godforsaken country filled with nothing. Not that Denver was much better, but it was there. I figured it gave me time to implement the next phase of my life.

Miranda Blanche was coming to Denver.   She had rented an apartment almost six months ago, and now it was time to *become* Miranda Blanche.

Chapter 2

"Miller. Mail." Sergeant Pelimar tossed a plain white envelope with my

name and the precinct address on it. As I opened it, my spine tingled,

that knowing 'know' that preys upon your senses right before

something big happens.

I wasn't far off. The letter spoke of impending doom to me. Why

me, a peon detective in no-wheres-ville? I read it again.

Rage Edifying Dignity.

Ratrix Obsession Victimizing Each Recondite.

RED ROVER:

You can call me 'Karma'. This is all you need to know for now
... Ricardo Dillon, died: March 28, 2006. Monica Dillon, incarceration
date: Jan. 14, 2007. Leavenworth, Ks.

I'll be in contact.

Karma

I am Jennifer Miller, head of special division 3, homicide, Austin, TX.

Why would someone send me this letter? What did it mean? I read it again before looking to my partner, Wyatt Grant.

"Grant, look at this. Do we have any open homicide cases with ties to Kansas?" I gently laid the note down and took out a pair of tweezers from my desk. Carefully moving it so that Wyatt could see it, he read.

Wyatt moved closer, glanced at it, and looked up. "Well, Dorothy … might wanna consider that." He grabbed a chair and moved it closer to examine the contents. "It's not like you have a full caseload now, what's another crazy?"

I grabbed the note and read it one more time, careful not to touch it or damage it.

"I wonder if this has anything to do with the Cranston case. You know, the triple homicide …"

"Check it out." He looked me straight in the eye. "Why you? That's the first question I would ask. We should probably send it for analysis quick though. I'll go get Martin. He'll wanna glance at it too."

I sat in rudimentary thought. He was right. Why me? What case or was it something foreboding? There were questions circulating the innermost working of my brain. No answers readily available. The investigation began, but soon went south. There was nothing to credit the letter to anyone in ICS, ASB or NCIC. I was at a loss. His wife, Monica Dillon, had killed Ricardo and she was doing time in Leavenworth. Why did I get this letter?

Chapter 3

I shuddered as I walked out the door to the U-Haul. Locked and parked, fully loaded the night before, all I had was a fourteen-hour drive and I would slide into my new life. As I drove, I reflected on each moment of planning that got me to this point. The thrill of the game was, once again, tempting me to make mistakes. Mistakes I could not afford to make. I ran through the checklist in my mind.

-Liquid Gel-tex coverings, hands and feet-disposed of by fire.

-Wigs-disposed of by fire.

-Clothing-given to Goodwill.

-Money-shipped three days prior. No tracing.

-Plane tickets flushed in airport toilets.

-Luggage left in airport parking lot with tags removed and disposed of by fire.

I laughed a little to myself when I thought of the fact that I burned so much of me. A little pyromaniac, at least it was a title I didn't mind. In comparison to murdering bitch and a life sentence, I could live with it. That was the last thought of the life I had lived as Charlene McCant. The drive was so completely boring that I had a hard time staying awake. Even though I had a good night's sleep and felt fine, the miles and miles of destitution could be wearisome. Counting telephone poles as they went by was the only thing that kept me going from Colby to Russell, Kansas. What an ugly state. I couldn't believe that lack of trees, people were distant, cars passed on the Interstate, but the value of life outside that was literally devoid of personality. Finally, I stopped in Salina. A truck stop lunch and a stiff cup of coffee, riddled by the few passers-by traveling the Interstate made enough of a break for me to keep trekking. My destination was merely two hours away.

Topeka was a dirty town per the Internet blogs I had read. The biggest part of getting acquainted with a new town on the Internet was the ability to get reality over tourism and advertising. My solution was to go on the Internet and find chat rooms that hosted people who lived in the city. I was told to stay away from downtown and to find housing more central to a section of neighborhoods. Confident I could find what

I was looking for, I forwarded my information to my realtor and was happy with the five selections I would view in the next few days and the ultimate choice I would make.

Internet blogs weren't only useful in finding housing and neighborhoods, but finding my next victim. A success in finding my victim left me the last two hours to plan my deviant, but necessary behavior. I knew what deviant behavior was and knew it was wrong to a certain degree, but, I also knew that this was one of the most crossed-over forms of abuse that existed and my breaking point had been reached.

Just as in the last case, this one was severe and continual. The young girl, Rachel Johnson, had posted to a familiar incest sight. Her story was meek in the beginning and I had passed it over, a mere plea for pity. I didn't see the gumption I normally required to fulfill my duty call. It took over a month on the blogsite before I saw another post and had been interested in several other cases, but Rachel caught my eye with her second post. In questioning the group, she indicated that she knew she was not to blame, but the son of a bitch made her feel the guilt, laid it on thick and threatened her mother's career if she told again. When Rachel had spoken to her mother at the age of eight, it had gotten her sent to her room, yelling and fighting between her parents and the next day was if nothing had ever happened. Rachel continued to receive her caller in the night, she continued to be told how much he loved her, and continued to be told it was all because of her mother's cold heart and lack of attention. Her relationship with her mother had been all but destroyed now.

Rachel was now fourteen. She was in love with her father and she knew how to manipulate the game. She had already been promised the new car, just had to remember, "This is our little secret."

I fidgeted in my seat, trying to release the numbness in my legs. The hair on the back of my neck stood straight up underneath my wig, even though it was shaved so closely that it was considered bald. I hadn't used the razor yet; there was no need. Another thought of Rachel attracted my attention. She had posted a question. This was a question very few could answer and my post back to her would have been brilliant, but I couldn't afford to post on the site … the only mistake that would ever get me caught would be the one I didn't know I made. This plan had been thoroughly thought out, culminated and perfected. I had gone so far as to rid myself of DNA to the best of my ability. This was uncomfortable, but it was necessary. I shaved my entire body, laid a layer of homemade latex mixture over my hands to my elbows and from my toes to my mid-calf. Toe prints and fingerprints were not going to tie me up. Mucinex was great at drying out saliva and had even, in the high doses created a vaginal dryness and lack of tears. I never cried anyway, who needed that?

The latex mixture was a mess to put on, but it helped in the advent that upon disclosure of my identity they did not have my identity, only what I wanted them to know. I pulled along the next exit and found a deserted dirt road where I burnt Sherry Conrad ... complete with Latex extremities and reapplied another set. Changing the fingerprints was a challenge, but I had found a way and it worked famously. Proud of my new situation, I hit the Interstate again and finished my journey in peace.

It was my plan now to inform Officer Jennifer Miller, an incest survivor, as to each of my creative identities so that she might at least have a chance to one day stop me. I would not stop without someone else putting an end to this ... and I had chosen her. She was the only one who would understand and allow me the presence I deserved when

all hell broke loose in my world.

Chapter 4

The reception area of the office was lit like Joe and the Volcano. I couldn't think that working here would be much of a challenge. My resume had been submitted weeks prior, and I had two phone interviews before landing this third and hopefully final interview with Lancaster, Stephens and Jones, LLC. The organization was a financial advising and brokerage company and I fit in well.

My skirt was tight and almost to my knee, the blouse demure and thin but revealed nothing I didn't want seen and my jacket and shoes had brass buttons to insinuate an uptight demeanor. Once called into Mr. Randall Stephen's office, the climate changed dramatically. The richness and elegance of his office was a surprise. The large executive desk and his finely tailored suit a pleasant distraction. He was handsome and excellent in grooming and smelled delightful. This might not be so bad.

The interview went without a hitch. I had studied massive journals, taken university practice exams I found on the Internet, and prepared myself to be Miranda Blanche, financial advisor.

The interview questions were straight on. He slammed me with the first of seven very thought out areas of interest. "If a client asked about basic offerings of your services, how would you reply?" He focused, looking me in the eye.

Very astutely, I began, "Sir, I can assist you with building a financial strategy and help you select appropriate investments that match your portfolio objectives. In addition, I can help you focus on working with your business by helping provide you retirement plans for your employees, provide you with financial advice for your key management and help with cash management solutions to meet your business needs. If there is an area I have neglected to service you in, I am but a phone call away. My clients are everything."

He stopped, looked down again at what must have been my resume with my last two financial advisor positions, of which I had prepaid cell phones established with the correct area codes and phone numbers and had already given myself quite a nice reference from my 'last' employer.

He looked up at me, grinning. "Who am I fooling … Welcome aboard, Ms. Blanche. We offer a $120,000 base plus commission program. You will be very successful with us. I think you'll enjoy it here." He rose from the desk and shook my hand, beaming.

"Thank you. I think this will work wonderfully in my five-year goal." I pumped his hand appropriately.

He had his receptionist, Maggie Lendor, show me around and help me get situated in my office four doors south of his. The same dynamic office was present, with different furniture. No less beautiful, no more efficient than his own. I was going to be treated well and would begin searching for new clients and assuming current clients in the morning. To prepare myself to meet the Johnson's I set out to celebrate.

I had purchased a Mustang GT convertible while in Denver; all I had to do was pay cash and cruise the streets of Topeka, getting a feel for the city itself. Moving from section to section, I could feel the change in income, culture and safety. The lower end of the spectrum offered me drug dealers, right out in the open, homeless people, street urchins. In the upper neighborhood, I found my apartment quite nice. Safety was available from morning until night, special security, and a gated community and a pool. I had to make sure that the security was on the light side, no cameras, only lock codes. I loved being on camera, but had given it up in my line of work. New technology for facial recognition caused me great grief. It had taken me two months to heal from breaking my cheekbones in Denver. What I had to go through didn't matter. The result was to victimize my victims. A little pain now was so much better than what I went through as a six-year-old child and I would never forget it. The summers here were wretched, so water would have to come from the pool and it was a nice one ... no more ocean for me.

Inside the apartment, the amenities were as nice as the realtor had said and for the price I had gotten, quite a great deal. The difference between Kansas and a coastal area was almost half as expensive a cost of living. My cash was still bountiful and this job paid well. I took the apartment without looking any longer. The next stop was shopping.

I had traveled with barely the clothing on my back and now I would wardrobe. The mall and Goodwill and I would be set. There weren't any major boutiques here and I didn't want to be noticed anyway. I needed to stay in the crowd. I donned a baseball cap, ponytail and jeans and I was back out the door. The glue I used on the wigs was permanent and would last about 30 days without having to replace it. To ensure, I replaced it every two weeks and shaved my entire body except for my eyebrows and eye lashes. My trip to Korea five years ago, after killing the follicles of my original hair was painful and expensive, but it worked and my lashes could never contain DNA. Worrying about DNA was solid and real and I took it seriously. Of course, the new lashes had the ability to be dyed to match my wigs, and implanting 50-60 hairs one at a time was dutiful and beautiful. The two things I strove to live by, dutiful and beautiful.

That evening I settled in and cooked a gourmet meal. Culinary school two victims ago was quite a nice addition to my resume. I had enjoyed myself and that is where I met my victim's wife. You see, my whole goal is to get close to the wife of the man I will take revenge upon. This instance would be more difficult. Janine Johnson was a professor at Washburn University. I would have to take classes in the law school to meet her that way and I wasn't up for that. Too noticeable and too bold a statement. The country club was out and that made me sad, because I loved to swim and play tennis. Jannie wasn't into athletics much. Her husband, a lawyer as well and running for the

Kansas House of Representatives, was going to go down hard. This bastard made mockery of the American way.

Once I was settled and the dishes were done, my wardrobe put away and my bed prepared for entry, I headed to a nightclub. The Owl's Nest was a low-town favorite by the looks of the Wednesday night crowd. The place was packed. Maggie had told me that two of my new clients owned the place. I was now sure they were laundering drug money by the looks of things. No problem for me, hopefully the coke flew freely.

At the bar a cute tender named Judy took my order and slid it down the line. Faking a miss, it spilled and she came running.

"I'm sorry. I shouldn't have slid it. Let me make you another." She was already on it. Ice in the glass, a shot of Captain Morgan's and a splash of coke and she was back in front of me. "There ya go. I'm really sorry. It's on me."

I took a sip. "Thanks. I needed that." I gave her my cutest smile. She held out her hand and introduced herself. Through the course of the evening, I fended off several male advances and kept eye contact with Judy. She was hot, had a sexy body, nice long, straight dark brown hair and pretty brown eyes. Her lips were full and red and she was definitely kissable. I actually preferred men, but my intense desire to have intimacy when I arrived in a new place was left to the ladies. They knew more, felt more and were more passionate. She was straight, but I planned to change that in a couple of days.

At the end of the night, 'Last Call' belted out through the sound system. Judy was quick to see if I needed another Captain and Coke and, of course, I did. "Yeah … thanks."

She tinkered with everyone else's drinks, bringing mine last. "So … you new around here?" She smiled brilliantly.

"I am … what gave it away? I have all my teeth …" We both looked around at the other women in the bar … I was quite a commodity.

"That was it … the grill is the most important part." She giggled.

"It is … kissability." I took a sip of my new drink as she tossed my old.

I felt engaged immediately and continued the conversation. "So, where does a new girl go to get the skinny on this place?"

"Well, there's not a lot to tell. I'm surprised you ended up here?" She questioned and waited for an answer.

"Your bosses are my newest clients. I start tomorrow as their financial advisor."

"Oh, yeah ...? That's crazy." She moved about effortlessly cleaning up her bar and closing it down as the lights came on. Never making a move to collect my drink, she had everyone else out of the bar by 2 A.M. and sat down beside me as the waiters and waitresses filled their own drinks.

"I should be going," I cooed. "I have had my limit."

She didn't make a move to follow or watch me, but as I walked by her to get out the door, she handed me her number, written on a napkin ... "Call me ... I'll show you around."

I nodded and slipped her number in my jeans. At home I surrendered to the new bed I had bought and had delivered, and would worry about the furniture sitting in the living room tomorrow. I had all the plans in motion and now the fun of the pre-kill would keep me occupied and sated while I waited for the final day ... July 4. Peter

Johnson would go out with a bang. I was so tired, I dreamed of taking a vacation after this job. It might be nice to just disappear to Tahiti or the south of France and to not have to worry about the plan. I might just do that … I drifted off to sleep.

PART TWO

Chapter 5

Wyatt Grant moved about the crime scene, gloved, looking for homicide evidence when Jennifer arrived.

Jennifer, "What do we have?"

"It's definitely a homicide. Victim is female, early 20's, Caucasian." He looked up from stooping over the victim, blood surrounding the body. "M.E. should be here soon."

Jennifer began her work. Searching the site took over two hours and just before midnight they headed back to the precinct. "Damn, I'm already tired and we just got started."

Wyatt acknowledged. Pulling up a chair to his desk and dropping in it, ready to make sense of his evidence, he tried to organize the mess on his desk, knocking an envelope on the floor.

Jennifer reached down to collect it, hesitating when she saw her name and it was posted from 'Red Rover.'

"Wyatt. It's another Red Rover letter." She pulled gloves out of her pocket and snapped them in place before retrieving the letter.

"Be careful. This time we might get something." He watched diligently. "You ever find anything else on that first letter?"

She shook her head no. "Just the information confirmation. Pretty cut and dry, the wife was incarcerated, Leavenworth. Nothing out of the ordinary." She slit the letter open. They eyed it intently, reading:

Rage Edifying Dignity.

Ratrix Obsession Victimizing Each Recondite.

RED ROVER:
My Worthy adversary ... please, do NOT let me down. I will not stop
Unless you put an end to this ... you do the 'map'. PS Be sure to kiss
daddy for me.
Karma

The bottom of the letter was a map with the following cities written in the middle:

- Duluth, MN

- Lancaster, PA

- *Monticello, AR*

- *Bakersfield, CA*

- *Cincinnati, OH*

- *Toe-Toe?*

Jennifer sucked in air. Looking at Grant, she started to panic. What was this all about? Worthy adversary? What was this wacko aiming at? A chill ran down her spine landing in the pit of her stomach. Grant lifted her chin with his finger, an intimate gesture he used for her when things got too tough. He knew the signs.

"Look at me." He commanded gently. "We will figure it out. Let's close the book on tonight's case and then we will begin a full investigation. The bastard wants caught and we WILL catch him."

She nodded. In a fog, her brain could not catch up. Why her? It ran through her mind over and over, why me? Why me? What did we have in common to the case? Kiss daddy? Did he know?

"Snap out of it, Miller. We have work to do." He motioned for the letter to be put in an evidence bag he pulled from his drawer and laid it on his desk. "We have work to do."

She did as she was instructed and resumed the task at hand, each moment wondering what it was that linked this case to anything in the universe. Luckily the night's homicide was a week's worth of day-and-night, but at the end of the week they landed at their desks again, full night's sleep under their belts and clear heads.

Grant took control of the situation with a file containing the analysis of the letter. "Well, shit!" He tossed it to her. "Nothing."

Jennifer read the report. No prints, no DNA, no irregularities with the font or printer, nothing that might lead them to believe that the letter had a specific writer. She tossed the report on the desk. "Okay, so nothing there. What about postmark, delivery service, what?"

Grant grabbed another folder containing the envelope and the letter itself. "No postmark. Someone had to deliver it. I sent preacher on the prowl." The referral to James Prachter as the preacher had stuck from the moment he crossed himself over their first victim. "He got nothing. The letter was placed on your desk by Officer Davis at around 7PM, delivered by Racine's Errand Service. Preacher found out that the letter came in via email from an unknown router, no IP address, the account registered to a bogus name. The bitch of it is that the origin IP address had been scrambled. So, anywhere in the world, we have no idea. It mirrored the IP address to over six million locations. There's no way we can take that apart."

"Wait. What if we use the list on the bottom of the letter to see if we get a hit from any of the locations?" She thought it a good idea until he blew it out of the water.

"Already done. Narrowed it down to every single IP address coming from a location in one of those cities. How's that for narrowing nothing? They mirrored the IP to come from each city, no discretion, equal numbers, we aren't dealing with stupid here."

She exhaled. What would the next move be? She eyed the evidence, marinated the information and tossed herself back in her chair out of frustration. "Okay, let's start from the beginning ..."

Chapter 6

The Owl's Nest was relatively slow when I popped in and ordered a drink. Judy was rushing through a six-drink order, but smiled when she saw me. Her company was a source of joy, if there was such a thing for me, and our time together was pleasant. A couple of late night chats at the bar. A lunch here and there when I could pull away from work, it all seemed so friendly and so right. This was the only part of the job I enjoyed and sometimes I felt like taking a vacation would do me great justice, but resuming my old identity was nothing to toy with. It wasn't an option, so instead of thinking of it, I chose to think of the night ahead of me. Wishing my no sex rule could disappear, but mistakes weren't allowed. I would modify as I always did and everything would be okay.

Judy finished the drinks and brought my vodka tonic. Never could I stay with one drink or pattern in a way that might associate me to any sort of habit other than the plan.

Judy smiled, "Hi there. You look great."

"Thank you. You're hot as hell, as usual. Nice jeans." I replied.

Judy did a 360 so I could look and I liked what I saw. "What a day ..." I sighed and she leaned over the bar, propping her head in her hands, elbows planted.

We laughed. I liked her laughter.

She turned to the waitress who had arrived to replenish drinks. With a wink, she was off to the other side of the bar and I was left to my own accord. John Samuals, my client and owner of the bar, Judy's boss, rolled up beside me standing way too close for my comfort. He stunk of cheap cologne and bad breath, garlic. I wanted to slap him immediately, but niceties were necessary.

John said into my ear, "Like what you see, Miranda?"

"What's that?" I played it off.

"I'm pretty happy with the return on our investment last week. I've never seen a turnaround quite so quickly. You are a very talented woman." He leaned even closer.

To pay attention, to give my full and undivided payment to my client, I turned around and faced him. "Why thank you, Sir. I hope to continue to serve your needs."

"The commission was quite nice. I'm sure." He gave me a ruthless grin.

What a crock. Maybe emptying his bank accounts would be a real kick? Too bad it wasn't on the agenda. Someone else would have to rid the streets of trash like him. I was booked solid. While he made chit-chat, I thought of Rachel Johnson and wondered for a moment if 'daddy' had entered her bedroom yet tonight. He had plans of taking Jannie on a dinner date, to a movie and then home for wine and romance. However, the romance would never happen. He would drop her at the bedroom door with a kiss on the cheek and feign working late in his study. Ultimately, he would end up in the bedroom of 14-year-old Rachel. The blogs had been regular since the beginning of the year and as Rachel's maturation process had become imminent, the visits became even more regular. This man was insatiable. Rachel's latest blog had bothered Randi because Rachel had gone past the guilt, had really grown up in the incestuous situation and was now making the demands. She was preparing herself to deliver her orders of entry into adulthood. It wasn't about the fact that she was going to start getting anything she wanted, including a thousand dollar allowance each month, it was about the fact that moving to this point meant that the abuse didn't matter anymore. Rachel could fuck anyone from this point on and never feel one bit of emotion in it. She would transfer herself to another place to rid herself of the memories of a baby who was having sex with a full-grown man. She would isolate her feelings of inadequacy, guilt, shame and accept the disassociation that melds the id, a victim of incest.

"Hey … are you okay?" Judy had apparently spoken more than once and was concerned.

"Hey. I'm good. Sorry, just going over work in my head. I should stop doing that." I laughed lightly.

"You should, especially tonight. Do you have plans?" She had such a dazzling smile and the heart of a lion, strong and pure.

"No plans … drinking with you until some man sweeps you off your feet." I finally laid it out there. I asked the question, the answer was hers.

Judy failed to answer the question, but touched my hand briefly with hers and made me another drink and brought it back. It was only then that she answered, "I've already been swept off my feet." She walked away.

When I looked down, my drink had a swizzle stick in it that said 'be mine?' and I smiled.

Chapter 7

I awoke to my alarm and it took me no time at all to realize that Judy was in my bed and my running shoes were in the closet. I closed my eyes tightly before opening them again, remembering all the night before. Judy and I had drinks at the bar after she got off at midnight, early for her. She had made me aware of a special night she had planned and, on accident that I might show up, she had taken the rest of the night off.

We went to Lake Shawnee and sat outside in the cold, in blankets and she told me how much she enjoyed my company. I wrecked her world when she started to kiss me and informed her I was HIV positive. The look in her eyes touched me in some small way, but I tucked it neatly in place and made it clear that I enjoyed the relationship but that I would die a horrible, suffering death should I know that I had infected another person. She seemed to understand and we spent the night with her kissing my body gently, using my hands to touch her.

I heard her voice in my head, soft and sweet, as she looked at me intensely, "It won't hurt to do this …" and she slid her hands down my pants. Should I not have the ability to control my mind over my body, I would have been in trouble. However, I came on time, in control and had no emotional bond to her whatsoever. She, on the other hand, was not so lucky. I peeled the skirt she was wearing up to her waist, ripped off her panties and used my hands to make her scream. I was careful not to use my mouth, but my feet and hands were protected by the gel-tex and I had an amazing time. As if on cue to the thought, Judy rolled over and tucked up neatly against me, mumbling how wonderful last night was.

I touched my lips to her forehead and slid out from underneath her. "I am an avid athlete and I must go run or I am not right. Can I help you find your clothes?" I woke her with my hand to her breasts. No one could be alone in my apartment even though I didn't leave anything in my residence or car, but I could not take the chance. "Wakie, wakie, baby …" I kissed her cheek. "Let's get out of here. Want to run with me?"

She balked at the thought of a run in the dark and laughed.

"We just got to bed … Go without me and come back when you're done and all sweaty and I'll show you how much I like you again."

I led her by the hand to the restroom where her clothes lie on the floor and picked them up. "I can't, sweetie. I have to be at work at seven o'clock." I smiled graciously. "I had a great time last night, but work comes first."

She was finally awake, stumbling, but awake. "I understand." She began to dress. "Will I see you soon?"

"You will. Remember, I'm flying out this week for a conference in Tallahassee though … won't be back until Sunday night. How about then?" I wasn't going to Florida, but I did need to do some research in Austin and it was on the sly. I would show up in Tallahassee, feign illness and confine myself to the room and leave for Austin at that time. The conference was easily recorded with surveillance equipment that would shoot right back to my phone and laptop and I would monitor activity that I had signed up for. No one would guess that I hadn't been there.

"That will have to do." She reached up and kissed my nose. What a sweet thought, too bad it didn't hit a mark for me. I always wondered if he had ruined my ability to feel compassion, love and adoration.

Dressing for my run, Judy swept through the room fully prepared for departure. I smiled and walked her out. Compliance was the way to my black heart and so far, she was articulating beautifully.

After my run, I hit the coffee shop and then headed back to shower and leave for work. My morning routine was laden with checking the movement of Miranda Blanche, because she did exist, she was just out of country on a jaded assignment for the company she worked for out of Philadelphia. I had to know where she was in case it was necessary to abort the plan. She was, as usual, working and playing with habit. But, one day, just one day missing her movement could land her back in the states, reflect my actions of opening bank accounts and credit cards in her name and showing movement on her Social Security number. Being a step ahead of the game was necessary. Again, I felt the pang of desire for a vacation. I wondered what it would feel like to go and do without hesitation and without the plan in the forefront of every decision. Maybe I would take some time after this job was finished? It was a pleasant thought that led me to the shower and my daily masturbation ritual. I had to love myself, if I didn't someone would do it for me. Luckily, I had gotten past the rage of having to do this for him as a child. It was now for me and for the job. If I released all pent-up energy a couple of times a day, no one could strike up intense desire inside me and I liked it that way.

As I monitored Miranda's progress for the morning, I noticed that my mirrored IP address had been searched. Miller was working. Too bad she had so much going against her. When I had profiled her as my most worthy opponent, I realized her special skills and upped my game thousand-fold. Was she making progress? Or, had I stumped her enough to frustrate her with the idiocy factor? I would find out soon enough. The trip to Austin would be my fourth. And, in no way, shape or form would I ever meet her face-to-face willingly. She was worth the struggle to stop me and I had made up my mind ... I would take that vacation.

Chapter 8

The Omni dome was situated deep in the middle of the city and was blistering with industry leaders and those attending the conference. Men in suits, women making an impression, all gathered for one reason—to learn new technology in investing, the latest answers, and the most probable situations. The Tallahassee Hard Assets Investment Conference started at seven o'clock and I had fifteen minutes to get to the airport two miles away and head out for Austin and the real convention I wanted to attend. My profiling research, years of hard evidence on how to not get caught, let me to define when and where I needed to be and how I made sure that someone would remember me, how I could make sure someone believed I was present in a location, when, indeed, I was not. I needed to be in Austin at another conference and had one chance to make sure my cell phone not only rang, but that it was answered and a conversation occurred. Never did investigators question a phone owner that had answered his phone as being ten states away. The worst part of it was the loser I had to sleep with last night to do it. Jack Warren was the worst lay in the world and I suffered through it thinking of Judy, but it had given me alibi at the conference and a way to take his cell phone and leave mine. Good heavens, wasn't it just my luck that someone who owned the phone just like mine was a middle-aged creep with very little hair and a big ass? At least he was married and to my best knowledge would do anything to keep his wife from knowing of his indiscretion, in my favor.

I quivered, and not in a good way, as I thought of his ugliness and how it had touched me. Most of my ploy was forgivable, but something seemed amiss, not quite right that I could sleep with him and not with Judy. I actually liked this woman. Oh well, I would think of that later … for now, I headed out the maintenance door in my jogging shoes and backpack.

My ponytail flipped from side-to-side as I ran quickly through the parking lot and hit the shortest course to the airport. It gave me time to think and my favorite time to run was when I was in the middle of the plan. Enjoying the run was short-lived due to how close the conference was to the airport and in twelve minutes I was boarding the plane donning a new wig, new ID and new persona. Shooting the temporary Botox-like injection into my cheekbones and putting on the 'fat' suit was difficult given the boarding pass time and the sweltering heat of hurriedness. But, once again, I was on board and sailing through the air headed to Austin, Texas and the Criminal Behavior Profiling Conference. My new identity: Ruth Ganza from Gainesville, FL. She had been a police officer cadet and not made the grade due to weight problems and ended her career aspirations to become a floral designer. I had no problem registering via the Internet and creating the right identification necessary to enter the conference. I now looked like a twenty-eight-year-old woman with mousy brown hair, horn-rimmed glasses and weighed in at 270. I was less than beautiful and not one person seemed to notice me at all. Perhaps my next hit should be one where my beauty was not apparent? I felt as though I slid into a role that made me invisible.

Chapter 9

The conference had kicked off at noon and my late arrival made it obvious if I walked in on the lecture late, due to missing my flight this morning. I had but one option, waiting for the next presentation and sliding into the background. The weekend went off without a hitch. I listened to presentations by top industry professionals concerning: criminal profiling, behavioral analysis, investigative strategy, crime reconstruction, false confessions, serial rape, sexual homicide, and victim logy. Day two of the conference, Saturday, I chose to skip out on the morning and say hi, in my own very special way, to Detective Jennifer Miller.

My run in the morning turned from a four-mile jaunt to six, three miles to her house and an hour break while I watched her through her window before she headed out the door to work. It was intriguing watching the very person who would take all the credit for stopping my tirade. She was pretty, dark brown hair and lean. She was classy, a good gait and nice tan, wore her clothes well. Yes, Indeed, I thought: I

58

do approve.

    I ran back to the hotel and dressed in the fat suit again and headed, as Ruth, down to the workshop. This was the actual part of the conference that I wanted to educate myself with the most. I needed to know what new techniques were being used, how to catch a criminal, because, as a criminal, I had to know what not to do. The workshop was greatly useful and I learned something new. **Signature and Modus Operandi were still the two main standing lines that hooked a killer, so that police could reel them in.** I was very careful to never leave a signature no matter how much I wanted people to know that I was the one protecting these little girls, no matter how much I wanted people to know that I was the one who cared, not the mother or the pedophile molester, no matter how much I wanted people to know that these victims were suffering and with my help they were free ... I could not leave a signature. No job could ever happen the same, no motive could jump out at anyone, and leaving a mark was a mistake. Only Jennifer could know. It was hard enough to allude officers of the law without handing them clues I did not want them to have. Yes, it was getting old and the stress was often blinding and disabling, but I had to do what I had to do.

The conference workshop on Violent Crime Link Analysis (VCLA) was keen on breaking down patterns. It was difficult not to squirm in the workshop as they spoke of the distinction between crimes as the main link to solving. The difference between an organized and a disorganized crime scene made tremendous sense and was a vehement concern of mine. I had to make the scene look disorganized: the body could never be hidden, the weapon needed to be present, it needed to look like a crime of passion and it was truly difficult not to prove that I could organize the crime scene but I needed the conviction of the wife to deter the magnifying glass away from another source, namely me. I knew what I could do and the dichotomy that my crime scenes looked extremely disorganized, the crime of passion so easily believed and persecuted, worked well unless my ego came in. I had to have a clear head. It was an abatement that I had to sit in that room and listen to them make excuses for other's behavior in making mistakes. I wanted to yell from the top of my voice that there was no real creativity in the examples they used and if people just thought out the real situation ... anyone could get away with murder. I was proving it. I did not fit half of their profiling situation and that I was female threw them under a bus. Nowhere did they profile the single female from a well-to-do coastal family, who knew how to walk amid society and fall into any clique she wished. They were going to need all the help they could get to catch me.

I finished the conference with a wealth of new knowledge that I would put to work. The restoration of plastic absorbs blood was the highlight and the one thing I could never forget. I could never bleed anywhere near anything plastic, nor did I carry plastic on my person, nor did I buy plastic products unless absolutely necessary. Plastic was the enemy in many situations.

Criminal profiling is a four-phased investigative and forensic tool. To profile possible offenders, they follow a four-phase process: antecedent, method and manner, body disposal and post – offense behavior. I clearly educated myself to each of the four phase years ago, but hearing new information, vying for a position of offense rather than defense in my work, made it possible to defeat the process and beat it at its own game. Science, although as exact as it is, has its faults. Profiling alone is what I counted on as an advantage for me. Because no one knew I was serial at this point, they had no way of creating a profile.

My mixed crime scenes, some disorganized, some organized would confuse them profusely when they found out that the 'suffering wife' was indeed set up and deserved to return to society. To start a criminal profile on me would take intelligence only few exhibited, but in the end, when I was ready, they would catch me and I was getting tired. And that reminder was continually challenging me due to the fat suit and the heat that the group of conference-goers created. Sweating like this was crude and horrible and I hated it. My body couldn't breathe like I wanted and I felt trapped, a feeling my daddy taught me to fight mentally. The challenge was never whether I would make it, the challenge was what I could take from any situation to use to my advantage. Thank you, "Daddy".

I dropped down into my bed without letting go of my bag, falling onto the coverlet with sheer exhaustion. I was tired. There was only enough time to get some sleep and fortify my body with a B-12 injection so that I was ready to go to work tomorrow. Judy would have to wait to see me, and I her.

The alarm sounded at five o'clock and I slammed my fist on the top so it would shut up. My rage came out momentarily and I remembered where it centered, because I did not want to get up. Little did the thought of heading into the office appeal to me. On the way home I, had watched all the video I could possibly muster of the Tallahassee conference and I was running on sheer exhaustion. Days like this were the most difficult, but I made it through. On the way to work I was spooked by the thought of not having removed all the cameras at the conference. Backward thinking, moving through each of the cameras I had placed, all four of them, reminding myself that I had gotten all of them back and disposed of them on my run before I left for the airport. With that came the thought of talking to Jack, exchanging a few phone calls during the day with his phone to mine, apologizing, reminding him of the huge mistake we made and my horrid guilt for violating his marriage. It was enough to shut him up until I could meet him again Saturday night after flying back in to Tallahassee and returning his phone. He had done as I had asked and taken my calls, suggesting I was 'out of reach' momentarily. A real nice guy Jack turned out to be and when we exchanged phones in the lobby, I had no need to remind him that Shirley might take offense to ANY mention of the weekend. I was safe. He completely understood.

Work was buzzing when I arrived and immediately I went to my office and prepared a report on the financial access system and how the hard assets conference could easily identify three areas in need of repair in our office alone. I presented the paperwork to Randall Stephens and suggested I could lead training programs on each of the subjects should he warrant the change. His pleasure was intense and he told me that he would let me know. I loved it when their egos made them say things like that. He had no intention of handing me any training responsibilities and for the most part he and I both knew that my job was to bring in more money and that made me happy. My commission goals were incredibly high and if I even came close to challenging them, I would be their biggest asset. He needed me and I needed him and without words we had an understanding.

Judy was waiting for me that night at the Owl's Nest and was only mildly offended at my explanation of such a rough weekend of work and no time to call. At the bar, I flirted with her and appeased two men who decided to buy me drinks. About an hour after they sat down, Judy seemed to become moody.

"Here's your drink, Hon." Judy sat the drink on the counter and turned to leave until I grabbed her arm gently.

"Hey … you okay?" I rolled my eyes at the guys beside me. "I have to pee … up for keeping me company?" I knew she couldn't refuse.

"Sure …" she hadn't quite gotten back to normal.

"C'mon …" I raised and excused myself. "Excuse me, guys. I'll be right back."

The guy on the left, sloshed, whispered about as loud as a police siren, "Why they always gotta go in pairs?"

His friend, almost as bad off, said, "They are always better in pairs."

Judy came out of the stall as I was washing my hands and slid her arms around my waist from behind. "I missed you …"

I turned around. "Did you?" My smile said too much.

"I did … but, here you are and it's all good." She kissed my neck, causing me to feel something. I wasn't sure what this girl was doing to me, but I liked it.

"I'm glad you missed me. I certainly need a break from reality."

"Is that what I am for you, a break from reality?" She whined and then her demeanor changed. "It's okay if that's what I am. I'm cool with that."

"Hey," I said, "I have to run for now … I'll catch you later, okay?" I moved to leave, but she stopped me and kissed me. Because I was caught off guard, I responded and it made me angry. As soon as I realized what was happening, I pulled away.

She was breathless, "Wow …"

I had to leave so that I could think and I left her standing in the bathroom of the bar as I headed straight for the door to freedom.

Really? She would let me walk all over her like that? I might have to rethink my projection. I never stayed with anyone who was slightly torn in any way, twisted in sexual dimension; I was twisted enough for both of us and I needed grounded. That was the whole intent of having a semi-emotional affair. Something safe and easy, something dynamic and useful, but in the end, something I could live with and that filled me with nothing more than a desire to be close to someone. Even I knew that my distance from reality was unhealthy. Even though I laughed at that thought, me, unhealthy … a serial killer gone emotional and healthy, who would have thought?

I had just crawled in my car when she opened the passenger's door and climbed right in.

Breathless from running, she spoke quickly, "Look, I'm off, how about we hang out. I don't want our evening to end this way. Okay?"

I wasn't sure exactly what to do.

"Look … just take me to my house and if you don't want to stay, then you can leave. Okay?"

"Okay." I put the keys in the ignition, started the car and drove in silence. Neither of us said anything and I liked that about her. I was stumped that she fit in my world like she did. I found nothing intrusive about her reaction and I did like being with her. Sometimes I had to admit I was lonely and she was so beautiful. I gave up, there was no harm in having a friend … I missed my best friend from college and Judy kind of reminded me of Patricia.

We drove in silence and I decided to go in with her. I had

gotten sleep and was a little bored, so company would be great. Once inside, she tried to kiss me again, but I stopped her. "Baby, I have to say this. I would never let you be that to anyone, especially me. Don't let me walk all over you. Don't let anyone ... I might not like to admit it, but I like being with you ..."

Picking up the conversation from the restroom, she didn't miss a beat. I knew she understood. She smiled the sincerest I had seen in my long line of liars, molesters, cheaters and drug users. Maybe she was a keeper?

My mind snapped like a steel trap. What was I thinking? NO mistakes! NO crime could handle an accomplice. The ONLY way to perfect a crime was to be the only one who knew about it. I could NOT let this happen. I shoved her away and moved to the other side of the room.

"Randi ...?" She didn't move closer, but spoke softly where she stood. "Randi, I didn't mean it like that. Light and easy, no strings attached. That's what I want too ... but, to be honest, I do want to enjoy it."

I turned to her, the rage subsiding. Tilting my head, she caught the question.

"I know how it is to not trust anyone. I don't want that either. It will be a long time before I trust you, or anyone for that matter, if it ever happens again." She went to the couch and sat down, tears softly slipping down her cheek. It was apparent she couldn't look at me after opening up and that I understood. So, I went to her …

Stroking her hair, I pushed a strand behind her ear. "I'm sorry. And it takes one to know one … would you like to talk about it?

PART THREE

Chapter 10

Jennifer Miller sat under a pile of paperwork, the desk not big enough to hold it. As a picture slipped off the desk and slid onto the floor, she leaned to pick it up. It was a long night, but the facts were laid out before her. Two trips to Leavenworth and interviews with Monica Dillon, information was present to suggest that things were not as easily writ as it seemed in the trial. Jennifer had read every trial transcript, every interview, every piece of information she could get on the Dillon murder. What she had pieced together was that Detective Paul Rand had investigated the homicide fully. He presented in court and the findings were never questioned. The prosecution had presented 21 slides of the crime scene that included ballistics analysis, gunpowder residue on Monica's hand, fingerprints on the gun, they had the weapon, and the sexual assault on Ricardo Dillon was explicit. Monica had cut off his penis and left it lying on the bed. The emergency call had come from their daughter, Sylvia, then fifteen years old. She had found her father dead and her mother lying on the floor with the gun in her hand, in shock, passed out.

Sylvia had testified that two days prior to the death of her father she had overheard a phone conversation between her parents, quite terse. The daughter's recount the morning of the incidence, included another phone conversation in which her parents had argued. When the defense asked Sylvia about her relationship with her father, the minor child broke down and was removed from the courtroom. Psychological reports found an incestuous relationship between the father and daughter and the prosecution used this as evidence of motive. The defense used it as an excuse for protection of the daughter. Either way, Monica Dillon, with no recollection of the night in question, was found guilty of Murder One, aggravated circumstances with exceptional brutality and was sentenced to forty years to life in Leavenworth Federal Penitentiary.

Miller's interviews with Monica Dillon were heart-wrenching. She seemed so sure she was guilty, but when Miller questioned her memory, she had none. She remembered nothing about that night, but had vivid memories of the entire day's events. That day she had spent time at the Country Club with her friend Susan Roets. They had planned to meet with her husband for dinner, but she did not recollect if that was, indeed, what happened. She lost memory about two hours prior to the murder.

All the sudden, a hand was on Miller's shoulder and she screamed.

"What the hell …" Wyatt jumped back, scaring himself. "What's up with you?"

"Oh, my God … you scared the shit out of me." She fell back in her chair, relaxing after the fear. Her heart was racing.

"You were deep in. I thought you heard me ask you if you wanted coffee." He sat down across from her at his desk.

"I didn't hear a thing. Call it instinct, call it whatever, but something doesn't add up to the facts in this case." She grabbed a file and opened it. Tossing it on Wyatt's desk, she added, "Did you see this toxicology report?"

He scanned the document. "Shit …"

"Yeah. I think I'm on to something. I'm going to run it through the database again, this time with different criteria. That might drop down the number of hits."

"I think that might work. You think someone drugged her?" He sipped his coffee.

"I do … it's the only thing I can find." She pulled two more documents from the massive pile, knocking others out of the way. "Check this out."

She handed him the paperwork that showed her theory. She continued, "There are seventy-two female to male homicides with genital brutality. However, only sixty-nine of them are wife to husband. I can rule out the others. But get this … there was incest in this case. That was motive.

"I see. I do think you are on to something. Good thing life is slow here this week." He grabbed another file off his desk. "I fiddled with this … think you can use it?"

The paper he handed her had RED ROVER: Rage Edifying Dignity. Ratrix Obsession Victimizing Each Recondite. He had defined each word, giving full definitions to each letter of the acronym. "I think you hit it on the incest. Let's focus on that ..."

"Rage Edifying Dignity ... what does that mean?" She looked him squarely.

He smiled, "To edify is to instruct in a manner as to encourage intellectual, moral or spiritual improvement ... Rage edifying dignity. If you are dealing with incest, think of the rage, think of the incredible helpless feeling the victim has and the mother ... what do they do? They are accusing someone of something heinous and we've heard it a million times in sexual predator seminar and study, they never find out and fully fathom what their husbands are doing to their daughters. It's so inconceivable to them they ignore it. Rage edifying dignity ... let my rage teach you a lesson?"

It made perfect sense. This is what made him the best partner and the two of them the most successful team. They were smart and they thought outside the box.

"That's why he picked me ..." Miller got up and walked out of the room leaving Grant to watch in wonder. She never spoke of her childhood.

The tennis was good. The weather was excellent. The situation planned to the tee. It was time to meet the family. I was in a white tennis skirt, white nylon tank top, impeccably tanned and hair complete with ponytail in a ribbon. I looked twenty years old. Finishing with my instructor, Pablo Diaz, I saw Janine Johnson begin her warm-up on the next court. Her instructor, Mimi Hillier, began with stretching as she did each time they began Jannie's lesson. To get the proper perspective, I motioned for Pablo to hit a few more balls to me, just out of my reach. Sitting on the sideline stretching, Jannie was an easy target.

Pablo pounded balls at me. After the fifth, he gave me the perfect opportunity. So, near the sideline it was almost out, Pablo drilled a ball at me. I lunged, swung, missed and landed just inches away from Jannie, letting out a scream in pain.

"My ankle!!!" I grabbed at it.

Pablo came running and Jannie and Mimi were right beside me instantly. Mimi went into trainer mode, "Let me look ..." she began to check the status.

Jannie, who was much faster than I thought, was up and next to me, hand on my shoulder. "It's okay. She's great. I'll run and get some ice." And she was gone.

Within twenty minutes I was on the sideline, had two trainers working with me and watched Jannie finish her lesson. She only took thirty minutes, so it was short and she was nice enough to check on me after she finished. I saw her turn my way.

I dismissed the trainers. "Thanks, Pablo. I'm fine. I appreciate it guys. I think I can walk on it." They turned to leave as Jannie approached and I got up to walk, putting as much weight on my ankle as I could, but tripping, almost falling. I could use this to my favor. Not planning the turned ankle wasn't a problem, but rather, an asset now.

"Oh, hey ... be careful." She was right by my side, again, to catch me. "You need some help?"

"I was just trying to get to my car. My dinner plans are important." I probably looked like I could cry. I was a class-A actress and I knew it. Years of studying, years of acting like things didn't matter. This was a breeze. She fell for it, hook, line and sinker.

Jannie helped me to my car, where I keyed myself in and tossed my bag in the back seat. "Thank you so much. I'm sorry I cut your lesson short."

"Oh, no … it wasn't short. I only have a half hour. It's all I can spare, you know … busy, busy." She smiled.

"I take a full hour or I would work 100% of my life. I must have a release. Financial planning, forecasting, the whole thing can be so grueling."

"You work in finance? I never would have guessed." She literally sized me up, to her liking. "I'm Janine Johnson." She held out her hand. "My friends call me Jannie."

"Miranda Blanche. My friends call me Randi." I shook her soft hand.

"Well, Randi … it looks like tennis is out for you for a while."

"Nah … actually I hurt it before and just stubbed it a little. Give me two days and I'll be back on the court." I was confident, because I didn't hurt my ankle nearly as badly as I was playing it off.

"Two days? What miracle cure do you have? We should bottle it, patent it and sell it … quit the rat-race." She laughed heartily.

Joining her, "I know, huh? We should. What do you do?"

"I am department chair at Washburn Law School. I specialize in corporate law, but finance was my second undergraduate. I figured if I were going to bring in the money, I better know how to protect it. My husband and I were just talking about switching to a new firm the day before yesterday. Interested in meeting with us?"

Rarely did things go this smoothly, but I was a little miffed at bringing her into my job. I hadn't planned that part. Thinking on my feet was a specialty, so I let my mind snap into place. "How about one better … I don't mix business and pleasure and I need a doubles partner for the tournament next month. Up for it? I can recommend some wonderful advisors. I'll even give you the number of mine, Jason Porter. He does me well." I looked at my car and on cue she got it.

"I see. Let me get back to you day after tomorrow. I'll see if I can't get some playtime in. I have to change my office hours if this is when you play on a regular basis?"

"I'm actually good. I set my own schedule. Let's talk day after and set up some practice time. I really am looking forward to it. I just moved here a few months ago, and have met a thousand men, but very few women …"

"By the looks of you, I'm sure you are right. Most women would be terrified to be near you. You're beautiful."

I loved it when women looked at me and I loved it more when they weren't intimidated. She had tremendous strength and it showed. "You got it, and thank you. I find it difficult to make friends sometimes. I'm kind of shy."

She bit. "I'm not. Consider yourself having made a friend, Randi. I can't wait to play. By the looks of you, we might do well in the tourney. I could put a trophy on my shelf, how about you?"

"I can do that …" I slid into my car and we said goodbye. My loins ached with desire for her. She was beautiful--long, flowing brown hair with gold highlights, soft brown eyes, gorgeous white, straight teeth and she smelled so good. Her body was taught and lean, she was tall and muscular. She was one of those women everyone wanted to be and men wanted to own. I drove away wondering why it was that she couldn't take matters in her own hands.   Maybe I would give her a chance like I did Roberta Jones in 2007. Poor Bobby Jones ... Instead she buckled, backed away from him and let him continue ... for that I made her slit the bastard's throat. Jannie might just give me renewed hope.

Chapter 11

Judy placed the roasted lamb on the table and sat to join me for our late dinner plans. Cooking for me was becoming a habit for her and I tolerated it. I never let people own my fondness and it was difficult with Judy. She should be married, happy and desired. I took care of the desired part and couldn't wait to rip off her clothing and take away the insistent thought of Jannie by making Judy scream for hours.

"Did you hear me, baby?" Judy cooed.

I had missed it, in deep thought. "Huh?"

"I asked if it was okay. You aren't touching your food ..." She pouted.

Who needed to eat? I pushed the plates off the table, crashing to the floor and grabbed her, pulling her on top of the table. Kissing her as passionately as I had ever kissed anyone before, I made love to her expertly, precisely, thinking of Jannie Johnson the whole time.

Judy lit a cigarette in bed as we lay, having traveled through three rooms and ended up in the shower before we resigned to bed. Inhaling deeply, she toked on the fag. "That was amazing." She exhaled; smoke billowing into the air.

I grabbed the cigarette and took a drag, agreeing. Pretty proud of myself, I had to question the motive. Instead, I lay my head on her bosom and relaxed, handing her the cigarette and listening to her heartbeat. If I weren't so crazy I could enjoy this. I liked the day-job, I liked the company, I liked Judy and I had a new friend. Life was exciting and the thrill I got from the whole situation was orgasmic.

Judy finished her cigarette and stubbed it out in the ashtray on the nightstand before she quickly fell asleep and her breathing became slow and steady. I ran the plan through my head again. Each pattern of behavior and event I took great care to flowchart to the highest degree. If I had options, I could think quicker in a pinch and I had articulated each move the opponent could make and had at least three countermoves to retaliate. That's how I lived my life, a chess game of sorts. One move deserved another and if I detailed each day what might happen, I had more control over my universe.

Lying in the bed, my head on her chest, listening to the calmness of the night, it came to me that one day this would end. Each of the victim's faces flashed before my mind's eye and I began to cry—each baby that I had saved, each man I had killed and each wife I had imprisoned. Tears that had not come for years, softly fell down my cheeks onto Judy's naked stomach. I saw each of the girls whose parents I had killed and the weight of their freedom rung through my head. It was truly sad to know that they would still have to live as I did—never able to care for another, always looking for the lie in someone, forgetting that people believed the world might be a decent place, carrying around the guilt and the shame of having your father fuck you ... and telling you how much you like it.

I cried without shame and held on to the fact that if Judy woke up, she would understand and that I would lie to her, because that is what I did.

Chapter 12

Miller and Grant sat at their desks filling out paperwork. As Miller finished, she looked over the desktop. "You done?"

"Not yet. How come I have so much paperwork when you collared the bastard?" He laughed.

I shrugged it off and grabbed the 'Karma' file. Starting to read, Grant waived me off. "Not again tonight, Miller?"

"Why not? I never sleep when we make the arrest. The adrenalin pumps for hours. How do you do it? What, you go home and sleep like a baby?" She dug further into the file, laying it all out on the desk.

"I do. It's over and I did my job. It's celebratory sleep."

Miller caught the joke. "Oh ..." She forgot he had a wife and that they had a life outside of work, unlike Miller. She lived the job, lived for the job. When you put in the kind of time she did, you learned certain things and one was to be intimate, you needed the ability and her father had ruined that. She instinctively knew that 'Karma' had contacted her for this very reason. For the first time, she felt that prosecuting her father as an emancipated minor and making the statement public might have been detrimental.

"Snap out of it, Miller." Grant was putting on his jacket to leave. "I'm done here, clearly you are not. I'll see you in the morning?"

She nodded. "Yeah. See ya in the morning." She went back to stringing the documents across the desk, fanning them out to get a better look and then she picked up the list of indictments that were similar in nature. Grinding through the list took four hours and she was tired. Surmounting fatigue got the best of her so she rose from the desk in the stillness of the office and stretched her muscles. occasionally, someone would wander through the room, expansive and their footsteps echoed through. Occasionally someone would say something to her, but for the most part they left her alone to decisively derail this mystery. She narrowed the list to just under twenty and none stuck out any more than another. She stretched her hamstrings, making them sting and waking up her nervous system. There had to be a connection.

Her mind kept wandering back to the woman that Monica had spent the day with, Susan Roets. The only investigative report was that she existed, but she had not been questioned. As Miller dropped her body over her legs, stretching fully, the blood running down, it dawned on her ... did Susan Roets exist? Had her initial thought that 'Karma' was a man wrong? Who the hell was Susan Roets?

Chapter 13

Miller sat down at her desk with a full breakfast that she had purchased and not touched. Thoughts rolled in her mind in an organized and concise fashion. It was something she was used to, just part of the process. She knew the notes by heart and they plagued her mind, destroyed common thoughts such as hunger and pain and thirst. She was on autopilot.

The first letter said nothing more than 'you can call me Karma'. But, the second was filled with more information. I needed to understand ROVER: Ratrix Obsession Victimizing Each Recondite ... and I was her worthy adversary. She wanted me to catch her and put an end to whatever it was she was doing. She had to have something to do with the murder of Ricardo Dillon, but Monica all but admitted it. 'You do the map'. How creative. Jennifer's list was narrowed to less than twenty wives killing their husbands. She'd have to call for everything on each case … months' worth of work. What was the key?

Chapter 14

The phone rang and I fumbled through financial analysis charts to find it to answer. "Miranda Blanche ... may I help you?"

The voice on the other end of the phone was smooth and subtle, yet I knew instantly who it was. Jannie said, "Miranda ... I wanted to check and see how the ankle was."

"It's great. Almost no bruising left. How wonderful of you to call. So kind." I cooed.

"I really was worried about you, and a little selfish. I think I am actually excited about playing with you." She waited for an answer.

Meeting her enthusiasm, "I am too. As a matter of fact, let me grab my calendar and let's see what we have available to play. Deal?"

"Deal." She shuffled through papers to grab her calendar as well.

I waited until she stopped before I began my recondite mission. "I have Tuesdays and Thursdays at eleven ... Monday and Friday at two, and Wednesday and Saturday's all afternoon."

She flipped pages again, ruffling into the phone. "How about Mondays at two, Wednesdays and Saturdays at … well, two. That keeps it all tidy."

"It's a date … I'm free today at two." I said.

"Is your ankle strong enough?"

"Absolutely. We can just go over strategy and things like that and hit around for a bit. That works for me."

She was noticeably excited. "I'm in. Two it is. At the club. See you then."

"See you then, Jannie." I hung up and sat back in my chair. What seemed like a very nice lady, she was going to get ugly.

I broke back into my work and laid out a portfolio for two new clients. Around lunchtime I found Stephens and adjusted a meeting scheduled with him every Monday. It conflicted with our tennis. He was not an easy sell, but he changed it, and I happily bounced back to my office. My new assistant, Brenda Wang, had ordered my lunch and it was ready as I sat back down to contemplate gaining more clientele. I must appear to be busy or I would never have the patience to do my real job right. I needed six more clients and the game turned to creating sales for the company rather than the disembodiment of Peter Johnson, the bastard.

Chapter 15

I showed up at the court a little early so that I could survey the situation. The surprise of how our relationship would unfold got me physically excited. Dressed in a navy and white tennis skirt, a peach tank, my wig in a ponytail and my NIKE shoes. I looked the part. College tennis would help me with the game. No one could beat me when I was in form; problem was it had been quite some time since I had played at a competitive level. More information was necessary, so I trailed into the tennis pro's office to get what I needed. I hated flirting with men, but, it wasn't like I didn't get their attention easily.

"Hi. My name is Randi Blanche ..." before I could finish Lyle Preston was drooling over me. Young and stupid, a dumb jock, he wasn't going to know what hit him.

"I know who ju are ..." He looked me up and down. His accent was blatantly foreign, but I couldn't tell where and it didn't matter. "I wootched you with Paaalo … ju quite goot."

"Great … So, there is a doubles tournament in June and I would like to sign my partner and me up for it. Where can I do that?" I smiled brilliantly.

"Right hare." He handed me a sign-up sheet and I filled it out.

I left appropriate blanks even though I knew the answers in Jannie's life. Finished, I handed it back to him. "Do you have an information pamphlet or something? Rules … anything?"

He seemed to stall for a moment before he handed me the information I needed. Everything was standard. Tennis association rules; nothing out of the ordinary. The times were quite early, and that I was not a fan of, but it would have to do. Court time began at six o'clock in the morning …

"Well, you are on top of things!" Jannie had walked in behind me and I had not seen her coming. My spine tingled at how near she was to me. When she spoke, her breath tickled my neck. I turned immediately.

"I am. There are things I didn't know, so if you could finish it, we are registered." I handed the paper to her to finish.

As she was writing, she glanced at a pamphlet that Lyle had failed to give me: Adult Doubles Mini Camp. After completing the sign-up sheet, she handed it to him. "What's this all about, Lyle?"

"Welp, Miss Jannie, dat is our doubles camp. Grat preparashun for the turn-a-mat. Let me sign ju up." He opened the pamphlet and they both read.

"Look at this ... is there any way you can afford the time off? An entire weekend, June 8-10th. It's just a stone's throw away in Kansas City. What do you say?" She was truly sincere in pleading. "Please ... pretty please."

I laughed. "How can I turn you down? You might cry or stomp your feet right here."

"Are you calling me a big baby?" She didn't give me time to answer. "You'd be right. I always get my way. And, I could definitely use the time away before summer term starts. It works perfectly for me. My daughter is even going to cheerleader camp at University of Kansas ... what a better way to spend a weekend. Let's do it ..."

I contemplated my calendar in my head. Nothing came to mind. It shouldn't hurt anything. "Where would we stay?"

She thumbed through and found the answer. "At the PQR Hotel and Spa ... I love that place. Get this ... Each player may enjoy a one hour Swedish or Deep Tissue Massage by appointment for only $70 plus gratuity. I pay $140 here. Oh, I could use a massage." She looked up under her lashes, baiting me.

"You think I can miss two days of work for a deep tissue massage ..." I waited for a reaction just a few seconds before finishing, "And you are right. Lord that sounds wondermous. I'm in. What are the dates again?" I grabbed my bag to double check and only had to move two things around.

"June eighth through the tenth."

"I'm in." I wrote it down as she tucked the information sheet in her bag.

She chimed, "I'll register us and it's my treat. I know I can use it more than you can, but it will be fun. Girl's weekend. I am so excited."

On the court, we started slowly, just bouncing balls back and forth, but the competition in each of us became apparent immediately. After less than five minutes, she stopped one of my hits back to her and looked over the net. "Let's play? Best 3 of 5?"

"Done." I bent my knees and prepared for her serve.

She bounced the bright yellow ball four times before tossing it up, cocking her racquet and letting it fly. She aced me and it was on. In the next fifty minutes, we battled back and forth, very evenly matched. Her serve was tight and her aim was perfect, a definite strong point to my ability to canonize a ball back over the net on return anywhere I wanted to put it.

Pouring sweat, feeling the sting of playing hard, I walked around the net when we were done to my bag. We hadn't spoken much since we began playing but we had kindred spirit. I enjoyed playing with her across the net. The real question popped into my mind readily. "You think we will mesh as well as a team?"

She took out her towel and dabbed at her perspiration. "I don't know. If we do, we will be lethal and I'm looking forward to it. The last person that played me that well was my husband, but he's too busy to notice I'm alive in the last four years." She tucked the towel back in her bag and pulled out a water bottle and guzzled it.

I did the same with my Evian. Spent with effort, I was tired. I had to think a moment; she was premature on the conversation about her marriage. Deciding to blow it off, I focused on the tennis, just like planned. "We should do well. Maybe we should find some fresh meat to see how we do?"

She looked around the courts where people were playing with instructors or dabbling in singles. The six indoor courts were all in use most of the time, but nothing of our caliper. "How about I find Mimi and see if she can rustle us up something?"

I nodded. That sounded fine. "SO, I should get back to work after a nice, long, hot shower … we are on for tomorrow?"

"Monday, Wednesday and every Saturday at two … yes. We are on for tomorrow." She smiled and tucked her things in her bag. "Shall we shower?"

We both got up and I tried hard not to think of her question as we both entered the locker room to shower.

Chapter 16

I was completely disgusted. In my effort to find the six new clients I needed, an appointment had originated. It was, however, at two o'clock in the afternoon and no other arrangement could be made. I had to cancel on Jannie. Her disappointment over the phone was apparent, but I had to work. Just as I would take care of her family, I had the same commitment to my career. Maybe I was just as disappointed? Hanging up had left me in a sour mood and I took it out momentarily on Brenda and then had to apologize to her. She was one of those mousy women that let people run all over her. If she lasted if the last one, I would be surprised.

I hustled through my day, sold the new client a myriad of services, pleased my boss and already doubled my commission for the month before I headed home to shower and then out again to find Judy. At the Owl's Nest, I sidled up to the bar just as she saw me and shot me a grin. She poured the three drinks for her waitress and then poured mind and slid down to greet me. As was our routine, it went very smoothly and I spent the night at her house to rise early in the morning to head out.

Tennis with Jannie was as great as it could be. We played matches against other teams and rarely lost. On days, we didn't play others we hustled through drills with Mimi and worked our tails off until we were ready for the tournament. Back in the office the day before I was leaving I had to put the rest of my plan in motion. It was time to literally begin the final phase.

Judy was all business, "So, Miss ... anything I can do for you?"

I knew juxtapose of her banter and played along with her. "Well, I seriously could use that drink, but I have no money. I can offer a trade ..." I waited for her reply as I sipped on the drink.

"No money, huh? Well, now, that's a real problem." She leaned on the bar and nearly whispered, "I think we can work something out, but you have to understand that is the most expensive drink in the place ... hours of trade will be encouraged."

"I will be honored to give you exactly what you want." The

game was over and she trotted off to take the next waitresses order and fill it while I watched her wiggle her ass for me, glancing here and there, always making sure she knew exactly where I was. It wasn't altogether unappreciated. She made me wet when I saw her and I did so love to converse with her. Great minds needed the intelligent banter and she was a great conversationalist. Along with the great tits, she was quite a catch and I paid attention to the incredible amount of attention she received from the customers. At that moment, I knew what she saw in me versus any one of them. I didn't beg her and I didn't gravel. I didn't ask her what she wanted; I took from her what I wanted. It was amazing to see her in motion, not a care in the world. It was getting close to time to cut her off and I never mourned a loss in this way before, but this one might sting a little bit.

Judy slid back and forth behind the bar, mixing drinks, managing guests and wait staff. Her personality was so full of life. She tossed her head back in laughter and her hair bounced off her shoulders. Exquisite features and lean muscles, she was stunning. I was sad to see her go, but first chance was the best opportunity.

Chapter 17

The Owl's Nest was hopping for a Thursday night. Entering from the back, so I could keep my car off the street, I saw Judy pouring drinks from the beer tap and snuck up behind her. "Psssst … how's my girl?"

She jumped and turned with a grin. "Hey, baby. You're early."

I kissed her cheek in a friendly enough manner as to not direct suspicion. "I want you to leave early … I need to make love to you." I shot it out of the cannon.

Stopped dead in her tracks, she cocked her head to the right and eyed me for a minute before commenting. "Where did the word 'fuck' go? You always wanna fuck me, Randi." She was as serious as I had ever seen her.

I shrugged it off. "Never mind. I didn't know if you would want to or not."

She turned and walked away without a word to me. Damn, I had pissed her off. I must have misread her affection toward me. Well, I would sway her with charm and make her understand I was unemotional toward her. All the others had fallen for the emotional aspect, jumped at the jealousy and played right into my hand. At worst, I thought as I sipped a drink the waitress brought me, I would disappear and never think of her again. The fight was better, but that would do.

Fifteen minutes of silence ended with her tossing her bartending apron to a guy who walked in the bar area. She spoke a few words to him and then headed my way. Sliding up onto the bar, she swung her feet over and dropped to the seat beside me. "Sorry Nona had to bring your drink. It's busy for a Thursday. Huh?"

"It is." I waited to see what was going on.

"I'm just about ready. I need to make sure that they don't need me to get Jason up to speed, but he should be alright."

"Jason?" I quipped.

"The new bartender. I'm working too many hours and wanna

back down a few. I told Kahlil that I wanted some time off. Maybe we can do something? More making love ..."

Ah, she had fallen for it. "That would be lovely. Let's get out of here." I moved off the bar stool and headed out with her hand in mine. We landed at her house a half hour later and the sex began.

Judy was different in bed this time. She was softer, more meaningful almost to the point of annoyance. Falling for the bait, hook, line and sinker, she was putty in my hands. After we were done and lying in a coat of sweat, she lit a cigarette.

Deeply inhaling and then letting the smoke out, she said, "I could get used to this. What are you doing tomorrow night? I think I can get off and there is a great concert at the Lendal Theatre." She popped up on one elbow. "Can we go?"

I didn't budge an inch. "I already have plans. But the concert sounds like a lot of fun. Who is it?"

"The house favorite at Sunset Club, Peeling Justice. They sort of play a metal lyric, but way less harsh. Remind me of ole rock-n-roll feel to it, but very meaningful lyric. I think you will love it. Go with me,

Randi ..."

Was she whining? I hated whining and I hated this conversation, but I was all-in, "I told you, I have plans."

She perked up, not what was expected. "Let's go Saturday then. They are playing both days."

"I'm out for the whole weekend. I've had it planned for a while."

She leaned in to me, sought my eyes, "Where are you going?"

"I'm spending the weekend at a tennis camp with my new tennis partner. We've been playing and registered for a tournament. It's necessary if we are going to win."

"Male or female?" She interjected quickly.

I had to play this right. With some form of fake remorse, I implied, "Well, it's tennis, Judy. What are you asking?"

She tried to sound calm, but her voice was shaking as was her hand when she went to put out the cigarette. "I am asking if it's another woman?" Her soft eyes registered the pain.

"It is … but there's nothing between us. She's a friend from the club who asked me to partner up for this big tournament. It's about playing ability, nothing else. Promise. She doesn't even know I'm a lesbian." I moved to where I was partially sitting up and tried to stroke her cheek, but, once again, she played right into my hands. The fight was on.

"I can get off for the weekend. Where is the camp at?" She waited for me to answer.

"Oh, Judy … Judy … Judy …" I did this when I scolded her on occasion, keeping her in line. She winced, knew what was coming before I got there, but I went there anyway. "It's tennis. A weekend filled with tennis. There isn't room for distraction and I'm afraid you would distract me. That's why I didn't tell you what I was doing. I knew you were going to be jealous." When I said the word, she lit like a match.

"I am NOT jealous, Randi. I just asked if you wanted to spend the weekend together. YOU said jealous, not me."

"Yes, I did. Quite acting like you're jealous if you aren't jealous." I dared her.

She lit, "I'm not acting jealous. You changed the dynamics of our relationship tonight and then you blow this at me. Fuck you, Randi."

"No ..." I got up and started putting my clothes on. "YOU fuck off, Judy. I made it perfectly clear in the beginning I would not get emotionally involved. I didn't break my promise. You are the one who got emotional and I can't deal with emotional. Never could, won't now ... won't ever!" I finished putting on my shirt, pulling it over my head and reaching for my bag.

"Don't go, Randi." She was on her knees on the bed, naked and beautiful. "I'm not jealous. I am in love with you," she whispered, "but I'm not jealous."

I shook my head. I never wanted to hear those words and when I did I ran for the hills. This time was different for me. Honestly, I didn't know what being in love with someone was like, but my feelings for her were different. Looking forward to seeing her each time was exciting, not a job. When I was with her I felt safe and secure, like the world couldn't come at me, no one would hurt me. I looked deep into her eyes and took her face softly in my hands.

With all my energy, I did my job, "It's over, Judy ... I don't want you to go for the weekend. It was great fun while it lasted," and I kissed her lips before she knew what hit her and turned to walk through the door. Before I knew what happened a lamp hit me in the side of the head. Piercing pain ripped through my neck and shoulder and I felt the warm, soft goo of blood running down the back of my neck. I felt myself wobble and then down I went.

The papers on the table revealed the story. Jennifer sat, dumbfounded, staring at the find. She had done it; she broke the case. At that exact moment, she knew not what to do. Everyone was either out on the street, busy at their desk doing paperwork or off for the night. She wanted to scream in jubilation, dance a jig of happiness, but she realized the work just began. Help was necessary, so she dialed Wyatt's number and waited.

It rang three times before Wyatt picked up the phone, "This is Grant. What's up?"

She took a deep breath and then couldn't contain. The information flew out of her mouth, "I did it, Wyatt. I broke the case.

Get this … she is responsible for five murders. The cities she listed all

find the same exact case, the same exact wife convicted of a murder,

well one of them is still in investigation, but it's all the same. She led me

right to her. Problem is, I don't know where she is now. She must get in

somehow. I think there's more to the story, but the only thing I can find

in comparison to the cities is a situation where a wife has murdered her

husband, clear and concise forensics that reveal everything, with one

HUGE exception, the wife doesn't remember a thing. Nothing. So, I had

these twenty cases and tossed one out due to some information about

the motive, ran the other 19 through the computer relations database

and find a big calculated situation in five. And, I'll be damned. Can you

fucking believe that every single one of them had a toxicology report on

the wives and they were all under the influence of Prolanlol, the date

rape drug and didn't remember a thing? Also, I read through the five

cases and one other thing glares off the page … guess what it is?" She

didn't give him time to answer, but cut right back in, "There is a friend

to each wife. Female. That she hung out with that day and remembers

making plans with, but has no idea if those plans came to fruition or

not. How's that? Huh? What do you think?"

She took a breath and waited. Too much time passed for her, even though it was only a couple of seconds. Her excitement was like a drug. "What do you think, Wyatt?"

"Miller, damn, give me a chance to talk. Shit." He rustled through his drawer and picked up his gun and strapped it on as he kissed his wife and headed out the door talking. "What a break. You are amazing. That's what you are, amazing. Okay, I'm on my way in. Get all the information together. We are going on a fishing expedition. Get it cleared with Captain and we leave as soon as I get there. First stop, first wife convicted, where is she, get clearance to get in and find out who we need to talk to do a full investigation there. Then start on the second wife. My ETA is 22 min. See you in a minute. Damned good job, Miller. I'm proud of you. Let's go get the crazy bitch."

Miller was beaming, but the excitement took over once again. Phone back in her pocket, she took the paperwork and organized it impeccably. She made a list of the women in order and pertinent information:

1. Monica Dillon, incarcerated 1/14/07 Leavenworth. Husband-Ricardo. Murder 1, 40 to Life. Daughter-Sylvia-15. Duluth, MN. Date if incidence 3/28/06. Friend Susan Roets.

2. Roberta Jones, incarcerated 9/25/08 Lancaster, PA. Husband-Nathan. Murder 3, 10 years, out in 5, self-defense. Daughter-Hannah-16. Date of incidence 7/27/07. Friend Shawna Stevens.

3. Stephanie Rios-DeLaCruz, incarcerated 6/3/09 Monticello, AR. Husband-Tom DeLaCruz. Murder 1-Life. Daughter-Samantha-12. Date of incidence 1/25/09. Friend Elizabeth LeBlanc-10th Judicial District Court Assistant DA secretary.

4. Elaine Stanley, incarcerated 5/23/11 Bakersfield, CA. Husband-Ross Thibideau. Murder 1, life without parole. Daughter-Vanessa-13. Date of incidence 10/11/10. Friend Mary Jo Shriner, chef to the celebrities and the wealthy.

5. Julie Gerard, incarceration date: trial set for November 11, 2012. On Remand Cincinnati, OH. Husband-Evan Gerard. Murder 1 indictment under further investigation. Daughter-Amanda-14. Friend Charlene McCant.

With all the evidence cited neatly and succinctly, Miller waited the next four minutes for Grant while she was on hold with the Leavenworth Federal Penitentiary in Kansas. Grant popped in, she handed him the paper and before they could begin talking Miller came off hold and set up the interview with Monica Dillon. They didn't have to worry about jurisdiction on this one, because she was willing to talk to them. This was not going to be difficult in the respect of getting to the possible victims, but it was a matter of what they might remember.

"Did you pack a bag?" Miller quipped as they headed out, paperwork in hand, twenty minutes later.

"I keep a bag in my car. You know that." He was proud of himself.

"Your gym bag? That means you have one real outfit ... the one you have on?" She laughed as they headed for her house.

"What? You don't like my suit? It's this one or my blue one. Take your pick."

"You're a mess. We are going to authorize a clothing expense and I'm taking you shopping when we get there. As it is, we have about two hours from flying in and getting to the hotel in Topeka where her lawyer is. We will meet with the attorney and then he will authorize the investigative visit to Monica in prison. He didn't seem to have a problem at all when they called and asked counsel if we could visit. He welcomed our visit." Her Cheshire grin couldn't be stopped.

"I hate to put an anchor on your balloon, Jen, but you know we are just starting. We have information. We have nothing else."

She nodded. "I know. I know. BUT … and that is a big but, we do have information and I know the key. I know why she's doing it. There was very little in the case logs, but enough for me to put it together and I'm gonna lay it on the line, Grant. She picked me for the very same reason."

The lights of the city came and went in the darkness of the car as Jennifer Miller told her partner of her incestuous relationship with her father in grave detail. Once she finished, she paused for comment, looking straight ahead. Grant put his hand on hers on the steering wheel before he spoke. The comfort was a sign that this would be okay and Jen knew she could get through it. She had done well this far and she would take this to the end and grant 'Karma' her wish to put a stop to this nightmare.

Grant listened to the story his partner told him and cringed at the thought of how many times the guys in the unit had teased her about her dateless life. He felt the pang of guilt that came with his own teasing. "Man, Jen, I'm sorry."

The words bit like a snake. She stopped the anger that rose immediately and softened her words back to him, "It's okay. She picked me because of my situation. Problem is, there is only one place in life I have ever spoken about it. A website. How she found me is how she found the victims. I want to research it on the plane, but I think I'm right. She finds her prey on this internet site. I posted on it a couple of years ago, and sometimes go read the blogs of little girls. It's a place we are safe to tell the whole story ... sometimes it's not so nice. A lot of us are in love with our abuser and can't get out. We don't see what's wrong with it, because it's all we know. I want to talk to every daughter, every wife and every friend that was supposed to show up at these people's house the night of the murder. I think we can crack this. But, Wyatt ... where's she at now?"

They pulled up to her house and continued the conversation while she threw her things in her bag and they headed back to the car for the airport.

Grant pried all the information out of Miller as they boarded the plane where all Internet service stopped. They planned their course of action. Essentially, they mapped out the plan by which they would fill in the blanks and find out if 'Karma' had led them on a wild goose chase. When they were done, they had about twenty-five minutes left in the flight in to Kansas City, KCI airport.

Jennifer was getting nervous, second-guessing herself. "Do you think this is all real?"

"What do you mean?" Grant stirred from his attempt to get a few minutes' sleep. "Of course, it's real. Just don't get caught in the game of believing your theory before you prove it. Let's read the letters again. One more time before we land and let's see what we hear this time." He moved his seat upright.

Miller dug the letters out of the case and read aloud: "Rage Edifying Dignity. Ratrix Obsession Victimizing Each Recondite. Red Rover: You can call me 'Karma'. This is all you need to know for now … Ricardo Dillon, died: March 28, 2006. Monica Dillon, incarceration date: Jan. 14, 2007, Leavenworth, Ks. I'll be in contact. Karma." She stirred to grab the second letter and began again: "Same title acronym … then my worthy adversary … please, do NOT let me down. I will not stop unless you put an end to this … you do the 'map'. Karma. Then there's the map. Duluth, MN. Lancaster, PA. Monticello, AR.

Bakersfield, CA. Cincinnati, OH. Toe-Toe?" She turned to Wyatt. "Everything plays out. Rage edifying dignity ... Sometimes I think that means just what it says, she's mad and she's going to take her anger and make restitution by regaining their dignity. Then the Ratrix obsession victimizing each recondite ... Ratrix is primary and recondite is concealed or hidden ... so,"

Wyatt jumped in, "the primary obsession is victimizing each hidden situation with the incest. Look at this, it's all right here ... I'm with you." He grabbed the papers and looked for his answers. "See, here it is. There are all these women, who, according to the killer, are not victims, but perps as well. Think about it, what if she is punishing them, the primary hidden target? Think about it ... she punishes them for what they knew and did nothing about. So, in a sense, you are right, she has set them all up and she somehow changes her name or something and is this friend that has disappeared in all cases. You have a friend in every case. But never has this friend been reached or identified as having made an excuse to not fulfill the plans, the wives can't remember anything and for all they know, she was there with them. Is there anything that releases memory from Proplanlol?" He looked at her like she would know the answer.

Miller shook her head, "Dunno, but we can find out. Let's get a list together of all the places we need to check. How come no one used the toxicology reports of the date rape drug? I mean, wouldn't that flag something?" She was angry.

Wyatt wasn't as understanding, "They were open and shut cases, Miller. Look at them. This one here ..." He pointed to Monica Dillon, "Hell, she had the weapon in her hand when they got there. It was all laid out. She didn't leave the crime scene. No persecutor is going to dig that one out. And what defense lawyer is going to fight something like that with a tox screen? She would have stood a better chance copping a plea. No matter what, we should give them retribution if they were innocent. That's our job, Miller. You think you will have a problem with that?" He looked for the answer.

She took a minute to think just as the airline representative came on to tell them they were landing. With a clear conscience, she answered, "I think I'm okay. I have resentment toward my mom, sure. She picked him over me and I've never been able to salvage a relationship with either of them. But, that's just part of the deal. I don't know how I would have felt if it happened any other way. Right?"

"Right. I see your point. Just wanted to make sure." He smiled at her.

"I got it. You know I don't dig my personal crap out and lay it on the table with a case. It's why I'm here, not who I am."

The plane hit the ground and within an hour they were headed in a rental car to Topeka, KS to speak to Randall Livingstone, Monica Dillon's attorney. They were meeting for breakfast since it was only 4:40 AM.

iHop was plenty busy when they arrived at nearly six o'clock that morning and were guided to a table away from the crowd where Randall Livingstone anxiously awaited their arrival. When Grant reached for his hand, Livingstone stood immediately.

Randall introduced himself, "I'm Randall Livingstone, and you are ..."

"Wyatt Grant and this is Jennifer Miller, lead investigator on this case." They all sat down and jumped right in.

Jennifer couldn't wait any longer. "I got these letters from someone who calls them self 'Karma'. Through the course of investigating this situation, I believe that we have a serial killer, possibly female, and that she has sent women to prison, Monica Dillon and others, for revenge."

"Revenge?" Randall was confused.

"The father was possibly having an incestuous relationship with the daughter in each of the five cases."

"What?" Randall's face became red with rage. "That can't be true … They are my friends. I grew up with Ricardo, a very respectable man in every sense of the word."

Grant came to the table, "Mr. Livingstone. I understand where you are coming from, but there is only one answer and that is as plausible as any. If we are right, then we believe that we can overturn Monica Dillon's conviction. We need to talk to …" He dug into his notes, but Miller beat him to it.

"We need to talk to Sylvia. Is she local? She should be what, 21 now?" Miller was hopeful.

Randall let it all sink in. "Yes, Sylvia is 21. She's at school during the year, but comes and spends the summer with my family. She's at my house right now. I don't think she works until this evening. She's very fragile you know ... losing both mother and father, this has been incredibly difficult for this young woman."

Miller was empathetic, "Sir, we understand, but we may have the opportunity to move this case and strike it from her life ... that might help her have her mother back and lose the stigma related to the entire case. I would like to try and speak with her. I understand female victims, it's why I do what I do." She pleaded with him.

Finally, Randall shook his head in compliance. "I will arrange it. As well, I have arranged for an appointment to begin interviewing Monica this morning as soon as you arrive. I think you will find her very receptive," he coughed, "however, I challenge you to go easy on getting her hopes up on getting this conviction returned. She's already tried to complete suicide inside once. I really do not want to see her taken through any more torment. This case is personal to me. If you can give me any information you obtain, I will see about working with you on gaining an appeal. New information on the case can be introduced and we can ask for a retrial. I will not begin to get even my hopes up. A quaint suggestion, find another reason for being there to interview her. I'll be the one to break the news to her when and IF we get that far. Fair enough?"

Miller chimed in, "Fair enough, Sir. Fair enough."

They made niceties and exited, headed for Leavenworth, KS. Through the drive, they detailed their list of questions. Over and over they played scenarios through their minds, using each other to bounce their ideas, coming up with the most articulate set of questions for Monica Dillon.

Chapter 18

Miller and Wyatt went through the penitentiary protocol of searches, identification checks and were escorted to an interview room awaiting the arrival of Monica Dillon.

Almost ten minutes later, a male prison guard escorted Monica Dillon into the room. Dark hair, dark eyes, a beautiful smile with straight white teeth, Monica introduced herself to the detectives. Miller knew immediately she did not belong in Federal prison. As she sat down, her class and distinction was evident.

Miller started in softly, "Hi, Monica. I'm detective Jennifer Miller from homicide in Austin, TX. This is my partner, Grant Wyatt." Wyatt shook Monica's hand before Miller continued, "We have been alerted to the potential of new evidence in your case …"

Monica burst into the conversation. "How can YOU have new evidence in my case? Where is it? What is it? I don't think I did this and I haven't been able to prove anything … they caught me in the room with my husband, holding the murder weapon. I can't remember anything ... Nothing! What do you know?" She was standing, demanding, yelling.

The prison guard reached over and sat her back down. "I'm sorry." She said. "I really haven't heard anything in over four years. No one visits me but my attorney. No one believes me. I have no proof. None."

Miller tried to use kid gloves. "Well, let me explain something. I got a letter a few months back that alerted me to someone named 'Karma'. Do you know a Karma?"

Monica reflected and then shook her head no.

"What is the last point of the day in question that you remember?" Miller waited, but she could tell Monica was getting frustrated. She helped her through, "Monica, we are here to help you. Please, we have four other cases that are very similar to yours, let us prove something different if we can. Just answer our questions to the best of your recollection. Okay?" She touched Monica's hand.

Monica looked at the hand on top of hers. "Okay ... I remember my daughter leaving for school at around eight. After that, I went to work, left at noon and then it gets sketchy. I think I met my friend, Susan Roets."

"Tell us about Susan Roets." Grant asked softly.

"Well," Monica said, "I met her at the Country Club tennis courts about mid-July. She was extremely fun and full of energy. We had so much in common: the ladies club, our college, although I was years ahead of her, our love of gardening and well, we just had this great friendship. I finally had a best friend after all these years of women just looking at me like the competition. She was a good friend. We used to go shopping, the one thing I couldn't find anyone to go and do. She showed me how fun it could be. Before her, I dressed like the pauper I grew up as. My husband hated my beauty, and Susan understood pretty. Ya know?" She looked at Miller for the answer.

"I know. Pretty goes both ways, doesn't it?" Miller helped chide her forward. "So where was Susan that day? Did you have contact with her?"

Monica looked off into space, trying desperately to remember. "I think we went shopping. The whole day becomes blurry at some point, but I think we went shopping and I had bags from two local boutiques, very exclusive: Charlie's and 45th street Shoppe. My daughter's room had two bags in there from the mall. I have sketchy memories of the afternoon, but the murder happened at 4:35 PM. From about noon on, I really have very little recollection. I have tried and tried, wracked my brain, and nothing."

Wyatt beat Miller to the punch, "Where did you eat lunch?" They chimed nearly at the same time.

"Wallie's on 34th and Kennedy. I had the cob salad and a cheesecake … you know, I was watching my weight so a salad and dessert is better than … well, anyway. I remember work and I remember lunch, but I don't remember leaving the restaurant." She waited for the next question.

Miller drew, "Are you aware that you had Prolanlol in your bloodstream at the point of arrest?"

"Yes. I don't know what it is, but someone said something about it maybe stunting my memory."

Miller continued, "They found significant levels of a drug called

Triazolam in your system. Do you remember taking the drug? Were you prescribed the drug? Who was with you at lunch?"

Monica lurched forward, "What is Triazolam? I had no medications. Never have, even in here. I use meditation and relaxation techniques, but have never had a problem. I wasn't sick a day in my life except for the flu when I was 23. What is it?"

Grant said, "It's a drug that erases memory if given in high enough doses. Sometimes it's used as a sedative. Did you have sleeping pills in any way?"

She was shaking her head no.

Grant continued, "Did you have lunch with Susan? Could she have put something in your drink? What do you remember?"

She tapped her fingers on the table until Miller placed her hand atop Monica's. "It's okay. Just relax and think back. Who were you with?"

"Like I told you, Susan and I had lunch. I had a Cobb ..." she looked up and stared into Miller's eyes. "I went to the restroom half way through lunch. Susan stayed at the table. I don't understand. Susan and I were great friends. I trust her."

Miller put both elbows on the table and leaned forward, "We haven't seen anything about her being interviewed, about you having anything in your case about her other than her name and that you had been with her at some time during the day. Because you held the 'smoking gun' so to speak, I don't think anyone interviewed her. Where can we find her? What do you know?"

Monica held fast, "Well, she worked for the Duluth News Tribune, our newspaper. She was a journalist."

"Did you ever see her ID? Driver's License, work ID card, anything?" Grant asked.

"I saw her byline a few times, no picture, but she said that she mostly researched and worked on contract for magazines and newspapers across the nation. Her home post was the Tribune. I didn't ask many questions. The Tribune was right across the street from my office. I sold real estate and I was quite successful. That was the start of our problems. It wasn't hard for anyone to believe that I murdered him ... I hated him."

Miller, "Did you murder him?"

Monica, "I don't think so. Honestly, I don't know. I was holding the gun when the police showed up. Have you seen the pictures of the crime scene? I set it up, tied him up and tortured him over probably a two-hour time period. I don't think I have that in me. They said that I had motive, because I was cheating on him and I couldn't be with my boyfriend if I had him in the way. That's not true. He wanted to divorce me, but I didn't want that. My affair was short-lived, but they used it against me; Bradley, my boyfriend, if you want to call him that, testified against me. I had told him I wished my husband was dead one time and they declared motive from that. They threatened him that he was an accessory if he didn't testify against me. I didn't want to divorce Ricardo. I'm not an idiot. I would have had to pay him, split half of my fortune with him and he wanted to take my daughter ..."

"Was he having sex with your daughter, Sylvia?" Miller said the words, stopping Monica in her tracks.

"I think so." Monica stared Miller down.

"What was your assumption based upon?" Miller was down to basic tactics. Let her talk.

"Our relationship stopped sexually when my daughter turned eight. I caught him in her room one time and the next day she acted very oddly. I didn't want to believe it, but over time, it was difficult to deny it, and believe me, I tried. If I wouldn't have told Bradley any of it, I might have had a defense, but he tore me up in court."

Grant interjected, "Did Sylvia testify?"

"No. At least we saved her that. It was never fully brought up in court. What they said was enough to blow me out of the water. Even I think I'm guilty. I just don't know for sure, so I have reasonable doubt. Too bad I wasn't on my own jury, huh?" She chuckled lightly. "What doesn't make sense to me is that I have never been a violent person. And, this has always bothered me … if I tied him up and all that, why didn't I have any marks of him fighting back? He was a big guy. I know at lunch, as of that time, I did NOT have plans to kill my husband. How did I think all this out, have time to plan and initiate the plan, when I hadn't for one moment before lunch that day thought of doing it? Oh, well … This is what I get to look forward to for the rest of my life. Prison … Federal penitentiary with maximum security. At least I ain't nobody's bitch." She laughed again and her beauty was apparent through the dark circles under her eyes. "They are all afraid of me. Great reputation, huh? And I thought that my property skills were what I was known for?"

Miller softened and said, "I will do what I can. I don't know what's going on, but here is what happened." She filled Monica in on the letters, the reference to her case and the fact that they needed to talk to Sylvia. Miller asked one final question, "Do you have or know of a picture of Susan Roets? We need to know who we are looking for."

Monica gazed off to the side for a moment as if she were roledexing information before she spoke. "You know ... she worked for the newspaper, but they never ran her picture. Wait ... we were members of the Country Club and you had to have an ID. I know that one time I lost mine and I went in, they did not have to take a picture, they had my original on file and just shot me out a new ID. Try them. The Duluth Southside Country Club on Hamden Road."

Grant asked, "Can you give us a quick description?" He readied his notepad and pen to detail the information.

"Sure. She was tall, almost six feet, probably, dark brown hair, very pretty. It was long and straight and perfect every day. Sometimes she wore it in a ponytail, but most of the time just straight. It was past her shoulders but not long, ya know? Ummm … blue eyes with really long eyelashes. She did have a scar on the side of her neck, just below her ear. It's in the shape of a half circle."

"What side of her head?" Miller blurted, trying not to get too excited. Scars were great, you couldn't get rid of them.

"Left side, just under her ear. You can't really see it unless you are up close. She had gotten her hair caught in her tennis racquet on an overhead small one time and I had to help her. That's the only time I ever saw it."

They left Monica with hope that they would return in a few days and fill her in with more information. As Miller and Grant walked out of the prison, they traveled in silence. It was mind-blowing to think that this woman might be in prison on a wrongful conviction. Their job was magnanimous in relation to the usual case. Getting to the bottom of this was no less a priority than breathing.

Chapter 19

The rental car sat outside a small coffee shop in downtown Topeka, KS. Ushering in ten to fifteen people at a time, the place was packed. However, Sylvia had requested that Miller and Grant meet her at that establishment, because she was familiar with it and wanted a friend to be with her. They gave her that and were seated when she walked in, looking for them. Miller waved to her from across the room, she ordered her coffee and joined them.

Sylvia was mature beyond her years. It was apparent in her demeanor and her mannerisms. She was very articulate. "Good afternoon. I'm Sylvia Dillon and this is my friend, Danielle Patterson. She will be sitting in with me for the mere fact that this is very difficult for me to talk about, even now. So … what is it you want to know?" She cut right to the chase.

Miller, being female and knowing what she felt was the truth would be the communicator. Based on her and Grant's teamwork in the past, they knew when to hold back and when to burst forward. They felt hesitation with this young girl would suit the interview more appropriately. So, Miller began the questioning. "Sylvia, we have logged all the case files and read everything we can find on the incident with your parents in 2006. Because this is so difficult, we are going to just ask very pertinent questions, giving you time to answer. That will cut down the time you spend with us and dredge up as little as possible. We believe that there may be a different story than the one presented in court, but we must, and I stress, we must have more information. There are two pieces of information that I need from you with grand explanation. I know this will be difficult," Miller approached the young lady very calmly and in a very matter-of-fact manner. "I need you to tell me if you ever went on an incest site and told your story?"

Grant and Miller waited for her to be completely shocked, but she wasn't. She answered swiftly. "Yes. I did. The site was called incestsurvivors.org. I had started blogging in a forum about six months before my father was murdered."

Miller stuck to the subject. "On that site, did you tell anything about your father, your mother, your name, anything that might pinpoint who you are or where you live?"

She shook her head. "No. I was very careful. Although I was young, I was smart and I knew better. I didn't want another crazy bastard doing the same thing to me."

Miller caught her reference and homed in. "Did your father molest you?"

"My father had sex with me four to five times a week from the time I was eight years old until my mother sent me to boarding school eight months before she killed my father." She finally looked as if she were in pain. "I knew my mom knew at that point and so I went to boarding school. That is where I met, Dani. Right?"

Dani nodded and took her hand. They were not just friends, but girlfriends. Miller understood. She took her time and asked another question. "Did you ever meet Susan Roets?"

"No. Who is she?"

Miller filled her in. "She was a friend of your mother's, but seems to have disappeared the same day of the murder. No one even bothered to question her. I'm looking for her right now."

Sylvia looked confused.

Grant took charge. "See, your mom had lunch with Susan Roets, a woman she had befriended after you left, after you posted on that web site about incest. The woman and your mom were very close, shared intimate details about your life as a family and the day your father was murdered is the last day your mom or anyone else knows of her existence in Duluth. Since you moved to Topeka after you graduated from High School? We wondered if you had heard from her."

She said, "No. I never met her. They drug me home from boarding school for the funeral and then the trial. I just stayed and went to public school. When my mom got sentenced to Leavenworth, I thought I might as well move down here to the pit of hell, rather than live where I can never go see her."

Miller said, "But your mom said you haven't ever come to see her?"

"Nope." She said, "And I won't. It's not necessary. But, for some reason, I don't feel as alone here and the Livingstone family is good to me. I didn't want to be in Duluth where everyone knew what happened. Everyone looked at me so funny. My mom killed my dad ..."

"I understand." Miller said. "Did anyone ask you about your relationship with your father before the trial? Were you deposed? Did a team of lawyers sit down with you and ask you questions to use in court?"

"Yes. I was deposed, but they said since I was only fifteen that it wouldn't be introduced unless it was absolutely necessary. Since I heard my mom argue with my dad so much her team wasn't interested in bringing up my testimony and the prosecution didn't need it."

"You think your mom did it?" Grant asked.

"Not really. If she did, she had good reason. She's not like that. They fought all the time, but she didn't care about him enough to kill him. He was in love with me and I think she knew that. I used it against her all the time. She was odd-man-out, but it didn't bother her. She had Bradley and they left each other alone. I just put it in my mind that whatever the court said; I would trust. It took the guesswork out for me and I was so young that I needed that. I guess I still do. It doesn't matter. Whether I believe it or not, my mom has been in prison for six years and she will be there until she dies. Either way, they both left me to fend for myself, and I do. I don't know what I would do if my mom didn't do it. I have no emotions. They ran me dry years ago. When my dad came in my bedroom and stole my childhood; he deserved to die. I wish I would have done it. He stole everything from me. Maybe my mom loved me enough to kill him? That would be the best thing for me to think right now, because then my life wouldn't be for no reason. I'm okay with it."

Miller's heart broke into tiny pieces and yet she understood completely. The calling you a liar when you tell is the worst thing that can happen to a survivor of incest. If this little girl had to believe her mother loved her enough to end the torture and the abuse, then that's what she needed to do. Miller replied, "I am the product of incest as well, Sylvia. I do understand. I promise you, we will try and come to terms with what happened and if Karma had anything to do with it, I'll make sure she pays. That, I promise you."

Sylvia looked at Dani and for the first time, Dani spoke. "Who is Karma, the one who wrote the letters, right, but who is she?" She looked at Sylvia and continued, "Do you think she murdered Sylvie's dad?"

Grant took the challenge, beating Miller to the table. "We have reason to believe that Karma knows something. It is in our best interest to not summate or accuse without evidence. We are on that quest for evidence. You will be one of the first to know if we find something of substance. Right now, everything stands as is."

Sylvia's eyes lit up. "I might be able to help you … Do you think that this Susan Roets, you called her …? Do you think that she found us on the incest site?"

Miller was impressed. "Damn, girl. You're smart. Yes, we think it's a possibility. We have to have evidence though."

Sylvia nearly whispered, "There was a lady or girl, I don't remember, a girl who talked to me on the incest site one time. I had posted something about how my father was in love with me and I felt guilty using it against my mother, but I did. I got what I wanted. At fourteen it was easy, but the longer I did it, the harder it was not to feel guilty. Even though my dad told me this was a normal thing, I knew it wasn't normal and I knew that I had them both by the balls. In short, I used it and this lady encouraged me to talk, get it out. I kept the log …"

Miller and Grant shot each other looks. Sylvia caught it and laughed. She added, "Not only that, but I still have the computer that I used to blog with. It's at home. Some old laptop that has my journals on it and I never let it out of my site. When I got home from boarding school for the funeral, I hid it at my friend's house and then when everything was over, I brought it with me. I've still not touched it since the day my father died. Will that be of help?"

Miller was quick to reply. "I might be able to have our computer crime team pull the sites and IP address of the person you spoke to. It's been a long time, but I don't see why the information shouldn't still be on there. Your computer memory is insanely ingrained on a computer system and we have analysis tools that can tear into it … I think we might have a chance. Can we have it?"

Sylvia looked to Dani for assurance. "It's yours. Just don't make it public, please." She pleaded.

Grant softly spoke to her. "We will do our best to keep you and your family from any more harm. That is our promise to you. It's a hefty one, but we will try and honor it."

They thanked Sylvia for her time and broke the meeting. As they headed for the hotel, Grant perked up and became very talkative. Miller was caught in her own issues, but listened as his verbiage began to make sense to her. The minute they got back to the hotel, they both busted out laptops and began their investigation into Susan Roets.

It was hours before they actually found something. Grant jumped from his chair beside the window. "I got it! Check it out."

Miller came running from where she was lying on the bed. "What?" She looked at what he was showing her.

Grant said, "Here is Susan Roets." He slid the computer toward her so that she could see better and the picture in front of her was of a homely woman with short blonde hair, almost obese and not six feet tall. He pointed to the caption, "Look, it even says she works for the Tribune, it's her byline picture."

"Wait," Miller slowed her breathing so she could think, "If she is Susan Roets, who is the tall pretty brunette we were looking for?"

"Okay, let's talk theory." Grant made his way to his handy-dandy note pad and started making marks. "We have letters from 'Karma' that we think we have attached crimes to places on a map. The causal link is enough to investigate. But, we know nothing about this Karma character. There are, with each case, a friend who disappears from radar after the murder. Where are those files?" He started to search the room with his eyes as Miller jumped to get her case and easily withdrew the files.

Handing the files to Grant, she sat beside him so that they could both look. She had files faxed over detailing each one of the cases she put together and she had read them until her eyes nearly bled. She knew them by heart. Pointing to a page in the Dillon file, she highlighted Monica's first statement. "Look. Right there, she states the name Susan Roets and that she could alibi her whereabouts. She never remembered leaving Susan. Flip to page three there ... right there." She pointed again. "They have a phone number for the Tribune and nothing else. Nowhere is there any contact information, nor do they even insinuate that they attempted to contact her."

They looked at each other. Grant took charge, "Jen, get on the phone with the Tribune and find her social. From there we will run her through the database. I have a sneaky suspicion that we are barking up the right tree. She's given us enough information to hang her ... my question is, where is she to put the noose around her neck?"

Chapter 20

"Whew, am I sore." Jannie fell onto the bed in the hotel.

I was right behind her on my own bed. "I never sweated this much in my life. What a grueling experience. Where's that deep-tissue massage they promised us?"

"I think we had to schedule it in. The problem was ... how we knew that the schedule they gave us was nothing in comparison to the offering of tennis. We've been playing since nine this morning. We had two breaks ..." she growled as she shoved her head in a pillow.

"Who are you trying to convince? I can't feel my legs. Those drills were killer and I thought I was in decent shape. Lord knows I was wrong." I sat up. "Hey, Jannie ... good news is, we won!"

We slapped each other a high five for the fiftieth time that day. Playing like champs, as if we had been a team for years, it seemed we had an uncanny knack for knowing what the other would do and there was no beating us.

Jannie sat on the side of the bed rubbing her thighs. "I cannot believe how good we are. How good it feels to be this good. You're an awesome tennis player. I'm flattered to be your partner."

"That will be great. A stick it up your ass trophy to those bitches in Topeka. I hate the way they treat me."

"What do you mean?" I pried.

"Oh, the social scene is horrid at home. Ever since Pete had a sexual advance slander at work a few years back, it's never been the same. We don't go to parties, we aren't invited to events unless we are 'giving'." She was not shy about opening to me. "And, because my marriage sucks so much, it's nice to have something positive. Even if I can't feel my body. Is this what they call an out of body experience?"

We both laughed as I replied, "Girl, you could only wish you were out of your body right now."

"No kidding."

I wondered if I could get any information out of Jannie, not something I ever tried, but I was curious with this one. "So, what's wrong with your marriage? I gave up on relationships long ago. Who needs that torture?"

"Oh, dear. It's been so long. My daughter, Rachel, is seventeen and I think it's been since she was about eleven years old. One day he just stopped looking at me, stopped talking to me, and my daughter and he began a very close relationship. Prior to that, he had been too busy working. He's a partner in Robinson, Taft & Phife law firm, very elite group of men. He's always been jealous of my position at the university. As department chair, I spend a lot of time working. I never really minded. We had a loving relationship, he was kind to me and I felt valued. Crazy, huh?"

"It just stopped?" I grabbed my bag and was digging through for clean clothing so that I could shower, but through the story, I stopped and sat on the side of the bed. Interested in what she had to say, I was all ears.

"Yes. It just stopped. I was too busy to notice it. By the time I realized it; it was too late. My marriage was over. Now they both just treat me like I don't exist."

"God that must be awful, Jannie."

She sighed deeply. "Not really. I have my work and my daughter is just a teenager, like all the rest."

"Is that really how you feel?" I baited her.

She laughed. "You sure you aren't a lawyer?"

I shook my head no. "Hell no. I lie about finances. It's much easier to con someone than to bold-face lie."

We both got a kick out of that one before I added, "Why don't you tell someone the truth? I tried it once and it worked out okay. Sometimes you just have to lay it on the line and be honest about what's going on." I got up and headed into the bathroom, flipping the shower on.

Jannie followed my, leaning on the doorjamb. "I never tried it. Always knew dishonesty was the best policy." She waited while I climbed in the shower, pulling the curtain closed. Washing my body, careful to not get my hair wet. The new application of glue stuck well before we left and my shaving ritual had been complete. I shaved again, always concerned with leaving hair. The geltex was not noticeable unless it began to peel and I was good for three days; it had never peeled before a week's time.

Jannie spoke softly, but loud enough I could hear. "I think my husband is abusing my daughter …"

I sucked in air, shocked. The shower thankfully hid the formidable reaction. I continued washing my body, waiting for the next sentence. It seemed like hours.

Jannie wasn't embarrassed. It was a fact. "I don't know what to do about it, Randi. My mind is abuzz. I find myself reacting in all kinds of ways. I tried talking to my daughter about it a couple of weeks ago. She blew me off, told me I was crazy and to mind my own business. She told me to get the f- out of her life like I usually am and things would be just fine."

I finished my shower and pulled the curtain, grabbing the towel and beginning to pat dry. Usually I air-dried due to the geltex. "What are you going to do?" I put on my boxers and tank top and walked right past Jannie into the other room.

"I want to kill him" Jannie came back into the hotel room and sat on the bed across from me. She wanted a reaction.

I gave none, gave Jannie the respect to look her in the eye. "Are you going to?"

"Would you?"

"Yes."

Jannie wrinkled her lips, biting the top one. "I have a plan."

"That makes it murder 1."

"I'm aware of that."

"The only perfect crime is one in which no one knows but the criminal. I suggest you keep it that way, my friend."

"Understood." She nodded her head, a continual gnawing on her lip.

"How about we schedule in those massages or ... even better, go down to the bar for drinks?" I said.

"I haven't had a good drink in months. Since the Christmas party. I could use a couple of Mai-Tai. Let's do it. I'll jump in the shower and, well, maybe you should change?"

"What, you don't think we can get some guys to buy our drinks with this hot number?" I laughed.

"I saw the black dress in your bag. Might do you a bit of justice and yes, the goal is to not buy a thing." She left the room.

Miller was deep in conversation with the Tribune staff again. This was the third time she was on the phone trying to get a supervisor. "Look, asshole. If I have to fly in to Duluth to get this information from the courts, I will fry your ass in paperwork for so long that your balls will shrink to the size of peas. Do you understand me? I've proven my credentials, everything has been faxed to your destination and all I want is a return fax of this employee information. I suggest you have it burning through my phone line in the next ten minutes or I get on the next flight, leaving at 11:21 and your ass is mine, Joshua Ford. I know where you live ... comprehend?"

She waited to hear a response and did. "If it's not here in ten minutes, I'm booking the flight and your mine. I hear your promise, but I want to SEE your promise fulfilled. Done." She hung up with finality.

Grant was laughing. "Is there really an 11:21 flight?"

"Yeah. And my ass is on it if he doesn't come through." She laughed. Even though she hated flying, she would go and wring his neck if he didn't send that fax. She had been waiting for hours after the clearance and he just had not sent it. Getting pissed was stopping her thought process. Her patience was non-existent. She wanted that information so they could continue. While they waited, they had unscrewed the rest of the caseload from each file and had similar information coming from: Lancaster, PA Shawna Stevens who worked at the mayor's office as an assistant; Elizabeth LeBlanc, Assistant to DA in Monticello, AR; Delores Shriver, Pediatrician in Bakersfield, CA; and the newest case, Cincinnati, OH's Charlene McCant, no other information available.

The fax machine started buzzing. Miller ran to pick it up, watching as it came across and there it was … the picture ID of Susan Roets. Her Minnesota driver's license and social security with a copy of her initial hiring photo …

Chapter 21

We were late as we hustled to the elevator in the hotel. Each dressed in slacks and a lightweight shirt; we were ready to accept our awards from the tennis weekend. The ceremony lasted all of twenty minutes for the thirty-two people who attended the camp and not only did we win the round robin tournament, but we won the most congenial couple. As the luncheon wound down, we were more than ready to hit the road and return home.

In the car, Jannie drove, we talked about the tournament until the time was right and I brought up the subject of the night before.

I went roundabout and snuck into the conversation. "I guess this weekend was a success, huh? We beat their asses."

"It was a success. I had a great time." Jannie glanced over at her.

"So, if you don't kill your husband, we have a chance of winning the Topeka Classic, right?"

Jannie was just sipping on a soda they had gotten at the gas station and spewed it all over the interior of the car. "If I don't what?" She laughed so hard she could barely keep the car on the road.

"Sorry, I just had to toss that out there. It's sort of weighing heavily on my conscience." That part was not a lie. How the hell could Jannie blurt out she was going to do my job? It threw me into a tailspin and I had spent the better part of the night going over the plan. It was infallible, unless she killed her husband. And, if she did, what retribution would I get from Jannie? For, no matter what Jannie did, Rachel, a fourteen-year-old child, had been severely abused and rousted from childhood by these two-horrible people. Jannie had to suffer as well. If she killed him, would that be enough? It would achieve the results I wanted, but the plans were in my hand and I felt resentment for Jannie wanting to do it on her own. Something was wrong? Something was greatly wrong! I was getting very angry, inner rage was devouring my emotions and making it hard to think, hard to breath. Something was wrong. No one had defied my plans. In thirteen years, from the moment I had decided to kill my father and blame my mother, no one had defied my plans and I had not given thought to the one person who dare to try.

"I was just kidding. For Christ's sake, I am a beacon of light for the law. I cannot break it. I'd like to rid the world of the waste of oxygen, but I could never, ever kill anyone. I hope you understand that?" She kept looking at Randi, making her uncomfortable. Driving was the priority on the heavily traveled interstate. "You believe me, don't you?" She waited for an answer. "Randi ... it's important to me that you believe me. It was just a sick wish that I don't really want to happen. God, listen to me." She was becoming frantic.

"I believe you. But I know the feeling." There was complete silence.

Jannie took a couple of miles to register what had happened. Before she spoke, she calculated the content of her words before she let them out. "Explain to me what you mean?"

"I am a victim, well, survivor of incest." I let the words ring through the silence of the car. I concentrated on the sound of the highway slipping underneath them. Jannie wasn't saying anything and I felt the brunt of vulnerability. I started to panic. No gun, no weapon, I opened myself up to the world at large and I had no weapon.

I started to freak out. The 'what if's' started to ring in my thoughts; when Jannie finally spoke. "How did your mother know? What did she do?"

I heard what she said, but didn't quite hear. "What?"

"How did your mother know? What did she do to help you?"

Laughter tore from my gut, an explosion. "Help me? You're kidding, right?"

It then hit Jannie what I had been saying. She barely whispered, "I'm sorry."

"Me too, Jannie. Me too." It was the most honest thing that had ever come from my mouth without vengeance. "Me too."

"Okay, okay … Randi, can you help me?" The opportunity to take an exit that looked as if it went to nowhere was exploited. Jannie exited the interstate and pulled over and parked. She turned in the seat. "I don't know if what I feel is true, but if it is, I must do something." She saw no challenge from Randi. "You have to help me."

"What are you afraid of?" Randi turned as well. She could lose nothing if she spoke to Jannie. And if it didn't go well, she would kill her and end this journey now. Someone had defied her and she wasn't afraid to take this woman out, even though there was a part of her that was truly interested in what she could do for her daughter, another answer to 'the plan'?

"What am I afraid of? Good question. I think that I am afraid I am wrong, either way. If I do nothing and it is what it seems to be, then my daughter is victimized by both of us. If I go to battle, and believe me I will wage a war of battles, and I'm wrong, then I accuse someone she loves of a heinous crime and I victimize my poor, innocent daughter. What do I do, Randi? How do I know for sure?"

I already knew. How could I explain? What if I let her in on the secret? This time I would take the chance. "Jannie, I've never been honest with anyone in my life, but you, you are different. I know the truth and what I will share with you will make your skin crawl, but you are of the right frame of mind to deal with it and I hope you do better than my own mother. When she ignored what was happening to me, it tore the very core of my being out and left only a black abyss. I hope for Rachel's sake, this works out for the best."

Chapter 22

Jennifer Miller waited on the last fax to come across the machine's face and placed it in the organized pilings that Grant was tearing apart. They had gone through each and every one of the sequences of events to find the most information, given the philosophy they held and it was all coming together.

Grant was moving sheets in order. "Okay, so … we have five cases, five lost female friends and two already backed with evidence of identity fraud. This last set of information ought to give us the evidence on the last three. You take those two and I'll take the big one."

Miller started with the first pile Grant pointed to and began her search for information. Through pages and pages of documentation, she found nothing on the fourth killer's friend until she got to page 69. "Here it is!" She moved so that Grant could see. "Here it is. Dr. Delores Shriver, pediatrician. Are you fucking kidding me?" She kept scanning the document. "There's nothing here about interviewing her. There's nothing here about having her on the witness list. What the fuck are these people thinking? Look, right here." She pointed to the part of the page she was referring to. "Right here it says, and I quote, 'Alibi for the accused fails to fall in order on only one situation: Dr. Delores Shriver could not be reached for interviewing purposes." Miller threw the paper down on the pile and dropped back into her chair.

Grant made light of it. "Okay, so they had an open and close case, Jen. Don't get all hot under the collar. We have probably done the same thing when someone stands there holding the gun when we arrive. Good news is, we might have a different set of rules now and perhaps these women can go free. Let's just keep plugging away. Document it and finish the file and then move to the next. I haven't found anything on number three yet. Let's keep reading."

"Got it." She did as he told her. That was the great part of this team, they both took orders from each other and emotions did not count. They grounded each other well. She hit the file again, documenting every time they mentioned the good Dr. Shriver who disappeared off the face of the earth in the investigation. Perhaps the doctor just disappeared off the face of the earth period? She was mentioned only two more times in the file. Miller quit that file and moved to the last file, Evan Gerard and his wife, Julie. Although it had not gone to trial, the investigator on it was more than willing to look to see if they could correlate a connection. She read through the file, it played out much in the same manner as the others did. Julie remembered nothing past an afternoon of shopping with her friend, Charlene McCant. She remembers pouring a glass of wine at home and answering the door after that, but it's all she could come up with. Contact information for 'Charlie' Charlene McCant was included in the investigation, but they had no luck in finding her. She was employed at The Museum of Natural History as the curator, but never showed up for work the next day. Miller had several questions she started firing at Grant.

"Hey, so what if the killer was the wife and she killed the friends too? I'm just saying for the sake of saying." It sounded ridiculous, but had to be explored. "Like they were having affairs or something ..."

"It doesn't make sense. No bodies have turned up. Let's keep going on this track and look for evidence. We can kill the evidence later, but let's just work on finding it. Okay?" He was very kind and very skilled. He knew her too well to let her get away with getting off task.

"Right." She went back to her documents and made all the accurate notations until she was finished. Grant had finished twenty minutes before and had gone for coffee and donuts. It was almost one in the afternoon.

They sat down with their information and started charting it on paper. They took all five cases and took the causal links, gathering as much information as they could. What each and every one had in common was the friend that the wife was with prior to the murders and none of the wives remembered parting way from the friends.

"We need descriptions of each one. We have to interview each of the wives. While we wait for planes and make plans, check in with the Captain and I'll start looking for information on each one of these. Let's put the research team on them and see if we can get reports from all airports, bus stations, and routes out of towns in each case and see what we have. I'll call mine in, you call yours."

"I'm going to run down and get some soda. I'm coffe-ed out. Want anything?" Miller headed for the door.

"Na. I'm good. Coffee is the sustenance of life." He laughed.

"Whatever. Kill yourself. I need something else. Maybe even water. Oh, I hate the sound of that. Healthy." She headed for the vending machine out in the hall. On her way, she passed two other motel guests. They were headed the opposite direction, bantering back and forth. And then she heard it …

The first guest thought he was funny as he said to his wife, "Okay, Dorothy, get all the bags together and grab Toto, we're in the heart of Kansas."

It hit her like a ton of bricks … Toe-Toe … Karma was in Kansas. Miller, on a dead run, headed back to the hotel room screaming, "Grant! Grant! I got it!!!"

Jannie and Randi pulled off the interstate and headed for the club where Randi left her car. They had discussed the situation for hours. Randi opened up and told her everything that had happened to her and the plan was to catch Pete in action and get hardcore evidence to prosecute him. Even though this was going to hurt Amanda, it was going to save her life and they were going to get her help.

Randi had to modify her plan. However, when she heard the caring and the compassion, the love this woman had for her daughter, she realized that there was an alternative to this situation and she was going to let it play out. In her mind, it was inevitable for the situation to be resolved and she was so tired of running. She liked what Jannie said and she was all-in.

They pulled up to Randi's car. The silence from the rest of the drive was comfortable. When they stopped, Jannie got out and the two women looked at each other, before Jannie put her arms around Randi and bawled like a baby. Once she was finished, she pulled away and tried to talk.

"I just can't tell you how much I appreciate all that you told me. I never really understood it and that's why it was so hard to determine if it was going on. My daughter just didn't seem to be all that affected by it. I didn't understand that she was in love with him and yet holds so much guilt. It makes perfect sense. Her anger at me, everything makes sense. I don't know how to thank you. I love you, Randi."

The sincerity nearly knocked Randi off her feet. It had been a long time since she let anyone say those words to her, but for some reason, she believed Jannie. It would be a game of waiting. If it wasn't resolved in a few days, then Randi would take it into her own hands. The tennis tournament wasn't even an option at this point. The only thing that mattered was nailing this asshole and saving Amanda. For once, she might be able to face the child she saved and have the outcome less devastating? She would have to think about that one. One great thing about sociopaths, they didn't really care. Randi knew she was sociopath, but this caring was a little new to her. Maybe there was a chance she could lead a normal life? No. She had killed too many people in the past and she had sent the letter to Jennifer Miller, Austin Texas police department. It was time to contact Ms. Miller again.

Chapter 23

Grant waited by the motel lobby as Miller finished her phone call. They stood outside in the heat of the day, the Kansas sun beating down on them. Miller was excited, the adrenalin had been pumping on and off all day long.

Grant said, "If you are right, she could be within a couple hundred miles from this very spot we stand in. We don't have enough information for this, Miller. You must listen to me. You are gonna send her on the run."

Miller fidgeted. She wrestled with the plan, answering Grant's concerns. "Wyatt, she's different. She's not like you and me. She reasons differently. This is the only chance we have of possibly stopping the next killing. She's a serial killer, Wyatt. She's probably with her prey right now. We can't work fast enough, but we have a good team. Let's let them do their work."

"I don't know, Jen. It doesn't feel right." Wyatt was ready to believe her, but still hesitant.

"Look, we have one hour before going on the air for the first time. Let's see what the update is. Every fifteen minutes we get the update and we postpone until the nine o'clock news if you want, but we have to do this. We have to stop the next killing."

He still didn't want to say okay, but he was compelled to stop another crime. "Okay."

Miller pulled her phone from her pocket and they headed back up to the hotel room on the second floor. It had been turned into a home-away-from-home investigation room with wipe-erase boards, computers and technology. The Topeka, Kansas police department had set them up and kept them away from the precincts just in case there was a leak in any way. They had their own homicides to worry about.

She spoke as soon as Henderson answered, "Jake. What do you know?"

Jake Henderson was the best researcher they had in Austin. He knew his way around the computer systems and he nailed everything he could as fast as anyone in the FBI. He was excited. "Charlene McCant had plane tickets for San Diego, CA the night of the murder. An 11:15 PM flight from Cincinnati, connecting in Dallas, with a thirty-five-minute layover. I pulled the airport video for that night and went through it myself. I found someone resembling the description you got over the phone with Julie Gerard."

Miller had made necessary phone calls and got in to every prison and talked to each of the victims explaining what happened. They had all given similar descriptions for their 'friend' and it was easy to believe they were all the same woman. She was very tall, nearly 6', lean and agile. She had blue eyes from what everyone could remember, however the hair was different in each instance. It could be coincidence, but when they sought ID pictures for each of the names used, they were all different. It was uncanny how this woman took on their ID. She never used their credit cards or their real employment, but she would interview from the get-go and took on their name only. She had jobs from all walks of education. She had been Susan Roets, journalist; Shawna Stevens, assistant to the Mayor of Lancaster, PA; Elizabeth LeBlanc 10th Judicial District Assistant Deputy Attorney's assistant; Dr. Delores Shriver a pediatrician and Charlene McCant curator at the Museum of Natural History.

Jake continued, "She had a different style of hair so we used the facial profiler software to scan everyone that came out of the San Diego airport, nothing. We then took all of the airports with connecting flights within three hours and scanned their video. BINGO!"

Miller was beyond excited, "What? What did you find?"

Jake was energetic, "You might just be right. A female exited the Seattle airport, we believe she was using the name Sherry Conrad the same night. Nothing else matches, but the facial profiler software is rarely wrong. You can't change bone structure and we had a near 100% hit on Sherry Conrad. We haven't been able to question anyone at the airports, but my best guess is that she had tickets in the original name of Charlene McCant. Somehow, she checked in on the plane, boarded and then left and changed into the new outfit and the new wig, our assumption from viewing the video, and boarded the plane to Seattle, flight 1540 United Airlines. She exited the airport rented a car and drove to Denver, Colorado. There we checked records and she had a residence. She lived there until February 4 of this year. When she moved, she left no forwarding address. However, she purchased a car off the street and that car was found ... drum roll please ..." He just stopped talking.

What the fuck? She waited for him to continue before yelling into the phone, "Jake, don't you dare. Tell me!!!"

He laughed, "Topeka, KS. No shit, Miller. She ended up in your back yard. She made a lethal mistake, Jennifer. She rented a U-Haul and dropped it off in Topeka, KS. She rented it Feb. 2, 2011 and returned it Feb. 5th. She might be in the same town you are in. Go on the network and plead to her. We are still working on the other. I have three people scanning every incest site, checking IP addresses and trying to find anyone coming in from Topeka, Ks or any surrounding area. Finding every kid in Kansas that ever blogged on an incest site will take days. However, we are keeping it narrowed down to the last year. If she preyed upon them during the last year, I am confident we will find them by IP address. I'm on it as fast as I can. Now, say something. You are never this quite."

"I don't know what to say. Let me fill in Wyatt and then I will call back in fifteen. Keep on that list. Get to me as fast as you can. I'm praying we come up with it." She hung up the phone and ran for Wyatt.

He was working in the other part of the room and she had fallen behind, still in the hallway. She ran in the door, barely open and started talking ninety-to-nothing. When she finished, he stood up and was as flabbergasted as she was.

She said, "Now, see what I mean about asking the public for help? I know she's here. I can feel it. It's the strangest thing, but in my gut, I know she's here and she wants me to find her. How we ended up here, I have no idea. Call it fate?"

"It's fate. But, I'm going to argue the population help again ..." Before Grant could finish, Miller's phone rang.

She answered, "Miller."

Miller's face deflated as if it were a balloon popped with a pin. "Yes, Sir. No, Sir." She paused. "Yes, Sir. Yes, Sir." Another pause. "I understand. Yes, Sir. I'm on it. Thank you." She hung up and slid the phone back in the pocket of her jeans. "Well, you don't have to argue it at all. That was the Captain. Apparently, the Topeka police department made a big fuss about us taking this public. They think we have been made a fool of by Karma and that she has us by the short hairs. They want nothing to do with it. I couldn't tell them we have proof that she might be here."

Grant interjected, "We don't have proof. We have suspicion. IF we knew she was here, we could arrest her. That is what we must find. Screw 'em. We don't need to go public. I think she will run. I know you think she's straight sociopath, but I want to argue that. My gut tells me she's not as sociopath as it seems. She is too calculated. What if she really is an incest survivor? She has rage and anger that will turn her upside down. What we really need is her real identity. I think you need to think deeper. Let's take just a minute and let's make like we're her. Let's play this out. Let's start from the beginning and take a deep breath, slow down and let's calculate what we know and think like she does. If she's here, she's not going anywhere this second. We have to work through this."

Miller nodded. They sat down at the table and started in. Miller first. "Okay, so she was a victim of incest. That I know, so let's go back to my childhood."

"What happened when you told? You did tell, right?"

Miller said, "Yeah. I told. Blurted it out one night at dinner. My mom said I was a liar, essentially, and my father was too embarrassed to try again. So, I won in one sense and in another, I've never felt the same with my family. It's the big pink elephant in the middle of the room." She slowed herself down again. "I see where you are going though."

"What if her murder spree started with her own family? We know nothing about her. I wish we could make that call."

Miller agreed. "I do too, but we can't. Okay, she's smart. Her letters were to the point. Toe-Toe … where would she have started from? Is there something we could put together to run through the case database? How old is she?"

Miller's phone rang. "Miller." She waited and then said, "Jake, do this for me … approximate her age from those photos and then go back from the age of ten to say right before the first homicide in 2006 and run the database and see if there are more killings of husbands by wives that had daughters between 8 and 25. Can you do that for me?"

Miller waited again, "Great. Get back with me, prioritize for me."

She hung up again. She immediately redialed a number and waited for an answer. "Lieutenant Wiler, please." She took off the button up shirt she was wearing as she pinched the phone with her shoulder, stripped to a t-shirt. "Yes, this is Detective Jennifer Miller again. I have a favor, let me explain my situation. I believe our perp is in Topeka, KS. I have information that shows her trail ending here and I believe she is preying upon one of your citizens. I need you to pull all quarterly employment tax information. What I'm looking for is every female new hire in the state in the month of February, March and April of this year. She seems to like having a job and I need to find her." She paused to let him speak. "I know it's out there, but I have to narrow down my search." She scratched her nose, a habit when she was nervous. "You can do it? Great. Get back to me at this number as quick as you can. Can you get it tonight?" The answer was shortcoming. "I'll give them anything they want. Thanks. I appreciate it." She hung up.

Grant asked, "Well?"

"He's going to get a subpoena and work with us. He needs our information and asked if we wanted to share the control room with them. It's pretty detailed and would be better than this room ..."

"You mean give the case to him?"

Miller knew he was right. "Yeah. It's out of our jurisdiction and the answer is to stop her as she asked me to do, Wyatt. They might have her in the back yard. Let's let them put her to bed."

"That's fine. It's usually you fighting for the collar. If it's okay with you, it's okay with me."

They packed everything up and headed out the door. As they got ready to pack up the fax machine, it started gunning. In came two articulate photographs of Karma at the airport. Two airports, two pictures ... each one clearly showing her facial features. They had their girl.

Chapter 24

Miller and Lieutenant Wiler were going over the case files again. Wyatt was handling phone calls to Jake and taking all information from the investigating cities they had notified of the potential for a wrongful conviction. He hadn't been off the phone for more than two minutes the entire night. Round the clock, the information was starting to come together.

Wiler said, "So, if we get information on these one thousand, six hundred and forty-two women, you think we have a match?" He was holding the sheet faxed from the Department of Revenue for all new hires in the months they requested.

Miller was more optimistic. "Narrow it down. They have dates of birth, we know she's between the age of 25 and 40. She's white. She is new to the state, compare it with the requested state ID's issued in the months of Feb., March and April and we have a smaller list. She's on that list. I just know it. We have to see if we can find a visual of some sort to compare it, and then home in on her."

"We can look at it and see what ones might have photo ID's of some sort and try and go from there. We should bang out every chance possible. Let's tear it apart." They sat down together and looked at the lists, comparing the two. Preparing a phone list for each and every company that had a new hire that month, they had to determine a plan of action to get the information. They narrowed it down to fourteen within the hour.

Miller said, "Okay, so we have names and numbers, how would it best serve us to ask for the information without letting someone know we are on to them?" She looked at the list again. Fourteen names:

- Regina Thomas- Washburn University adjunct professor; English Department.

- Phyllis Preuter- Topeka City of, Water Department. Clerk.

- Emily Chu- Whittier, Wayne and Reynolds, Accounting. CPA.

- Brenda Vixon- Eastside Elementary School. Second Grade Teacher.

- Miranda Blanche- Lancaster, Stevens & Jones, LLC. Financial Planner.

- Sheila Ford- Sixteen and More. Retail Store Manager, White Lakes Mall.

- Diane Granger- Pet Supply and Products. Retail Store Manager.

- Louise Ralston- Dillon's Grocery Store. Clerk.

- Penelope White- Dillon's Grocery Store. Clerk.

- Sharon Watson- Kennedy & Sorenson, LLC. Financial Analyst.

- Olivia Elliott- Perkins. Restaurant Manager.

- Leona Donaldson- Pier One Imports. Store Clerk.

- Elaine Palmer- Sharkey and Company. Import/Export Manager.

- Tina Lassiter- State of Kansas Department of Corrections. Corrections Officer.

One more look at the list and Miller knew she was on it. They looked through the throw away names and tried to make sure that they had not eliminated someone of substance.

Miller, "I think she's on here. Let's start the calls. I'll do it. How about I go in as a State Representative verifying employment. I can say that we have the threat of identity theft and just need to know if they have the capability of photo employment IDs. If they do, we will subpoena them? Good enough?"

Wiler was thrilled. "That should do it. Get on the phones. I'll help Wyatt get things together over here. The thrill of the chase!"

Chapter 25

I sat in the library and worked diligently. With only forty minutes to my next meeting destination, I had to get the proxy to work for me on the library server. Breaking into the server was always a challenge, but once I drew up my email, I encrypted the access log and handed over the site mirror for display. Having done this on the other two occasions to send mail to Detective Miller, I had it down, but for some reason I wanted extra precaution. A dream I had last night had her on my ass and it was too scary to even believe possible. It made me feel better to make doubly sure that things were okay today. Once I had the Proxy, well, in this case the VPN, I had to connect through another access log. This then denied the cookie and made it crumble. The only way they could find me would be to subpoena the proxy owner and ask for the logs, but when I sent it spinning in 600,000 different directions, they would be searching whole cities and must go through hundreds of thousands of proxy logs before they came up with the university library as the host home. It was fool-proof.

Once I was in, I laid out the letter and got in and out. It was sent and I leaned back with a sigh of relief for only a second before I was out the door. Purposely I dressed differently today and wore my hair shorter. I would change wigs in my car and toss this one in a dumpster I sat on fire. Plan in motion, I was out the door.

As I headed out, by huge coincidence, Jannie ran smack, dab into me. Literally we bumped into each other.

Jannie was as surprised as I, "What are you doing on campus, Randi?" She smiled brilliantly. "Were you looking for me?"

It was the only way out. "I was. Your office said you were out and I thought, huh, professor out of office ... in class or in the library. I was right. Well, I thought I was wrong, but here you are."

She grabbed my arm and pulled me back in the library with her. "Your hair is sooo cute. How did you get an appointment this early in the morning? I love it." She spun me around so she could get a good look. "I like it much better than the longer. It makes you seem even classier, more grown up."

"Thank you. My stylist had an early appointment and I didn't have a client until 11 this morning ... in and out and viola ..."

"Cute, just as cute as a button. Here, let me turn in this book and then I'm headed back out. I never come to the library. You have a keen sense of presence." She walked up to the desk and handed the clerk the book. I ducked behind a couple of students, faked looking at a flyer hanging up and scooted out the door with Jannie when she was done.

Once we were out the door I relaxed some, but Jannie was overly chatty. I would have assumed just the opposite given the desperate plan we had developed. It was challenging for me; how could she be so calm?

She chimed into my thoughts, "SO, are you going to help me?"

I had challenged her to let me think about it so that I might have time to perfect the plan, but it was good as it stood. "Yes. I am. And, I think what we came up with is the best that there is. Can you set it in motion? I can pick up the equipment if you can get me in to set it up. You are so lucky that my brother, Thomas, is a genius at this. He's going to talk me through setting it all up."

"I am sure this will work and I can get you in as early as tonight.

Rachel is free and so is Peter. I will take them to dinner to celebrate my tennis trophy. They will hate it, but they will go. Here's my key ..." she started taking it off her key chain as she spoke. "You just go get another key made and then drop it off here before four o'clock when I leave. I stopped at the ATM this morning and got cash for the equipment, just in case I have problems and don't want to own up to it. I have a spare account and so I took out ten thousand dollars. Walk with me to the parking lot of the Law School and I'll give it to you."

I checked my watch. I was running behind, but I had to do this. "Sure. We must hurry though. Guess we can't jog in these shoes, huh?" We both laughed. Walking quickly, going over the plan once again, we were there in no time. She gave me the cash and I headed out.

Once I got to my appointment with my client, I sold the package of investments. They not only gave us what we asked, but put in 20% more than asked and shot my commission through the roof. If life were really this easy, wouldn't it be wonderful?

Why was it so easy for me to succeed? Something wasn't right. Nothing I had done in the last year had gone wrong and my life was never like that. An omen followed me like a black cloud all day long. I couldn't shake it. Was it just that the plan had changed and I had rescinded control? Was it that Jannie was taking matters into her own hands and I felt ill at ease with that? Whatever the problem was, I was comfortable walking through my fear and shooting it straight back the other direction. If it was anything other than misjudged feelings for the change, I would deal with it as best I could. Never did I make spur of the moment decisions and I had thought this all out. Other than Judy calling me fifty times a day on my cell phone, everything else was crystal clear and moving in the right direction.

Miller checked her email and had a message from Jake to call her ASAP. He had tried to leave a message, but her box was full. She saw the 'urgent' marked and made the call immediately. Within minutes he faxed her a copy of the newest letter from Karma:

Dear Detective Jennifer Miller:
I have had a change of heart. Hopefully you are on task and gathering information. This project will be my most difficult, if not the most gruesome for me. Good luck. The baby & baby are taken care of.
Karma

Her mind abuzz, Miller read through it three times and picked out the information she thought best gave clues. What was 'change of heart'? Her most difficult project? Gruesome? And the biggest indicator of something out of context was 'baby & baby'. She completed her thought process with the fact that the mirrored sites again gave them no indication of a location. It would take weeks, if not months to find her and pinpoint the send location. She had to think like Karma. What would be the point of sending her a letter?

Miller found Grant. "Hey, new letter from Karma. Read this." She handed him the fax and let him register the information.

As he read his facial expression showed everything he thought. He had the same questions. When finished, he looked up. "What the hell? As if we needed more puzzle to solve."

Miller wasn't of the same mindset. "At least she's contacting us. It gives her a chance to make a mistake. That's her problem; she wants to get caught. Somewhere in here she's given us exactly what we need."

"What if her change of heart is to not make this hit?"

Miller thought about it. "No. She's here and she's with her prey. Somewhere the clue is right before us. Read it out loud to me." She sat down and closed her eyes. Meditating on the words alone, nothing more, she heard what was written. After he was done, he handed her the fax back.

"I think we just need to gut it and make a list. I'll grab some paper." He moved to the desk and readied his notepad and pen. In midair, ready to roll, he paused. "Wait, baby and baby … that's the big one. What if it's twins?"

Miller grabbed the file with the small amount of information they had on the blog sites. "Right now, all we have is names of sites. The team is still searching for IP addresses in Kansas, Missouri, Nebraska and Iowa. Let me get him on it." She grabbed her phone and dialed Jake's number.

He answered. "Hey, anything new?"

Miller said, "No. But I need those IP addresses from the incest sites. Any chance you can bump that one up?"

"Sure. Let me see where Lopez is on it and get you a partial if nothing else."

"Cool. We are tearing apart the letter now. Thanks for keeping up on it all."

"No problem. I saw it on your desk and just knew. She's smart, but there's something wrong with hiring a service to send over the email. I'm checking on it now. The guy who took the order is in at noon today. I'll get with him as soon as I can and find out if there is any traceable evidence. I'm sure there won't be, just another dead end, but we are working every angle we can find."

"I know you are," Miller offered encouragement. "This beast will be tamed. There must be something in here of importance. She wants to be caught."

"Go get 'er, Miller. We are cheering you on."

"I'm trying. Get me that list ASAP." She hung up the phone and turned to Grant. "Okay, let's brainstorm."

Through the next half hour, they derailed the message. Hidden information had to lie in the words on the page. They had everything from the possibility of twins to baby product names to towns with infant-like business. They took the map of Kansas and looked at every little, tiny town surrounding areas and county names to see if anything rang a bell and then the fax came from Jake.

Miller could hardly contain as the paper came out of the machine. The websites were all listed and it narrowed down the incest bloggers to eight from Kansas and roughly the same from every other state. Iowa only had four.

"Oh, my God …" Miller was stunned.

Grant grabbed the paper and saw exactly what Miller was slapped with. "Baby & Baby … Johnson & Johnson. Holy shit. And, gruesome … Tina Gross."

On the page, listed Peter Johnson from Topeka, KS and had a local address and Tina Gross with an address in Talmage.

Grant caught the weight of the news, as he looked her in the eye. "Cowgirl up!"

Miller was caught up in the emotion of the moment. She knew this was heavy. "I'll call and get a copy of all posts she sent. Give me ten minutes. Get the addresses nailed down and any contact information."

He was already on it. She spent two minutes on the phone with Jake and had paper spitting out the fax machine before she ended the call. He was already a step ahead of her with any name that came up.

Thirty-four pages later, she was deep in reading the posts from two young girls: appleofmyeye1998 and duddyslilgrl09. She scanned the posts looking for anything that might have led Karma to one of these girls. It was heartbreaking to read through their stories and their communication. She tried to find dual response posts, but found none. She looked at everything they said, what they identified as markers and what was merely chat to pass time. Miller tore through the posts and found them to be of little help until she got to page 31 and there it was. A conversation between appleofmyeye1998 and cameLION. The song Karma's Chameleon came to her immediately. "Grant! Grant!!!"

She shoved the post in his face. "Read this."

He read and looked up. "It could be. Let's have them trace out on the other side." He was on the phone to Jake asking for the results as she finished reading. They had limited contact, but cameLION was insightful of this fourteen-year-old little girl. She promised her that everything would be okay and that she was a survivor. If she wanted a way out, just ask. The little girl's post back seemed to be an answer:

> appleofmyeye1998: He won't stop unless
> someone makes him and no one makes my
> dad do anything.
> CameLION: He can be stopped. Just look to
> the day he is. I'll be there for you.

Wiler touched Miller on the shoulder and nearly brought her out of her chair. "Rough night, Detective?"

"You scared me. No, actually, good night." She pulled up a chair for him and started to fill him in on the newest information. When she finished, she said, "I need some more work from the field crew. This list of new hires is narrowed down and I just can't find time to make the calls. And, there are two possible IP address registrants that fit the family profile possibly. I need them checked out. Grant is making calls to get pertinent information, but we need field surveillance. Think you can set that up?"

"I'll go to the DA now and see if he can get us whatever it is you need."

"I'm not quite certain how this should play out at the moment." Miller was already planning tactical strategy.

Wiler was thinking of something completely different. "Hey, have you eaten today?"

"What? No? No time ..." She went back to her thoughts and was making notes.

"You have to eat. Look, there's a little diner about a block from here. Let me buy you lunch." He smiled.

Miller stopped what she was doing and felt an inner struggle beginning. She did not mix work and pleasure. Well, she just ignored pleasure. "Are you hitting on me?"

"Hell no. I just wanna collar this bitch and if you pass out on me or die of starvation, I'll be left alone to fend for myself and Karma doesn't write me letters. My Captain said I'm supposed to take care of you, guard you like a dog ..."

"Dog is right." Grant was right behind him. "But, we do need to eat and I'm going along. Let's go, Miller. We have to put all this together." He laid a big smile down for Wiler and slapped him on the shoulder.

"Good suggestion. I am hungry. They have sweet tea there?" Miller asked.

Grant answered before Wiler could. "You know they don't and if they do it's not real sweet tea. This godforsaken place really lacks class and distinction. No comparison to Texas whatsoever." They laughed and headed out the door leaving the handsome Detective Wiler to follow behind as they chatted the entire two block walk.

Once in the diner, Wiler took control again. "LOOK, I didn't mean anything by it. I just thought she needed to eat."

Grant was relentless. "LOOK at her ..." he said, mimicking Wiler, "she is gorgeous and unavailable. Just know she's one of the guys and that's that. You didn't bother to ask to feed me ..."

Miller saved Wiler some face value, "No one can afford to feed you. Leave him alone. No offense taken. Let's just get some food ordered and get cracking here."

Grant viewed the menu and huffed and puffed his way through ordering. Wiler got a kick out of it. "You southern folk sure don't understand the Midwest a bit, do you?"

Miller quipped, "What's there to understand? Dirt, a tree every mile or two and fields and fields of dusty crops that when the wind blows no one can breathe ... just like home. I'm clicking my heels together right now."

Wiler got a kick out of her. "I see. So, Texas is home?"

Grant slapped his forehead, "Here we go again ... get a room!"

"Stop it, both of you." Miller was too busy thinking about some serious pancakes with butter pecan syrup and that pitcher of water. "Okay, so what do we KNOW ... Grant?"

"Latest update ..." he got out his notebook and started to recap. "We have two possible names from incest websites that could lead us to the family in question. Information complete, we need to investigate fully. Secondly, we have a list of 14 names for new hires in this community between the ages of 20 and 40, female, from out of state. We matched those with DMV records and have narrowed that down to five names: Emily Chu; Miranda Blanche; Sharon Watson; Elaine Palmer and Tina Lassiter. We are fetching employee ID pictures from a warrant now. Hopefully we can come up with something Jake can scan and see if there is a facial profile match. Right now, we know that she uses wigs heavily ... airport pictures of these women ..." He thumbed through his notebook to find the right page and then continued. "Yeah ... she likes to fly. Uh, Susan Roets, Shawna Stevens, Elizabeth LeBlanc, Dr. Delores Shriver -no airport pictures for her- but luckily the hospital she spent some time in the ER on shifts had some surveillance footage of the ER and ta-da!!! We have pictures of her as well. The last one is Charlene McCant and she gave us a beautiful smile for the camera."

Miller asked, "So, out of all these pictures ..."

Grant was pulling them from the file and laying them on the table as they spoke.

She continued, "We have no possible ID? Were there any other fingerprints at the crime scenes?"

He shook his head yes. "We found several prints, but get this, they were all different. Chase is looking at all identifiable evidence from the five cases and there are stranger prints in the homes of each one, but ... and this is a big but, and I'm not talking big ass, get this—two are male, three are female and they all come up in the criminal registry."

"What?" Miller was confused.

Wiler gave his two cents, "So, you have crime scene prints from the 'friend' of each of the convicted wives, but they come off as registered felons?"

Grant was excited, "They sure do. Registered SEX offenders. See ..." He laid out a new set of pictures over the old ones ... "In case number one, the Dillon's, we have Susan Roets. Here is a set of the prints from that scene: they belong to Tony Bates. Bates is a convicted child molester, did time in Minnesota, and had an alibi when the occurrence happened. Second case ... where is it?" He fumbled for the information. "Right here ... okay, second case is Shawna Stevens, friend of Roberta Jones. The set of prints that came up belong to Josephine Hernandez, did time in Pittsburg, PA for felony indecent liberties with a minor. Case three: Elizabeth LeBlanc, the friend. They find prints belonging to Sally Weathers, again, felony conviction for statutory rape, did time in Little Rock--again, had an alibi. Fourth case, my favorite, Dr. Delores Shriver, pediatrician ... No record of a medical license for her in any state, mind you the person checking these things should be shot. Not only does she not have a license to practice medicine and was a PEDIATRICIAN, but her fingerprints on record were never checked, they found them in a folder in HR. We ran them, they are the exact same prints from the crime scene and belong to ... the million-dollar answer. Any takers?" He looked up, joking with them.

Miller, "Come on, man ..."

Grant laughed, "Spoil sport. Okay, belonging to Samuel 'the ice man' Riggs. His crime of choice, three counts of murder 1, doing time in Pelican Bay—no chance of him practicing medicine as a female, in an

ER, and at the mercy of the wife, Elaine Stanley, psychologist while he was in Pelican Bay reaching for the soap. AND! Big and here, he did time for sexual battery. Again, a sexual offender."

Miller saw the connection clearly but it didn't make sense. "So, what about the last case? Charlene McCant?"

"Prints on her came back just the same, registered to felon Vicki Torres, statutory rape. Ohio State Prison, Youngstown. Her alibi says she was not in Cincinnati to lay her prints down on that crime scene. So, where does that leave us?"

Miller dodged a plate as the waitress sat it down in front of her. She pushed it out of the way so she could think. "Here is where we are ... She's smart. There must be a way she laid down those prints, like a machine or something that could impress the prints onto the scene, or we are wrong and these people were there, their alibis a joke. How could she do that in a fit of murder? It's as if she wore the prints. Is that possible?"

Wiler saw where she was going. "Wait, so you think she could have gloves or something that had the prints impressed? Where would she get the prints?"

Grant chimed in, "She has to have access to prints. Who all has access?"

"Not only does she have to have access, but she must have a way to use them once she gets them … Damn, I'm impressed and it takes a lot to impress me. Let's not worry about it now. Let's figure out where she is. I want to ask her."

They all sat for a moment, gathering their plates, taking the first bites, and putting it all together.

Miller was the first to speak, "What the hell was wrong with the detectives that found additional prints? That wasn't in the reports? Did you read that?" She asked Grant.

"Nope. I found it on the evidence page of every case. They never even ran them. The prosecutors had open and close cases … they didn't need anything making a mess of their case. They suppressed evidence that wasn't necessary to the trial."

"Stall out the Gerard trial for me?" Miller asked him.

"Sure."

Wiler spoke with a mouthful of food, "You really think she wants us to catch her?"

Miller thought about it. "She does, and I think I understand why. But, what did she actually do?"

Grant saved her from spilling her guts. "She's sociopath. She likes playing this game. I'll put my paycheck on she has an exit plan and she's already out of here."

Miller didn't buy it. "I don't. I think she thinks she's smarter than we are and she has no clue. That's our advantage here. So, our surveillance must have due diligence. We are a step ahead of her; I can guarantee it. We have to stay that way."

Chapter 26

Randi settled in to lunch with her client and prepared for her afternoon of fun. This was a challenge she had not foreseen. A chance to do good, instead of murder the bastard. It wasn't something she had readily come to, but she was settling in to the thought. Maybe if he went to jail and suffered through the rancid behavior of fellow inmates, child molesters were candy, she would feel the retribution she so desired? It wasn't a bad thought. It was pleasing to witness her mind's eye detailing their rapes and sodomy.

The client bored her to tears and she sat in awe of herself that she could multi-task as well as she could. Not once did she give thought to the client, but rather, she detailed her equipment purchase, making mental note. She figured her in and out points at the house and estimated all points of interest for camera and audio surveillance. If she took one hour, Jannie keeping the family busy, she should have enough time to place all equipment and set up the arsenal of media to capture the footage necessary to put the bastard behind bars for a very long time.

The lunch meeting finished and the client said they would think about the proposal she offered them on paper. It would do the work she was not interested in doing at the current time. She flashed a brilliant smile, shook the man's hand and headed out to the equipment purchase right after she dropped off the key to Jannie. Pressed for time, she had run to have it copied and dropped it back off. The plan was set in motion for 7:15 that evening. Jannie had made dinner reservations and the family would be gone. All she had to worry about was neighbors. Going stealth was the only option.

Prior to that, she stopped by home and changed clothes, wigs and her appearance to the best of her ability. She would not need ID, so she left everything at home. In her jogging outfit, complete with padded ass and shoulders and a flabby stomach, she hit the pavement and jogged three miles the opposite way before she hailed a cab to purchase her goodies. In her backpack was everything she needed to complete her mission.

Randi's first stop was a local residence she had called from a pay phone that morning, inquiring about a van for sale. She needed the mobility and needed to be able to set up her monitoring room. This van would do nicely and was already complete with the sides painted in bright red: Sam's Carpet Cleaning and Fire Restoration. She batted her eyelashes, begged for a better price, and because she was so poor and even asked if she could use his tag until next week because she couldn't afford to register the van until then. He was an idiot and let her do it all. She was virtually without responsibility.

She drove an hour-and-a-half to Kansas City and found her way. At the store, she picked out several pieces of luxury equipment: telephonic intercept, video camera, video and voice transmitting devices, vehicle tracking equipment, night vision systems and recording device transmission equipment. Because the ten thousand dollars wasn't enough, Randi had brought an additional twenty-five thousand. She got everything she needed, including the van she purchased for less than the thirty-five thousand.

She was careful not to disclose anything about her whereabouts or the case she was working on. In the van, she had changed into a 'detective look' and was sure the gentleman helping her was more interested in the twenty pounds of ass she had put on than anything she might be using the equipment for. The baseball cap covered her hair and eyes and she kept her head down so the surveillance equipment in the store couldn't ID her.

Back in the van, she headed to Topeka and took the time to go over the plan, step by step, detail by tiny detail to make sure she knew what she was doing. Jannie had offered to send her pictures of the house, but she knew that would get her into trouble later and chose to have her describe it while they drove home from the tennis camp. She had a visual idea of what she was up against, but until she stepped foot in the house, she would not know exactly where she would place the equipment. It was an opportunity for her to learn something new.

Chapter 27

Miller and Grant were discussing the venue in preparation for their surveillance. On the phone, all afternoon, they had information on both Tina Gross and Peter Johnson. They had a task force behind them and 24-hour stakeouts at the houses and places of employment. Tina Gross looked to be the best opportunity until they examined the fact that she had divorced her husband three years ago, and there was no male living with them or near them. They were secluded in a small town near Salina, KS and Jake had posted to her about her current situation. She had said it stopped months before and that her mother had moved them to a safe place. They still opted for surveillance, but ruled that out as the most causal link. They then focused on Peter Johnson.

Upon examination, they found Peter's office, the Country Club, two golf clubs, several restaurants, his home and his favorite drinking establishment and meeting place for clients. With that information, they put the surveillance in motion. Miller and Grant would take a shift that night, but now they had more informational necessity.

Grant had mulled through the human resources challenge on finding ID's and employment verification. He had narrowed the five women down to three. Emily Chu was Asian and 5'1", ruled out. Tina Lassiter was African American and that ruled her out. Karma was good, but not that good. They had three suspects left. Miller had Wiler put a tail on each one of them and he had just walked in the door for a report.

Miller said, "Hey, what do we know?"

Wiler greeted her with his wide grin and warm handshake. "We know a lot. I put a tail on the three women; two are on right now. We haven't found the third yet. Two are financial managers; the third is an Import/Export Manager. She travels quite a bit, but she's in the city right now. They are staking out the one we can't find--at her work and should pick her up before the day is out. We called in and she's expected in and out of the office today, has already checked in and left. We know we have some things to look at."

"So, we are in a holding pattern?" Grant said.

"We are." Wiler moved to a seat next to Miller. "How many pictures do you think we need before we can use the facial profiling software to compare these women?"

Grant took the question. "One. Two to make sure. Do you have pictures yet?"

Wiler shook his head. "They will text me as soon as they have a full-on front of the face."

Miller helped. "It's harder than you think to get a facial picture. Most of us on stakeout can't get past the 'look too close, if they see us we are busted feeling '. But they aren't looking for us most of the time. However, she knows we are near. We have to be careful."

Miller was exhausted and yawned twice before Grant said, "Hey. We need to go get some shut-eye. If we are taking the surveillance tonight, we need to be fresh. How about we call it quits for a few hours? You look horrible."

"Thanks. You're beautiful too. You know how to flatter a girl." She laughed it off, but knew he spoke the truth. "I think we should hit the hotel. I can't keep going without some sleep."

They parted ways and headed back to the hotel. In the car, on the way, Grant laid it on the line. "I know you want this, but we have to be certain we have the right person. We have no evidence at this point that our perpetrator is even in the city, let alone one of these three women we are tailing. Let me play devil's advocate here. What reason do you have that puts either of these new hire women able to be Karma?"

She pursed her lips as she thought about the question. "I have to say that with the information presented by Karma, we have a keen sense of depth to this case. We have detailed the investigation to the five cases and their commonalities. We have Karma living in Denver, Co and making a U-Haul rental in February of this year in which she paid cash for the U-Haul and dropped it off here in Topeka, Ks. That leads us to this part of the country."

Grant weighed the information. "What if these letters are to throw you off, not help you catch her?"

Miller fell into psycho-social mode to answer this one. "Okay, so there are two things we know here. One, we have no profile analysis on a female serial killer--too few of them to analyze. Two, Karma is potentially a sociopath and we must consider that when investigating this case. She emits primary evidence of a psycho-socio pathology. Criminal profilers have worked diligently over the years to find reasoning to serial killers. What they know is that certain things remain constant in each case. They don't want to mix it up; these killers want to follow the same routine. When they follow this routine, they sate this desire, sick as it may be; they fulfill a desire. Karma's desire is not so different from any other incest survivor story. She's in a quandary. First and foremost, Grant, she is an incest survivor. My question there is how did that story play out? If I could only ask that question … There are only a few options and I'm going to say that hers was one of the hard cases. So, let's devour that information. Her father was sexually preoccupied with her, as an adolescent regressive. He was an instrumental sexual gratifier, meaning he took what he wanted sexually without consideration to another person. No care of Karma, not her mother if she existed, not other siblings … he was only interested in sexual gratification. IF Karma survived the abuse until she hit a maturity level, the abuse would have most definitely stopped. Daddy likes his LITTLE girls and the maturation process in incest brings about a power of its own. Rarely does it go into an adult situation. She got blamed for this. Somehow, someway, they end up making the child feel as though this was her fault and it does serious damage. The reason she handles these murders in this particular way is that she feels unworthy of love. This isn't going to ruin anything for her, quite the contrary. She is to blame, so she takes it in her own hands and comes out of it with a sense of satisfaction about how, when, where and why these abusers suffer. I truly believe that she incites the wives of this order merely because her mother denied her the truth."

Grant questioned that. "What do you mean denied her the truth?"

"When she told, potentially she could have been called a liar, a trouble-maker, a drama queen. The mother has a very difficult time understanding or wanting to come to terms with the fact that her absence of intimacy in this relationship caused her daughter harm. This is classic in father/daughter incest. The mother is a victim, but she is also a perpetrator. When she is faced with it, she denies the allocation, giving the father another sense of power. No one will believe the child. From there, the abuse usually increases. The second problem with this particular type of incest is that the daughter is typically in love with her father. We saw that in the blogs, correct?"

Wiley said, "I really found that interesting."

"Interesting is a good word. When the daughter is used in this way, there is an element of love. She is, for all intent and purpose, the wife of this man. She loves her father and incestuous sex only hurts the first couple of times. When a child is small, it might hurt worse, but the victim gets used to it. Only when they begin to mature and realize outside social mores do they become uncomfortable with the situation. Does that make sense?"

Both men looked at each other, but they tried to understand. Wiley took the question. "So, the sex isn't unpleasant when it's used in a loving sense?"

"Basically, you are on the right track, but it's not about the sex. The abuse is much more psychological. This kid is made to be an object of the man's affection in many ways. He lavishes her with gifts to get her silence, but it backfires, because the daughter often misinterprets it as to a love affair. When she tries to enforce the power of the relationship, then the abuse becomes cruel in every way."

Grant said, "Example?"

"Ummm ... okay, I want a new car as a 17-year-old daughter of father/daughter incest. Do I get one?"

"I get it." Grant had the epiphany necessary to understand what she was saying. "She has the power then. Without giving her the car, he is pushed to the point of blackmail? Am I right?"

"Yes. That's it. So, she has this power and abuses that power in every way. Then the anger and resentment comes because the dysfunction in the family becomes very apparent to her. She's usually socially intimate with friends at that point and finds out that this is socially wrong. She then starts a myriad of feeling associated with the filth of participating. She doesn't remember that she was not a willing participant in the beginning. This abuse goes on for years. Typically, it starts between the ages of 5 and 10. The social impact is often seen at the onset of adolescence. The man just can't seem to keep his eyes off his daughter. Instead of just molesting her, he begins having sex with her. Showing up in her room in the middle of the night. These men usually demonstrate low sexual arousal toward their victims, instead they use the source of their anger to focus on and the assault on the victim takes on a whole new life. If we knew where she came from, the type of abuse she experienced, we could talk to her."

They were completely silent as they digested the information.

Chapter 28

Randi took a cold shower and rustled up her system. It was necessary to be on her toes and alert. She fixed dinner, listened to music, relaxed on the couch to ready herself for the mental journey ahead of her. She was going into the lion's den and she needed to be prepared. Her nerves were jumpy. Every sound from outside made her jump. That would keep her alert and she needed it. She tried to meditate all noise away and become one with the universe, to disappear as a person so she could handle the situation.

She wondered how Jannie was doing. This must be hard. Never had Randi thought about what it would be like if you had a child in this situation. She remembered her mother screaming at her, telling her what a dirty little girl she was, shredding her with words about how she ruined their marriage right before she drank another bottle of vodka. It made her shudder, to the point she had to shake off the thought. She wished that Jannie had been her mother. Maybe things would have turned out differently.

The phone rang and nearly made her climb out of her own skin. It was Judy. Another four rings before it went to voicemail, but she didn't answer. She missed Judy. It had only been five days and she really missed the closeness, the smell of her hair as she slept with her ... what was wrong with her?

She immediately stood up. It was as if she broke and moved into a new personality. She paced, her anger intense. "What the fuck is wrong with you?" she screamed at the top of her lungs. "Why are you so fucked up, Carolyn? What are you thinking, you stupid, stupid, girl!" She started swinging at things that were not there. She was trying to hit things that weren't in front of her. "You shut up! I mean it. Shut your mouth!!!" Tears streamed down her cheeks before she began yelling again. "Carolyn! Carolyn, I said come here ... daddy wants to play house. Carolyn ..."

Randi began looking around, as if finding a place to hide, before she ran and hid behind the couch. She kept watching to see if anyone was coming, huddled with her legs drawn in and her arms holding her in a little safe ball, whimpering.

Chapter 29

"What do you mean no new news?" Miller paced. "I need something to go on and this feels extremely important to me ... does it to you, Sir?"

The Captain was as angry as she was. "I am well aware that you received a letter, Miller. However, need I remind you this is NOT our jurisdiction, not our state and we have no business in Kansas. NONE!!! Get your asses home. Personal days," He was furious. "Personal days my ass. Both of you get back to Austin, now. That's a direct order."

Miller was furious. She continued to listen as her blood pressure rose. There was nothing she could do until he was done chewing her ass. She waited. Tapping her foot, Grant watched in pain as well. He knew what was coming; they both knew it would come to this.

"Yes, Sir. May I make one request?" She waited for the clearance to ask. "Thank you, Sir. May we have 72 hours, just 3 more days and then I'll get my ass back to Austin and do my job like a good girl. Just like you said, Captain."

Grant could hear the Captain yell over the phone, "Don't you condescend to me, Miller! How dare you. Tell sissy pants to get his ass back here and you have three days. And, you better be in here with fresh clothing, 8 good hours of sleep and be ready to close cases. Do you hear me???"

"Yes, Sir." She hung up the phone and threw it on the bed next to her. "So much for getting any sleep, huh?"

"Not for you. I'm getting some sleep now and I'll get some more sleep on the plane ride home and then I'll go home and sleep some more before I go back to work, the bastard." Grant pulled his pillow over his face and tried to go back to sleep.

Miller was done. She'd been woken to the call from the Captain and it was bad. They were out of jurisdiction on a case that had nothing to do with Austin, or Texas for that matter, and she knew it was coming. But, she got three more days. Three more days to find out who Karma really was and to stop whatever it was she had in the works. All through her sleep, she was plagued with the letter from Karma. Change of heart ... most gruesome yet ... what did it all mean?

It didn't matter now. She had to get more work done. She left Grant in the room and headed down the hallway, ear to phone, waiting for Wiley to answer.

Ten minutes later she was in the car with Wiley, on their way to the Johnson house to watch what the family was doing. They could not interview the family and alert them to the possibility of prey, and they couldn't alert them to the fact that whether or not Karma was involved, there was the suspicion of incestuous abuse. Either way this guy was down for the count, but they had to be careful. The evidence they had was not obtained legally and it could not be used against them.

The ride to the Johnson estate was filled with explanation. Wiley couldn't believe her Captain, but she knew he was right. At least Wiley was sympathetic. It was going to be a long night of just her and him, so they stopped and got some snacks, sodas, and water before they found a place just down the street from the Johnson home.

Chapter 30

Randi snuck out from behind the couch, crawled to the door where she grabbed her backpack and slid outside. Once outside, she resumed the normalcy that she carried daily. It was as if the raging fit was gone. She jogged ten minutes down the road to where she left the van and climbed inside. Checking all the equipment, she realized it was getting dark, so she checked the batteries in her headband flashlight. She couldn't turn on lights in the house, so she would use her headset.

"Damn it!" She stomped her foot. "Wouldn't cha know?" She tossed the flashlight gear in the passenger's seat and headed out.

She stopped at a convenience store and purchased the flashlight batteries and was out in the van, replacing the bulbs when sirens started wailing. Passing her and sliding into stalls in the parking lot, three cop cars surrounded the place. She about peed herself.

Once they stopped, they got out of the car. One cop ran right up to her door, scaring the shit out of her. "Get down!"

"What?" She said.

"Get Down! We have had a report of a bomb inside the office next to the store."

"Can I leave?"

He waved her away and she was gone. The van was already started, she slipped it in drive and peeled out and headed down the street, heart pounding.

She let out a breath and tried to relax. SO, that is what it will be like if they catch me someday? She laughed to herself. That was so real. She almost wished she cared about someone enough to call and tell them what happened. But she didn't and she kept driving to her destination.

Miller and Wiley were two blocks from where they were set up to stake out the Johnson's house when a call came in on the radio. All-points bulletin for a bomb threat. Wiley was on it in a heartbeat. "Sorry, Jennifer, we gotta go."

He slapped the siren on the top of the car and hit the button and it gave her that familiar feeling of being at home. They hustled over to where the bomb threat was. They pulled into the parking lot, sirens blaring and Wiley saw a woman sitting in a van, looking down. He pulled up right beside her and shot from the car.

"Get Down!" he yelled as he neared her van.

"What?" She said.

"Get Down! We have had a report of a bomb inside the office next to the store." He focused in on the storefront they were weary of.

"Can I leave?" She squeaked out.

He waved her away and she was gone. Miller jumped from the car and they headed closer to get an update from the first officer on scene. After an hour of checking, watching the bomb squad and gathering information, they determined it was a juvenile prank.

Miller said, "Well, I guess it was as much excitement as I can handle for the night. It's not like we will happen upon Karma and arrest her in action, stop a murder and be the big hero. She probably isn't even in Topeka."

"Now, now … you gotta be optimistic. We can set up at the Johnson place and see what's going on. If nothing else, remember, we can try and stop this abuse. If we find any indication that something is going on, then we can use it against him. That little girl really said a lot. We might even get to subpoena that information in the future and get it legally; then we can use it. You're just tired."

"I'm just tired and pissed. But," she patted the bag next to her in the seat, "I have Twinkies and life can't be bad if you have Twinkies. Right?" She busted open the box and took one out for each of them.

Chapter 31

Randi had parked two blocks away, down the street, close enough that when she turned on the equipment she was within range to record. Her plan was to spend the night in the van, hoping the celebration of Jannie's non-threatening award would spur Pete to put the moves on his kid. She would record it and then they could go from there. She worked as she thought, placing bugs all around the house, especially in the little girl's room.

Amanda's room was neat as could be with posters of Justin Bieber and Twilight all over. She was really into ballet, a frail little thing by the looks of the pictures in her room. A beautiful girl, she looked just like Jannie. For one brief second Randi wondered what it would be like for the three of them to steal all his money and run away. For one brief second, she thought of living her life as her own self. What would that be like? It had been years, since she was 17, since she had heard her own name, except for the flashbacks she could not control. They were few and far between now and not like they were when she was in college, under an assumed name. People just thought she was crazy and they were right. She was a loose cannon. If it hadn't been for the tennis coach, she would have killed herself. But, Noreen Werner saved her life. She hated her from that moment forward and used that anger as her fuel to win the college tennis circuit three years in a row. Noreen was now dead.

There was a sound outside and Randi froze in her tracks. She went to the window and watched, listened. Nothing. Just the wind. It had spooked her though. She moved a little faster after that. It was easy to install the cameras and the audio equipment. Every picture had an eye now. Every corner of the room had audio surveillance and even the ceiling fan above the bed looked down on the possibility of catching this man in the act.

Randi left Amanda's room and for kicks, went into the master bath and planted an eye in the shower. She wondered how Jannie looked when she was naked. What a pervert, she thought to herself. She had marked the garage, the kitchen, Amanda's bathroom, and the living room. Really those were the only places she thought Pete would try anything with Amanda. She then moved to the kitchen and was almost ready to exit the back door, as planned, when she heard a noise again. This time it was right outside the window.

She peeled back, hid behind the island counter and watched. A flashlight beam traveled the back yard. She could see it work its way to the house. Some guy was reaching above the back door, looked like he was trying to find a key. Without luck, he ended up putting something on top of the glass door. IF she had to guess, it was a surveillance camera.

"Shit!" she whispered. If it were a camera, it would be on at this point and someone would be manning it. She heard the ladder from against the back fence raise and hit the side of the house.

"FUCK!" she uttered. Someone was bugging them. "What the fuck? Shit, fuck, damn ... how am I going to get out of here?"

She got on her belly and slid backward to a door just adjacent to the kitchen. It was a utility room. Once inside, she could breathe for a moment and think. No windows, no other door, but she knew the garage was on the opposite side of the wall. Two pieces of sheetrock and some insulation attached to 2x4s were between her and freedom. Randi felt for the studs, knocking softly against the wall. This was the only way out and she had to figure out how to get through this wall and to the garage, to a car and have Jannie drive her out under the carriage. She moved the washer and dryer carefully, quietly and sat down between them.

"Holy Shit!" she breathed in deeply. Turning her body to face the wall, she kicked her boot against it as quietly as possible. It gave some. She put her boot higher up on the wall and jammed her feet against it without making any noise. She could not get caught. Not right now. She had no explanation for any of this. Using the Mucinex was not working to its fullest potential. She didn't want to leave any DNA. She had geltex everywhere that she could get it, but there was always the inevitable piece of sweat or something that could drop on the floor. Speaking of, she was starting to pour sweat. She had to hurry.

One more kick and the wall gave way, on the one side. A hole big enough that if she broke through the other, she could wiggle into the garage. Through one side, she cleared away the debris carefully and quickly, putting it back into the wall and into her backpack. She placed her boots on the other side and kicked again. This side broke through, but it was a much larger hole and would be noticeable. She was thinking while she was acting. She slid the washer and dryer back in to place as much as she could get it and still give herself room to crawl through the hole. Maybe no one would notice that they were two feet away from the wall? You never knew what people could overlook. However, once inside the garage, insulation and drywall in her bag, the hole there was much larger than she even expected. With her headlamp, she scanned the room. There were three more cars, one a Range Rover. That was her car of choice, but she had to fix the hole in the wall first. She scanned again and there it was.

Against the opposite wall was a piece of plywood with a target on it. Who knew what it was for, but she ran and grabbed it and laid it against the hole in the wall. If she could have made the mirrored match more closely, she would have been surprised. It looked as if it moved directly from one side of the room to the other. She was running out of time and her DNA was at risk of being left behind. It was nothing to figure out where the spare keys were to the vehicles, but she couldn't take the car. As much as she was beginning to panic and she wanted to be out of there, she couldn't.

What could she do?

Chapter 32

Wiley was on his fourth bottle of water when Miller had to comment. "Are you serious? Have you ever been on a stakeout before?" She laughed.

"Actually, no. Why?"

"You will have to go pee. You keep drinking water. Where you gonna go?" She eyed him seriously. "Ever think about that?"

"Actually, no ..." he laughed with her. "I did not think of that. I guess I will just have to hold it, won't I?"

"Oh, Lord. Anyway ... so, what's your story? How did you get into homicide?" She decided against making fun of him. He was a nice guy and she was enjoying herself. She was close and she knew it. Something was going to give. She just knew it.

Wiley wiggled in his seat. "I always wanted to catch criminals. My dad is a cop. He's a traffic cop, but same as. I thought he was the coolest guy growing up and still do. You?"

"Well, I don't really know. I was born with the desire to look at dead bodies and then solve the equation. It's just what I was meant to do."

"Why did she pick you?"

Wow. That was a low blow. She had already said that she was an incest survivor. Maybe he forgot? She was trying to defer the question and head a different direction when she saw a flashlight beam in the Johnson's back yard.

"HEY!!!" she pulled down in the seat. "Ten o'clock, flashlight beam in the back yard." She whispered.

"I see it. Is it one of ours?"

Miller was confused. She hadn't scheduled anything, had he? "I didn't do it. Did you?"

"Shit. No. I didn't do it. We gotta go get 'em. You think it's her?"

They opened the door and climbed out of the car. "I'll call for back up. Don't do anything stupid. You take the east side, I'll go west. Be careful, Miller."

They headed out in opposite sides of the estate. She could see down the street. The sky here was amazing. It was lit up enough that you could see where you were going as if it had a little nightlight. Crystal clear, the sky led her on her way. She scaled the fence and slipped down in to the yard, hoping there were no dogs. From her vantage point, she could see a guy by the back door; he put something up and then walked toward her. She scrambled behind a trellis of roses and wanted to scream when she grabbed thorns, but she was quiet. He was so close when he reached down and grabbed the ladder. He took it, flexed it out like he hadn't a care in the world and leaned it up against the upper window where he stuck something there too.

She was too scared to talk to Wiley on the system, so she just watched. He finished that and moved it to one other window and stuck something on it too. A heavy-set guy, he didn't look like a cop, but he seemed to know what he was doing. Once he finished the second window, he put the ladder back and escaped through the back fence where she followed.

The backup unit was waiting for him on the other side of the fence and had him face-down, in cuffs before she got out of the yard. They had him in the back of a car and on his way downtown before anyone broke a nail. It was their job to go down and question him; it was Wiley's case now. And, she looked forward to it. They headed back to the car through the yard two doors down and got to watch the Johnson's pull into their garage.

The Johnson's car slowed at the drive and pulled in as the door climbed up, the light flipping on in the first unit of the garage. Pete pulled the car in, parked and got out and went into the house. Not a word spoken between them until Jannie spoke to Amanda.

"Sweetie, grab your bag for me. We don't want to be looking for it in the morning when it's time to go to school."

There was no answer. They moved inside the house.

Chapter 33

Randi's hands barely held her in place as she pulled herself up to the side of the Range Rover. It was the last car in the garage, farthest away from the open space. When the garage door started to open, she pulled herself up by the windowsill of the car and put her feet on the front, passenger side tire. She couldn't let anyone see her. The family moved into the house without incident and it seemed no one noticed the movement of the plywood target. She breathed a small sigh of relief before she made her call to Jannie. Help would be on the way soon.

Randi dialed the phone and waited for her to answer.

"This is Janine Johnson; may I help you?"

"Jannie, its Randi, don't say a word. Just listen to me." She waited for a second, Jannie said nothing, so she continued. "I need you to come down to the garage, drive the Range Rover out and get me out of here. I'll explain on the way out. You had more company than just me tonight. Delete this call and my number from your phone. I'll see you in a few minutes. Hurry."

Randi hung up and waited. It wasn't five minutes before Jannie was out and fired up the Range Rover, unlocking the doors; Randi climbed in on the floor of the backseat.

"Go. Get me out of here, but don't get a ticket or we are busted. About five blocks from here, pull over and let me get off the floor and I'll fill you in."

Jannie drove. After a few moments, she pulled over and spoke. "What is going on? Are you okay? My heart is pounding."

"It's okay. Something happened though. You have cameras on your glass doors in the kitchen and on two windows upstairs. I think they are on the master bedroom and Amanda's room. I don't know what' going on, but I tried not to get caught by his cameras. Some fat guy in black planted them. I snuck out the utility room, put a hole in your wall." She winced.

Jannie laughed, "You what?"

"I put a hole in your wall to get out without being seen. The washer and dryer now sit a few feet off the wall instead of directly against the wall and I moved that plywood target in the garage to the opposite wall to cover the huge hole I kicked in to get out." It was funny and I laughed too. Now that I could breathe again, it was funny.

She laughed with more gusto than I had ever seen from her, even when we won the tennis tourney. Passion was present now.

"Okay, so you got our stuff planted?"

"Yeah. Drop me off at that white van you passed a block or two back, better yet, I'll go on foot. Crazy. Who do you think could have planted on you?"

She wrinkled up her nose ... "I don't know, but watch me go home and find out. I know how to do this. He's always called me hawk-eye. I must be losing my touch, because I didn't notice the target moved. Usually I can pick up anything amiss in the house. Tonight, I knew you had been in, so I wasn't looking for anything. I will find the one on the window upstairs. We had a nice dinner, Randi. It was weird. It's like I could read their minds and I was in complete control. It was the greatest feeling. I have no remorse putting him away for life, if he's touching my daughter. How long do you think it will take to get something?"

Randi was caught up in the excitement too. "I don't know, but I'll let you know as soon as I have something solid. I'll turn it over to the police once I do, then they won't have to look at you for evidence tampering. It makes it much smoother in transition from us to the police." She thought about it. "If he's like most assholes, he will have some sort of resentment at you for making him go to dinner and celebrating your own victory and he will take it out on Amanda tonight. Let's pray it's as easy as that. I don't know how many nights I can stay awake and work during the day. We will just have to have faith."

"How will we keep in touch, Randi? Sometimes I'm scared." She was truly being sincere.

Before it was clear to me, it was out of my mouth … "If we get something, we can run away to a tropical island, just you and me and Amanda, where no one else can hurt us."

"You mean for a vacation?" Jannie didn't get it and Randi could back out of it easily, and she did.

"Yes. Let the drama float past while we are sunning on a beach. What could be better? Something to look forward to."

"I could use a vacation …" She drifted off into her own thoughts. It proved to me how little I knew about her.

"All right. The plan is still in action for tonight. Don't fuck up. Someone is watching you. Any reason to believe the cops are after you?"

"The police? What in the world for? We are pillars of the community. There's nothing …" it hit her like a ton of bricks. She looked me in the eye with a newfound truth. "Oh, God … Who could it be?" She started to cry.

"Oh, shit. C'mon, Jannie. It's not the end of the world. Rarely do the cops come looking for you. They usually just break in and take you. It's something else. Who is it? Think. Think about it. Does your husband think you are having an affair?"

That hit the spot.

"Does he?" I asked.

"He said something about this weekend. It was weird how he kept asking if you were a dyke. If I really went with a woman and questioned why I was in such a good mood. He has begged me to stay in this marriage. If I divorce him, he loses everything. Our money is my family money. He had nothing when we met and we have a prenuptial agreement. The only way I lose anything is the clause that says if I cheat then he gets half. That might be it?"

"That's it." I literally took the first deep breath since the guy showed up at the door. "Okay ... plan as usual. You need to go get whatever you said you needed and get home. Business as usual. Call me from the school tomorrow morning. No contact any other time unless you use a pay phone. If you need help, call the police. Okay? Jannie, you got that?"

"I got it. Okay. I got it."

I got out of the Rover and ran to the van. Jannie pulled off in the opposite direction. As I ran, I saw something very interesting, a woman and man walking back to the car parked on the block adjacent to my van. It was the same man, the cop that told me to leave the parking lot at the convenience store. What the fuck? And then she saw the woman and froze in her tracks; hand on the door of the van.

Randi yanked the van door open as calmly as one can yank something and got in. They had not seen her; they were deep in conversation. Her mind raced ... Did she lie down on the floor and hope they passed, or start the engine and draw attention? That was the decision of the hour. The wrong decision would land her in jail, for life ... Jennifer Miller had found her? She did not have time to applaud her future captor. She started the engine and pulled the van away, backing into the drive next to her and pulled out.

Chapter 34

Miller and Wiley walked back to the patrol car after collaring the man who was in the Johnson's yard. Headed back to the station to interview the trespasser, they were on their way back to the car, when they heard an engine start and the same van that had been at the convenience store parking lot bomb scare pulled out and drove away. They were less than a block away from their car.

Miller questioned it first, "What's that van doing on this block, in this neighborhood? You think it was someone with the dude we just collared?"

"I bet it is. No sense in a carpet cleaner being on the street at this hour. Shit. I'll call it in. Get the tags!"

She started running as hard as she could to get close enough as the van pulled into an alley and ditched her. She got nothing. Huffing and puffing when Wiley pulled up, she climbed in the car and they headed in the same direction.

"You get it?" He asked.

She shook her head no. "Damn it. It was a woman though."

They headed down to the police station in silence, letting it all sink in. Right before they got there, Miller said, "I never thought she had a partner. It never crossed my mind. Might make sense. We have to re-evaluate everything."

Wiler was ready to interview and held the optimism. "I can get sap out of a stone. We have a Kansas way of doing things, let me work my magic on this guy. If I don't get anything, you can try the Texas-Technique I've always heard of." He grinned.

"What technique is that?"

He laughed, "You beat the shit out of him and I'll cover for you."

They both roared with laughter. The whole day's stress let loose on one lousy joke. They laughed for a full two minutes before pulling into the precinct. And there is where the magic happened.

Chapter 35

Officer Greg Blane pulled up next to the white panel van with the business logo: Randall's Carpet Cleaning and Fire Restoration. He called it in immediately.

"Officer 1218. Please advise. White panel van with Randall's Carpet Cleaning and Fire Restoration located at 29th and Hill. Need backup. Noted--approach with caution. Please advise. Over." His heart was pounding in his chest, his gun drawn as he stood beside his car, the door shielding his body.

"Dispatch to 1218. Be advised to wait for units responding. Reply?"

"10-4. I have the van in sight." He waited.

Within a few moments, he heard the sirens of the approaching backup units. Soon they sped to the location and screeched to a halt, officers flying out of the three cars that came in response.

One officer moved forward screaming, "Come out of the vehicle with your hands in the air. Acknowledge."

They all waited.

He yelled again as he approached the vehicle, "Come out of the vehicle with your hands in the air!!"

Another officer threw open the door to find no one inside. The officers combed the van with gloves on, seeking evidence when the original officer found the handwritten note from Karma:

> *Dear Detective Jennifer Miller:*
> *I am very impressed. It caused me a moment of excitement to see you walking the street near the Johnson home. I did not give you enough credit. That was good police work. However, I am not here any longer and will be gone before you get this. Please use the surveillance equipment in this van to monitor the progression of abuse in this family. Janine Johnson is not involved in the incestuous relationship between her husband, Peter Johnson and her daughter, 14-year-old Amanda. I was here to take care of this situation, but Jannie will take care of it. Whomever it was who put up the cameras on the two upper-*

level bedrooms and the kitchen sliding doors is not with me and blew this gig for me, believe me, he will pay.

It will behoove you to continue to chase me, but you will never get this close again. I must have let my guard down, but thanks to Jannie's willingness to disclose the abuse, my job here is done. Please prosecute this bastard.

Again, accolades to you, my friend ... great job.

Until we meet again,
Karma

Chapter 36

Miller was getting tired. This guy kept saying the same thing; over and over, the same ole story. Peter Johnson hired him to keep tabs on his wife, because he thought she was having an affair. She threw her hands in the air just as there was a knock on the glass and they were called out of the room.

Outside the interrogation room Miller was given handwritten note in an evidence bag. She read it through the plastic.

"Are you fucking kidding me?" She wanted to beat a hole in the wall, smash the glass on the two-way, thunder into the room and kill the guy sitting there who caused her to lose her suspect. "She was right here … I was that close to her, Wiler." She looked to him for support.

"What does it say?"

She handed it to him. After reading, he too was upset. "I can't believe it. That was her? I stood three feet from her." He rolled his eyes and felt that he let Miller down. What could they do?

Miller was ahead of him. "She has to get out of town. We need and APB. Where is your Captain?"

Wiler said, "It's the middle of the night? He's at home in bed. What do you wanna do?"

"I wanna catch her! Shut down all the exits out of here. Put checkpoints on all the interstates. How long has she been gone? How much time has she had? How far can she be? Where are the major airports, minor airports?"

"I got it." He moved into the other room as she stood by, incredibly remorseful of the mistake she made not chasing the van. Wait, how did Karma know who she was? Karma knew what she looked like, who she was. "She's been gone for four hours. She could have flown out anywhere." Patrolmen and investigators had crowded around. "Excuse me, please." She exited the room and found a corner that was private and dialed Grant's number.

He didn't answer, probably on the plane. She was completely

discouraged. Even though the Johnson family had been spared, it was a horrible feeling to have been that close to her and not to have even known it. Not once, tonight, but twice, Karma had slipped through Miller's fingers and the brunt of that sunk in hard.

Five minutes of alone time, pacing, planning, calculating, and she was off to find Wiler. He was in the interrogation room again with Jimmy 'the blob' Pate, the PI who was planting cameras for Pete Johnson. They had him on nothing.

Through the rooms filter, she listened outside while Wiler filled the blob in on the fact that they had nothing on him and he was free to go. He also told Jimmy that we preferred that he keep this to himself, however, we all knew what would happen so it was of no use.

Within a few minutes, Wiler escorted the blob out of the room and he was free to tell the Pete Johnson what had happened. They let him get out of earshot before they consolidated their thoughts and calculated the last bit of information until they had a plan of action and they headed out to the Johnson's house.

Chapter 37

The cabin floor creaked with my weight as I finished unloading the last of the cases from the trunk of the car and deposited them on the floor beside the bed. If only I had more time, I could have told Jannie to meet me and she could have made her escape as well. Now they would never catch Pete Johnson. Damn, Miller!

My fingers nimbly flipped the silver latches on the black leather case and I was ready to assume my new identity. This one was the emergency I had hoped I would never have to assume, but it was time.

First, I took all the information in the green case, all documents, clothing, any item I felt would be evidentiary and carried it out to the fire pit in the yard. Once inside again, I gathered wigs, geltex, razors, scissors and cosmetics ... anything I had touched or used to prepare my disguise and put it in the pot on the stove full of water and turned on the burner. Once boiled, I would bleach it to remove any DNA that might remain. As the flame started to lick the bottom of the pan, I headed outside to start the fire in the pit.

The deed to the land and the cabin was safely stored in the floor safe inside and I took a minute to breathe. My exit plans always included creating a male identity and an escape nearby. Most people would try and run, but that put the police at an advantage. She had purchased an old, beat up truck and had rented a garage. That's where she put her car and traded for the truck. By the time they found the storage unit and had uncovered my Miranda Blanche information, I would assume the life of Bradley Glassman, Fish and Game Commission Officer.

The Kansas sky blinked as the fire surrounded the documents and information that needed to be destroyed. I watched it; the thrill of the chase coursing through my veins. I needed to relax and become Bradley. Through the course of the next two hours, I took the ashes and scattered them in the lake, finished boiling the mechanisms used, poured the bleach on them and then rinsed them off four times. Now I could settle in to Bradley.

It was more difficult for me to become male. Not only did I have to shave again, but I had to complete the painful process of Botox injections. With technology what it was, facial profiling allowed the police to generate random samples of my location via camera. Everyone had cameras now-a-days. It used to piss me off, but now it was just another game to beat them at. I took the injections and in the mirror found all points of interest and marked them with brand new eyeliner. If I were careful and marked just to the side of the actual injection target, I could increase the size of my jaw line, my cheekbones would become fuller and my lips and eyebrow line thicker.

It hurt like hell, but the mirror reflected the difference. Immediately my facial features took on a new distinction. I cleaned up the area and packed everything back in the silver case. After I gathered all documents and ID cards, complete with blank driver's license and government ID card, I sat down in front of the micro-camera and got ready to snap my picture. Two outfits later and feeding it to the new laptop I had purchased, I had my IDs ready to mold the pictures and laminate. I laid the blue case with the silver case, phase two complete.

Now all I had to do was destroy everything left from my past life and lie down, get some rest and prepare for the next day as Bradley

Glassman. If I said his name in my head enough, I could become Bradley Glassman. I was so tired. The excitement of the night had me exhausted. It was always the same situation, once I was out of imminent danger, I would sleep for twelve to fifteen hours and make the bad world go away. My new world had a lot to offer me and all I had to do was hide the red case, filled with over $730,000 long enough figure out what I needed and then mail it, with my other necessary property to my next targeted home.

Everything else must be destroyed within the hour, including cell phone cases. I had broken down the phones, destroyed the GPS systems and left them smashed on the front seat of the car in the garage. The last black case, the Bradley case, was all I needed to convince someone I had been living life as usual for the last eight days. All I needed right now was a good week of testosterone shots to make my voice deeper, grow some shadowy facial hair and roughen up my appearance. Receipts, forged bills of sale and other items had to be scattered throughout the house so that if someone came in while I was sleeping, the first thing they noticed was nothing out of the ordinary. Although it pained me, the place looked like a bachelor lived here.

Finishing up the disposal process, it was almost ten o'clock in the morning and I needed sleep. I was ready to lie down and take the weight of the situation off my shoulders. Jennifer Miller was definitely a worthy adversary.

Chapter 38

Miller and Grant walked to their desks and fell into their chairs. The night had taken an early turn when they were called out to a triple homicide. With the investigation heating up, they had a long day ahead of them. Pages of information were coming through the fax machine and Jake was already on the forensics. They had met with the ME and were ready to see an autopsy report so that they could match ballistics to the gun they found nearly a block away. It was business as usual.

For Miller, the pangs of Kansas still struck a chord. Everything reminded her that Karma was out there and her latest neuroticism was that Karma was just around the corner, watching her. She had never felt this kind of over-the-shoulder hesitation. Grant had empathized with her, but essentially, she had to wake up and realize that everything regarding Karma had disappeared. They found out Miranda Blanche was a fake name. The real Miranda Blanche was on European tour with a symphony orchestra. Like the other situations in all five cases, Karma had assumed the identity of someone who was traveling overseas for an extended period. She paid their bills, made sure nothing would point to her negatively and lived their lives in America while they gallivanted across Europe or Asia. Miller credited Karma for such a sense of detail. They found her house, spotless and lived-in, yet no evidence that she had lived there. At night, lying in bed wide awake, Miller would wonder how hard it was to clean a house with bleach that thoroughly that investigators could not find one hair, one piece of clothing, nothing to implicate a real identity. It amazed her. She was beginning to move from frustration to admiration and that was a dangerous place to be. Miller would never rest until Karma was behind bars, waiting for a lethal injection. She hated Karma and would not allow herself to think about the one thing they shared.

Grant said it again, "Jennifer ..."

She finally came out of the deep thought. "Yeah?"

"Damn, thought you were sleep walking again." He handed her the latest fax, showing the test results.

"Just as we thought." She handed it back to him and moved her files so that she could neatly arrange them. "I think we ought to canvas Trinidad Ave. through 65th street and then comb the business district to see if we can get a gun sale."

"I agree. And, we need someone to check into the car. There should be record of that car being in the neighborhood before. If we find the answers, we find the killer."

She agreed with him and they went back to work. Something between them had strengthened in their stay in Kansas. They didn't talk about it much unless someone alerted them to new movement in the case and that agreement was the safest bet for success for Miller. Karma won. Plain and simple, Karma had won.

By three the next afternoon, they had nearly solved the case and were in the interrogation room with two separate suspects. Grant had one in room 2 and Miller had the other in room 6. They were deep in, asking all the right questions, needling the former convicts, drilling home the depth of the situation for each one respectively. Miller was moving the suspect to speak when the knock came on the glass divider.

She slammed her fist down on the metal table, causing the suspect to jump before she exited the room. Outside, she met the Captain.

"Yeah? Something come up?"

He was hard to read, never showing emotion unless he was yelling at someone. But he looked different.

"What's up, Captain?"

Hands in his pockets, jingling some change, he took a second before he spoke. "I need to have you look at something."

"Sure." Miller thought it was something to do with the line of questioning she was throwing at the suspect inside. But, she was wrong.

He led her to his office and moved behind his desk, motioning for her to sit down, which she did. He spoke softly, "We have a lead in the serial case from Kansas."

"What? What happened? Where is it?"

"Slow down, Turbo. She's contacted you again."

Miller's mind flipped a switch and she forgot about the guy in room 6. "What is it? What's wrong?"

Captain Martin chose his words, "I think this is to the point of unhealthy, but I know what you are going to want to do. With that, I'll give you the letter." He pulled open the drawer and withdrew an envelope. "It was delivered about ten minutes ago. It's from her."

Miller pulled gloves out of her pocket, snapped them in place, took the letter and held it. Her pulse raced. This one was handwritten again. The postmark was from Sweden. Carefully tearing off the left side of the envelope, she slipped the two pages from inside and unfolded them to read.

Dear Jennifer:

I can call you, Jennifer, right? It's been awhile since our last meeting and I just wanted to check in. You shouldn't have any new information other than what my past lives have been about. The trail should have come up extremely empty. For that, I'm sorry. You have been on my mind constantly, a much worthier adversary than I first thought. I love it. I'm really settling in to my new life, one you will not approve of, but, in all fairness, it's not for you to say. Maybe I miss our Kat-N-Mouse, maybe I'm just bored, we both know I'm sick, so that's a moot point, but I just wanted to heat up the chase. Janine Johnson will get a phone call from me today when I finish writing this and I'm going to ask her to run away with me. Amanda shouldn't have to testify at the trial and I changed my mind, I don't want her to go through

what we went through anymore. She's
safe now ... She has me. So, follow the
trail. I'll even leave one for you to find.
All the best,
Karma

"She's crazy," Miller mumbled. "She's really crazy." She looked up and Captain Martin was watching her every move. "She's bored, Captain. Because she's bored, she's going to leave a trail for me to follow. What should I do?"

He took a deep breath and laid his head against the back of his chair. "You're a fine detective, Miller and I want to encourage you to let the FBI handle this, like I should all cases out of our jurisdiction. But ..." He let the word hang in the air, "we all know she wants you to be the one who finds her and without you, they cannot capitalize on the mistakes she makes. I think you should partner with the Feds and bring her in."

Miller sucked in air. She had not anticipated his support in this case, ever. He wasn't made like that. "Why?"

"You question me?" He eyed her and then softened. "I had a case like this. Back in the day, I was in California working the Zodiac Killer. It wasn't my case, not in my area, but there was something about it that got my blood boiling and so I researched as much as I could. I always wondered what I could have done with it if I would have just had all the information at hand. You are hers by choice. She needs brought in and we have a great team here. We solve crimes, that's what we do and your head is so far up your ass from this case that I can't see you ever getting anything done until you bring her in. I called for a transfer to replace you while you are gone, and when you're done, I expect you back here, fulltime, without distraction."

She was jumping all over the place in her mind.

He continued, "Bag that evidence and get some rest before you show up at the Feds office making us look bad." He stood up and offered his hand. "Good luck and Godspeed, Jennifer. We will miss you while you're gone."

Jennifer was speechless, but her mind intact, as always, "Don't go getting all weepy on me, Captain. I'll be back." She pumped his hand wishing she could give him a hug, but didn't have time. She was out the door, evidence in hand, to find Grant and tell him what happened.

Chapter 39

Jennifer Miller sat in complete silence after having been escorted to an off-the-main-hall room. She could see everyone walking by, talking and going about their business, but she could hear nothing. The Department of Justice building, housing the FBI was immense, nothing like her home unit. The ambiance was luxurious and plush, versus what she was used to, concrete and cold. Half of the lights were burnt out in the station room, but here, the light was brilliant. As she was rifling through the rooms she could see, looking at all the factors that she was not privy to, when Agent Reynolds walked into the room. Encompassed by glass, Miller had missed the door behind her, and as Reynolds entered, was a bit startled.

Reynolds said, "Oh, sorry. Didn't mean to spook you. I asked them to bring you here, because it's sound proof and you wouldn't be bothered. It sounds like you've had quite a stressful situation lately?"

Miller stood and offered her hand, "Officer Jennifer Miller, Austin

Homicide."

They shook hands as Reynolds sized her up. It was a good minute before she spoke, saying, "Agent Melinda Reynolds, FBI special victim's unit. You are much different than I interpreted from your file." She was a beautiful Latino woman, tall and lanky with gorgeous, long, straight black hair and soft brown eyes with the longest eyelashes. She pursed her lips, again sizing Miller up. "I think we will get along famously. You?"

Miller hesitated as she did her own measurement: athletic, stylish, clean, aggressive ... as much as she could see, "We will get along fine."

"Great." Reynolds headed for the front corridor, opening the door and ushering Miller into the rush of traffic and the buzz of agents working various cases. "You can call me Mellie. All my friend's do. It's easier and I like the intimacy ... I'm not as girlie as I look and I can tell you, the first impression you get of me is usually wrong. So, I'll let you reserve judgment." She spoke over her shoulder as she led the way to the elevator. Once at the doors, she pushed the button and they both stared ahead.

Up the elevator to the next floor and down the hall half-way, they walked in silence. Miller watched Mellie carry herself with grace and distinction. Everyone they passed said something to her. She was polite and kind, seemed to be liked by everyone. That was not the case with Miller in Austin. She had stepped on many feet solving cases, although she was highly regarded, no one spoke to her in this manner. Not only did she feel like she could learn from Mellie's FBI training and recognition, but maybe she would finally learn some people skills. She almost laughed at the thought of Grant's chiding so many times about how she really needed to get out more and get a life.

Reynolds opened the door to a lavish office with two executive desks, more computer equipment than they would ever use and walls full of crosses and religious garb. Quite taken aback, Miller didn't have time to think any further.

Reynolds jumped right in, "So, this is where we will work when we are at home base. You don't have a problem sharing, do you?"

Miller shook her head and seated at the desk across from Reynolds, facing each other.

"I've read everything in the files and all documented evidence. Maybe I'm presumptuous, but I have a few theories I'd like to blow past you. First and foremost, we have certain malignant in discrepancies. I need resolution. Where were you when you got the first letter?"

Miller thought about it. "In my precinct. Just doing my job. You know, daily routine."

"Why you?"

"I think it's because I'm an incest survivor. We finally put all the pieces together and that is the one thing that remains constant. It wasn't right out in the open, but I did enough research and found it all. We have six women accused of crimes they did not commit. I'm working to get each one a new trial and find the answers ... Right now, the letter I got yesterday, gives us a new trail. She made a phone call to Janine Johnson. It was three days ago ... which would put her somewhere in the vicinity of a four-state radius from Topeka, KS. I talked to Janine and she was also questioned by Officer Wiler in Topeka."

"What did she say the call was about?" Mellie pulled Fiddle Faddle out of her desk drawer and started nibbling on it, offering it to Miller as well, who declined.

"She didn't want Amanda to have to go through what she went

through … she wanted Janine to take all of her money, quit her job and leave, and go AWOL in order to keep the girl safe from the abuse of testifying."

"She's not leaving, is she?"

"No. She wants to put the bastard away and has already been in counseling with the girl. Johnson believes her daughter can do this. It's all out in the open and she feels that the kid has enough support …"

"Do you?"

"Yes. However, I think she's still a possible target for Karma."

"I think you're right. I also think Karma is nearby."

"Here?"

"No. I don't think she left the area she claimed for killing." Mellie tossed the rest of the piece of Fiddle Faddle she was eating in her mouth.

A chill ran down Miller's spine. "What? How? Surely, she wouldn't stay still. We were on her. I saw her. I know what she looks like."

"No, you don't. You know what she wanted you to know. If she thought you were a threat, she would have never sent you this letter. You fell from the chase and she's heating it up again. She made a call. Did you trace it?"

"They are working on it. I asked that it be sent here."

"We don't have it yet. I'll check on that." She made a note in a booklet. "I also want to know more about the incest. The real key is why she chose you."

'I don't know ... "

"Trust me on this." Mellie smiled at her. "This is my specialty. Crimes of passion, crimes of distinction, special victims and sexual assaults. I know Karma. She's given you more information than she should have if she doesn't want caught." She got up and moved to a wipe-erase board, popped the top off a marker and started writing. She literally outlined almost everything Miller and Grant knew about the case in one, neat and uniform outline.

She turned from the board to address Miller again, "Anything I've left out?"

Miller saw everything from the moment she got the first letter; the deviant murders, down to the city and exact location and time; the alias; the mode of murder; the victim's daughter's names; the IP addresses that Karma used to prey upon them and more. Mellie had articulated more data and factual information in this neat outline than Miller could remember in the entire time she had spent on the case. Stunned, she didn't know what to say.

"I know. It's a gift. I try and use it to my benefit instead of playing the gambling game I started out with … that's how I ended up FBI." She laughed and sat back down at her desk, this time facing the wipe board. "I got caught and they offered me a job in exchange for my charges. How could I say no?" She spun around facing Miller.

Miller had no idea how to handle this woman. What could they do to team up? How would they best work together? How could they catch Karma?

Reynolds watched her intently. She knew nothing more than she had read in the extensive, yet lacking, file that had been brought to her when they had given her the case. This woman was smart, but not brilliant. She was trained, but no specialty. It was as if her instincts guided her in everything and with that, she solved cases.

"I guess you couldn't." Miller didn't know what to say.

"I didn't. But, what skills I have are very rustic. I use my head. They trained me, but I didn't fare well in the training. I always wanted to argue. BUT …" She smiled a wicked grin, "I did know enough to listen and learn."

"I have questions about this …"

"Me or this case?"

"The case. I trust you. They said you were the best and I believe them. I did my research too." Miller couldn't help but smile.

"What are the questions? I'll give you my best." She kicked back and listened.

"First, why me? Even if I am a survivor of incest, why me? Secondly, IF you think she's in the area, why? Why stay so close to the only thing we know?"

Reynolds waited to make sure that she was done before she answered. "First, because you are someone she can LET catch her. She told you straight up, she needs to be caught or she won't stop. This is a sickness for her. I can guarantee you that her IQ is above 150, genius. She's brilliant and she's skilled. Education and articulation, that's what her pattern shows me. She only wants you to catch her, because she can't make herself stop. What must it be like continuing to prey? What's it like to always look over your shoulder. AND ... the way she uses the other criminal fingerprints, she must be out of her element. I can't figure out how she's doing it, but gloves or stockings or whatever she's using can't be comfortable. She literally thinks of everything. Not one mistake on any of these crimes, because she plants what she wants us to find. Only in retrospect have we gone back and found even these things. They were right there under everyone's noses and she let it go. She knew that we wouldn't look for it, because it clouded cut-and-dry cases. She counted on our laziness and she was right. If you survived what she did ... then you can feel her pain and you'll go easy on her. If she lets you catch her, then she still scores one for the team. Easy. Secondly ..." She drew more Fiddle Faddle out of the box and began nibbling through her dialogue. "I have to have this ... sugar and protein makes my brain work better. Ha. Anyway, secondly, why leave the area? We had it cut off. We blocked airports, train stations, bus stations, and the interstate. We knew how to block her. Why bother? If she had it set up, an escape route, which I think she did, absolutely knew exactly where she was going, all she had to do was disappear. Since she's taken on other people's lives, I would assume she's done the same thing now ..." The phone rang and she picked it up and punched line 1. "Reynolds."

She waited for the person on the other end and then said, "I'll be right there."

She grabbed the box of Fiddle Faddle as she was getting up. "You coming? They got the trace. We are flying out right now ..."

"What?" Miller's heart rate increased and she quickly climbed to standing. "Where are we going?"

With a little laugh, "Topeka, Kansas ... To-To."

Chapter 40

The heat was nearly unbearable as they opened the airplane door and exited the jet. The heat sucked Miller's air out of her lungs. It was clearly different than the mugginess of Houston and the dry heat blew on her face as they entered the airstrip limo waiting for them.

Miller could see herself in the limo glass. Her hair had frizzed out and she was sweating already. Reynolds, however, looked like she just walked off the runway. Everything in place, makeup impeccable and her hair perfect; Miller was actually jealous. Beauty was always an advantage, but Reynolds passed beautiful and was truly gorgeous.

Mellie spoke, "You okay? It's hot."

"Yeah. I'm more used to this, but who can tolerate 112 degree any place? I'm allergic to sweating."

She laughed again, "Really? I would have thought you were truly athletic and loved to sweat … you know, when the time is right."

"I am athletic." Miller found that amusing.

"Really? What sports? I'm an avid tennis player and used to play pro volleyball. That's how I got into gambling. God, I love the thrill of winning."

Miller still had no clue who this woman was. She was so down to earth, but everything Miller had researched said that she gave 150% to her job and nothing else. "I like volleyball, but preferred softball and golf. Tennis is okay, but I tend to hit homeruns ... you know, over the fence. Not a lot of control in my swing. Softball is more a power sport and I like that more."

"I see. I see you as more graceful. Volleyball ... we should play sometime."

"I know a set-up when I see one. I'm not playing volleyball with you ... ever!" She liked Reynolds.

They got a kick out of the conversation that ensued, mostly about their college days and sports. How men viewed them and what they needed in a relationship that they could never find and how the job prevented real intimacy.

They arrived at their destination and Wiler was waiting for them. He had a huge grin on his face, but Miller knew the look he gave Reynolds when she exited the car. Never again would he see Miller in the same light. From that moment on, she knew that Reynolds overshadowed everything in the room, the moment she walked in, where men were concerned. But, she was here to do a job and who could be a better partner than this woman she was beginning to really like?

Chapter 41

I settled in on the porch, the sweltering heat causing the testosterone to burn in my veins. Control was burnt into my psyche by Daddy and yet this rage that built up with the hormone was almost too much to handle. I spoke aloud, "How do guys handle this? No wonder they are assholes ..." It had been days since I had called Janine and I relied upon my instincts to tell me when it was time to go, and it was time to go. I was like a moth to flame; it was time to go.

Sixteen minutes later I was walking out the door and out of this hell hole I had come to hate. The truck was packed, my money sent forward and I had to make the $100,000 I had kept out work in my favor. Miller should be in Kansas or at least talking to her team here. It would be exciting to get near her again ... wouldn't it be funny if I asked her out on a date? The daydreams kept coming of what it would be like to spend any actual length of time with her, talking to her, dancing with her, drinking with her and loosening up, just the two of them with none of this between them.

I chuckled at my sick brain as the rain started pouring in the open window of the truck. Popping my head out just enough to see, I realized a storm had blown in and it was a bad one. In Kansas, the weather could change in ten minutes, drop thirty degrees and get very ugly and it had just happened. The black clouds had broken and I had driven right into it without really paying attention. The highway was almost unseen; the rain was that hard. My heart raced as I fought to see where I was going and then it happened. Out of nowhere another truck crossed the yellow line and headed straight for me.

I screamed!!! It hit me, thrown about; the crashing sound so loud I was deafened; searing pain shot through my body and then my world went black.

Stormont Vail Hospital emergency room was hopping. People were rushing about with the disastrous storm that had just hit. Three ambulance were pulling in at the same time and the Life Flight helicopter had just landed. Shannon Denison heaved the empty gurney out of the way to make room for the Life Flight victim to be brought in.

On the roof, the helicopter landed and the two EMT lifted the patient to the gurney with the backboard. Jason Crable screamed orders through the rotating helicopter rutters and moved as quickly as possible. This patient had little chance of making it. "Grab the bag. I left it sitting on the bench." He pointed to his medical bag and Mike Ray grabbed it and tossed it on top of the patient as they ran inside the building, pushing the patient in front of them.

Once inside, the elevator took them down to the ER where the staff was prepared for what they were bringing. A trail of blood dripped to the floor when 'Brad's' arm fell free from the fastening and they pushed her in to the room that Shannon had prepared. She took over the moment they were in the room.

"Just leave this gurney, we don't have time to change it. Throw another bag of blood up and filter the IV into the channel there." She pointed.

They responded. Three nurses and a physician's assistant worked to get new vitals and to hook Randi up to the monitors. Shannon grabbed a pair of scissors as she started to cut off the clothing Randi was wearing, tattered and torn, leaving blood-soaked pieces lying on the floor, belting out orders as she tried to save this young man's life when she realized what she was dealing with. The last cut revealed that 'Brad' was not 'Brad', but a woman. "What the hell?"

Jason and Mike were witness and just as devastated. The facial hair made it hard to believe, but the female organ did not.

"Transvestite?" Mike asked.

"Doesn't matter, let's get to work ..." Shannon went back to her first love, saving lives.

Two-hours-and-twenty-minutes later, Shannon took her first break outside the room of 'Brad'. She was exhausted. The treatment had stabilized her patient, but the outlook was still grim. Dr. Athminis had brilliantly worked a miracle when this young woman coded and jumped her heart back on track. The blood loss had been minimized and all the cuts sewn up. Shannon pushed the button on the coffee machine and it was spilling black liquid into the cup as Dan Timmons walked up.

"Dr. Timmons ... coffee?" She asked politely.

"No. I'm good. Great job in there. You okay?" He was a sandy-blonde with an attitude, athletic and just plain fine in Shannon's book, but married. She always kept her distance. He was a player and she had no room for a lascivious affair at work.

"I'm okay. I just dropped off the package at the desk and headed here. What do you think is going on?" She sat down in the break room with Dan to discuss what had been bugging her the whole time. The more they worked, the more they found strange with this young 'man'.

"I think that the police should be notified. I had Barnes call ahead so they could see for themselves. Probably on their way now." He leaned back in the chair, stretching and yawning.

"What do you think that covering on her feet and hands were?" Shannon was very interested in finding out about 'Brad'. They had pulled off a gel-like covering and had bagged it in case there was a need.

He pursed his lips, "I don't know, but it was so durable. Nothing like anything I've ever seen and the levels of testosterone were excruciatingly high. It's a wonder she wasn't in a blind rage at all times; enough to kill a horse."

"I will fill the police in if they come. You go get some sleep, it's going to be a long night. The tornado must have hit just outside of town. I heard we got a call from general and they are rerouting all ambulance here; they're full." She sighed and knew it was going to be hell. No going home any time soon and her shift ended at 3 PM.

"Thanks ... I am beat. Let me know when the next one comes in. Turner is on the floor?" He stood to go.

"Yeah. He got here a little bit ago. We're good. I'll come and get you if we need you." She laid her head down on the table when he left. Last night's night on the town was catching up with her. One little bit of rest and she would go back out for the next victim ...

"Excuse me ..." Wiler spoke to the sleeping nurse. "Shannon Denisen?" He touched her shoulder and she bolted upright.

"What? Where ... Oh ..." Shannon flipped until she realized where she was. "I'm sorry. Can I help you?" She rubbed her eyes and stretched, looking at the clock. It was 8:15 PM.

"I'm Officer Wiler from Topeka PD and this is Detective Jennifer Miller and Agent Melinda Reynolds. May we speak to you a moment?" He was kind and low-key and killing Miller the whole time.

Jennifer wanted to scream "where is she?" She looked around the ER wanting to know which room so she could go cuff her. She was sure it was Karma. She was positive they had the break the needed. When the report came in about the she-man with gel coverings on her feet and hands with finger and toe prints they knew it was Karma. Wiler had heard the call come in from dispatch and in the middle of their informational meeting had jumped up and headed for the door, yelling behind him. She loved his passion. They were out the door and three minutes later at Stormont Vail. Now she was waiting again.

"Sure." Shannon was now awake. "Brad Glassman is what the identification she was carrying in her wallet says and if she weren't so bruised, I bet she would look just like the picture."

"It's a fake ID. I called for a fax to come in with the correct ID picture. Is there somewhere we can set up camp? I want to be here when she wakes up." Wiler did all the talking, charming his way into anything.

"Sure. We have the fax over there ... you can stay in here if you like."

Miller couldn't wait, "Actually, we would like to see your patient, please."

Reynolds stood beside her, just as antsy. This could be the break they needed to close this case. They were moments away from the truth.

"Sure. Follow me. Room 21. Right this way." Shannon led them to the room Bradley Glassman occupied.

Once inside the curtained door, machines buzzing and whirring and beeping, Jennifer got her first good look at Karma and she knew it. The bruised face, multiple stitches and the fractured arm, she didn't look too bad for what they said had happened to her. Miller immediately cuffed her to the bed.

Shannon spoke up, "Officer …"

Reynolds stepped in, "It's Detective … Detective Miller … and we are holding this patient for questioning and will be beside you with every move. We believe that this may be the perpetrator in a serial murder spree …" Even though she spoke softly and clearly, the nurse's registration of information clearly spooked her.

"I see." Shannon looked at the she/he lying in the bed and

wondered what kind of life he really led. "She's going to be transferred up to ICU for observation, there was some minute bleeding near her brain from one of the bruises. We will monitor her for at least three days. A bed should be ready soon."

Wiler was cuffing the gurney to the wall. Shannon looked at him funny as well.

Wiler, in his defense, said, "You don't know what we are dealing with here. When she comes to ... it's going to get really crazy."

Shannon realized the breadth of the situation. "I can take care of that. We administered a sedative, let me go request a larger dose so that we can keep her calm. I'll be right back." She excused herself long enough to get doctor's approval.

Reynolds moved like lighting, reaching in her briefcase and pulling fingerprint sheets and ink. "Hurry, I need her prints before they protest and I need them this second. Jen, help me, the more perfect they are the better. Hold the sheet." She inked the blotter and rolled each finger and thumb over the paper and as she was finishing Shannon walked back in the door.

"What are you doing?" She knew it was a violation of hospital policy, but she was honestly scared. The FBI was nothing to mess with.

"We took fingerprints. I'll let Miller explain while I send these off." She and Wiler exited the room leaving Jennifer and Shannon.

Shannon pushed the medication into the IV and deposited the needle in its disposal tank and turned to Miller. "And ..." She'd seen pushy cops before, but if this was something that could put her or the staff in jeopardy, she wanted to know about it.

Miller started out slowly, not allowing her passion to scare this nurse. They needed her and the staff on their side. "Well, we have been following this case for months. Linking it to six homicides and another attempted right here in Kansas." Her southern drawl very apparent as she had become extremely fatigued in the heat, Miller continued. "We have reason to believe this is our murderer. She is cunning, ruthless and a sociopath, therefore at high level risk to anyone around her. We are checking the ID for Bradley Glassman, but I would assume there is foul play. Is there a way we can seclude her and our staff is offering a 24/7 security plate? We will watch her 'round the clock."

"Sure. I'll check with admin. You'll have to wait a few minutes. But, I think I can get everything Okayed." Shannon left the room.

Miller pulled up a chair and sat beside Karma. She stared at the features, the bit of stubble on the cheeks and chin ... a man? She was right, Miller didn't approve. How ingenious. This woman was willing to do anything. When they arrived, the first thing they received was the gel-like coverings of hands and feet and immediately Karma fell in to place. Wiler and Reynolds were now issuing orders to find more information and they would, she just knew it.

Watching the bruised and battered body fight, Miller became very remorseful. What if she died? Would they ever hear the whole story? Could they piece it together enough to really make a sound case? Was this woman Karma? And, who was 'Karma'? She gently took the hand of the woman before her and held it as she whispered, "Hey, it's Detective Miller ... I'm here. It's okay. Don't worry about anything, just get better. Can you hear me ...?"

Miller watched the machines as she spoke for any indication that she might be getting through to the woman, but nothing changed at all. Her vitals had stabilized some, but she was still in grave danger. So,

Miller just sat beside the bed in the cold, lit room and listened to the rattle of the machines and the hustle and bustle outside the room, waiting for Wiler and Reynolds to get back with more information.

Miller watched and waited for another half hour before Melinda entered the room. "How are you doing?"

Miller glanced up at her, as she pulled a chair up on the opposite side of the bed. "How is she doing?" Mellie sounded sincerely concerned.

"No change. They did more tests, we're just awaiting the return. The doctor is supposed to be in shortly." Miller was exhausted.

"You doin' okay?"

"Yeah. I'm just tired. This is always how I feel when we collar someone." She lied.

Reynolds let that statement marinate before she spoke softly. "I'm not buying that one. BUT ... the doctor will be in and they said they would be moving her to a room. I arranged a corner room on the psychiatric ward if possible. The extent of her injuries will tell whether we go with ICU or the Garden of Eden." She eyed Miller for a response, but got none. No argument, no resistance.

Doctor Timmons entered the room and excused himself to the side of the bed. "Excuse me, please." He checked the monitors and then addressed both women. "Well, she has no internal bleeding, however, she has three broken ribs and multiple contusions. She lost a lot of blood, but seems to be responding with the immediate care. There is minimal bleeding on the brain, but having her sedated will only delay my diagnosis. I'm going to let her come out of sedation. Right now, the plan is to get her to a room in ICU so that she can be fully monitored."

Reynolds started to say something, but he hushed her. "I am making the decisions right now. She's not a flight risk. She is possibly comatose and we need to find out the extent of the injuries before we can fully treat her. I know you want her in tip-top shape prior to arrest. And, what are you going to do with the press outside?"

Miller responded first, "Where are they and how many? Do they know we are here?"

"They don't seem to. They are just interested in a statement as to the extent of her injuries. The other vehicle in the accident left three deceased. She's the only survivor. I have given strict orders to negate your presence as you requested."

"Thank you," Reynolds said. "We want to make you fully aware of this situation. Just to brief you, she is a serial killer, six deaths and the wrong imprisonment of six women regarding those deaths. She's ready for a lethal injection in Federal court now. I want to make this perfectly clear as a representative of the Department of Justice, the FBI is in charge here. To ensure that she remains in custody, and she IS in custody, we will be making plans for her removal immediately upon your word that she can withstand travel. Understood?" She waited for his response. When he didn't reply immediately, she continued, "An obstruction charge will look very negative for this institution. And, with what I know, it's a good place to be. Your job will be in jeopardy, as well as a personal charge for impeding an investigation. If you would like to bow out now, be my guest."

Timmons face was beet red. Miller felt sorry for him; he was just trying to do his job. His reply was more than adequate, "Whatever you say, Agent Reynolds. Let me meet with my team."

"That's perfectly fine." She rose from the chair and moved to the farthest corner of the room.

Miller felt peace-keeping was the key, "Sir, if you just keep me abreast of the extent of her injuries and any plans that you have to make a change, I'll be more than happy to make it happen in a way that lessens any obstruction to your wishes."

"Thank you, Detective Miller." He gave Reynolds a dirty look on the way out of the room after he finished assessing his patient.

When he left, Miller lit into Reynolds, "Mellie, why did you threaten him? She can't be a flight risk. She can't move at this point."

"To answer your question honestly, she IS a flight risk. If you think she hasn't planned for something like this, you are wrong. Do NOT underestimate your competition. This woman created finger prints belonging to someone else. We now must find out where Brad Glassman is and IF he is alive, moving our body count to possibly 7 and that's just the tip of the iceberg. You must keep your cool in this and not let your emotions get the best of you, Miller. That is why she picked you, you can't collar her. Luckily, it's in the hands of the Department of Justice now and JUSTICE WILL BE SERVED."

Wiler walked in the door just in time. He handed the paper to Miller first, which pissed Mellie off. Instead of complaining or demanding, she moved behind Miller so she could see as Miller read.

"When I got this in, I went ahead and took liberty to do some more research. She is Carolyn Riley, born into one of the wealthiest families in New Hampshire. An original settler in the nation, her great-great grandfather signed the Declaration of Independence. She's from good blood. Get this ... she attended school at University of Leicester in England on an International Baccalaureate scholarship at the age of 17. Apparently, her family has always studied medicine there. She was in the medical program and finished highest in her class. She did not attend post-graduate degree programs and dropped out of the educational system at that time. She did, however, while she was at the University, date an INTERPOL Forensics specialist, Dalton Wayne, the entire time she was at University. This guy specializes in Forensic evidence attainment, contamination and reliance. He works with DNA, fingerprints, disaster victim identification and heads up an International Forensic Science Symposium. Where better to get information on how to make a crime go away? She has had medical training and forensic training for the most part. She also has availability to INTERPOL agents that are not on the up-n-up, possibly an accomplice to the crimes? Maybe they didn't even know? She never left DNA, fingerprints were attained from known, convicted criminals; she has access to anything she needs somehow. She is intriguing. I did more research ..."

"And ..." Miller and Reynolds answered at the same time.

"And, she came back to the States after school and lived at home. The next two years, she attended, oh a little college in Hanover, NH called Dartmouth, on tennis scholarship. She studied there but never declared a major. Her line of study was mostly law and criminology. And, her only other extracurricular activity was ... drum roll please ..." He waited, for affect. "Okay, okay ..." they gave him looks that got him rolling again. "She was involved in integrated martial arts, boxing and fencing. She definitely has anger issues."

Miller read into the research and asked, "Where are her parents?"

Wiler was gloating, "I'm glad you asked that question. Matthew Thornton and Margaret Riley, of which she took her mother's name, a bastard, born out of wedlock, was in a quandary you would think. However, that is not the case. She was integrated into the family wholly and fully, various articles show that she was the sole heir to the whole Thornton estate ... billons, and guess what? Dad is dead, murdered by mother ... who is in prison."

Reynolds let out a gasp, "It's her. I knew we had her."

"Now what do we do with her? Do you think her mother knows? Is she alive? What part of her sentence is she in? We need answers." Miller felt the adrenalin attacking her system. Calm wasn't an option now.

"I agree. We need answers. Let me get the agency on it." Reynolds took the paper Wiler handed her and left the room quickly.

Leaving Wiler and Miller, the first time they had been alone, Miller felt uncomfortable. Their kinship was gone from her stay in Kansas prior. The awkward silence hung for a few minutes before he broke it.

"So, how you been?"

"I'm okay. How about you?" She asked softly.

"I've put a lot of thought into this case. It haunted me until I read that fax. Now I have a calm. Carolyn Riley ... now we know who she is." He shook his head, a personal affirmation for him. "I think it will be open and close from here. We have all the evidence we need. I'll let Reynolds handle the actual collar, but I feel more at ease now."

"Really?" she asked him.

"Yeah. Don't you? She's sitting right here in front of you." He didn't understand.

"What if she dies?"

"Then we know that she won't kill anyone else. She's a serial killer and we have her." He was proud of that.

"I guess you're right. I got too close to the case. I'll let Reynolds handle it from here. My boss will be glad I'm going back to work."

"Yeah, just in time to celebrate. Stay for our Fourth of July celebration. Take a day and relax." He was hopeful.

"I dunno ..."

Reynolds entered the room again. "Well, it's official. They are going for an indictment tomorrow here in Kansas. Wiler, it's your call. The assistant DA said he would handle it all and collar her here. You good with that?"

He nodded. "Sure."

"Great, because I am going to work up all the other indictments and deliver them to your DA so that they can follow through. I think we can get this all linked together and handle it in one fail swoop. Our only problem is that Timmons wants to keep her until she is out of danger. Without his release, we have no other option than to remain here with 24-hour security. Can you get that arranged? Technically, since I called in your DA, I'm out of it. What a stroke of luck. To think she had an accident or we would have dug for needles in a haystack."

She slid into a chair and faced Miller again.

Wiler was wild with excitement. "Who's going to handle the press? What do you think they will say to a six-count, maybe more, serial killer capture?"

"I'll handle the press until I leave tomorrow, but for the most part, you need to keep things under cover until you have your ducks in a row, so to speak. This conviction will count on detailing all the evidence. Linking them together, individually casting doubt on each other, you better hope she doesn't have a great attorney. I've seen the swindlers get people off on better evidence. We need more information. Who wants to stay here and who wants to dig up more dirt?"

Wiler answered immediately, "I wanna dig with you."

Miller was fine being left with Karma ... Carolyn. She wanted to talk to her first thing upon waking. "I'm good with that."

"Great," Reynolds said, "let's get rollin'. I'll be getting calls back within the hour and we need to start the process on the other work. I need to find Brad Glassman. He's probably out of country like the others she impersonated, but if not ..."

Miller hopped in, "I'll make sure that your Captain has security. Until then, I'll stay by her side. I would hate to see her walk out on us."

Reynolds said, "Deal. We'll keep in touch, but we need phones and computers. Take care of you. I'll make sure someone relieves you by 11 PM. Let's meet at the hotel then. Downtown Ramada, right?"

Miller nodded. "See you there at eleven."

With that, Reynolds and Wiler left the room to have the newest of nurses come in. She asked a lot of questions, "So, how are we doing? Has she stirred at all?"

Miller answered each question.

"The sedative should be wearing off soon and we will see what we have. The doctor just got back the blood work, nothing out of the ordinary. They have her scheduled for a brain scan in the morning and the plan is to now move her to a private room. Can I get you anything?"

"I need to eat. Can you send something in? I'm not picky." Miller hated the thought of eating, but she knew she must.

"Sure. I'll get right on that, Officer." The nurse left her alone with Carolyn again and Miller looked at her.

It was strange to see her in this light, fully. She looked so different, the facial hair and her jaw line was different. Almost everything about her was different, Karma chameleon befit her. This was drastic. From the jaw to the five o'clock shadow to the raised eyebrows ... she really had done quite a change on herself. Miller wondered if she had plastic surgery. How did she do it? The testosterone was one thing, but the change in the shape of her face, the masculinity alone, was not covered by the hormone. Miller uncovered her hands and saw the cuts and bruising from having probably tried to protect herself in the accident. She had long, slim fingers, very clean and very well-manicured. They were completely feminine. Miller slid her hand inside Carolyn's and prayed again that she wakes from the medically induced slumber. She desperately needed to talk to her. Right now, it stared Miller in the face that they were going to possibly put this fine woman on death row.

She must have squeezed her fingers as she prayed, eyes closed, because Carolyn winced.

Vocally, Miller heard her gasp.

"I'm so sorry." She dropped Carolyn's hand gently to the position she found it. "Carolyn ..."

Carolyn's eye lids fluttered for a moment before she regained control and they flew open. Immediately Miller uncapped her gun holster and placed her right hand on the butt of her handgun.

"Carolyn, it is Jennifer Miller. You are going to be okay. You are in the hospital ... you had an accident." Miller tried to soothe her.

"What?" Carolyn looked at her body, the room surrounding her and the panic set in just as Miller guessed it would.

"It's okay ... try not to move too much." She stood up and backed away from the bed enough she wasn't in jeopardy of being grabbed as she started to push the button for the nurse. That brief second of thought, when she decided she wanted to talk to Carolyn, could have been the split second that Carolyn tried to bolt. Miller knew she better be aware and never underestimate this woman. "You are handcuffed to the bed. We have arrested you and I will Mirandize you when there is a witness available, but Carolyn ... that is your name, right? Carolyn?"

Carolyn shook her head. Admitting defeat, her mind abuzz, she knew it wasn't the right time. It was time to play Miller for all she was worth. She would talk to the detective, the only one who would ever be truly on her side ...

"That's right. It's okay! Can we talk? Are you able? Before anyone else gets back?" Miller prayed she would talk to her so that she might help Carolyn.

She nodded her head. Her lips were on fire; she needed a drink. On the side of the bed she saw a Sprite can and pointed to it, realizing that her wrist was cuffed to the bed. When Miller noticed that she saw it, she explained further, "You are cuffed to the bed and the bed is cuffed to the wall. Look, I don't know how much time I'll have alone with you, they collared you here locally. You had an accident on the highway, someone hit you. Three people were killed in the other car.

When they brought you in by Life Flight, we were already here. They found your gel-covering and discovered you were a woman. I knew it was you when I heard it come over the police radio in Wiler's car. Can you speak?"

"I don't know …" croaked out of her sore throat, but she could understand her own words. "My throat hurts bad."

"You have a big bruise on your neck, three broken ribs, a stress fracture in your left ulna and a ton of cuts and bruises. You have to hurt like hell."

"I do, but I'm okay. I'm used to pain. What do you want to know, Jennifer?" She would tell her anything she wanted to hear, because there wasn't a hotel or a police station that could hold her alive. She was already contemplating her escape. The one thought she had hope in was that she wouldn't have to kill Miller to get out. "I'll tell you anything you want to hear before you Mirandize me, before my attorney gets here, but it's between you and me. Deal?" Carolyn held her hand out to shake, cuffed to the rail of the gurney.

"Deal. Okay … six murdered men? Are there more? Brad Glassman?" Miller held her breath until she answered.

"Seven … and Brad makes eight … well, I'm not sure I killed him, but he's buried in a barn on his property, but only ashes. I had him cremated. Sorry …" Little tears came to her eyes as she spoke of Brad Glassman.

"You killed him?"

"I don't know. I sometimes lose time … I woke up in his house … he was dead, but from a coronary. I don't know. I couldn't escape the state, you had all the exits closed off, too tenuous. I hid in his shack on the lake. What else?"

"Did you kill your dad?"

She nodded her head, looking away.

"I know it's not your fault, Carolyn. Can I help you?" Miller felt her heart go out to this woman, so close to her own age, so close to her own life. "Anything?"

"Let me walk out the door …"

"I can't. I can't do that. This is my life. I love my job. It was wrong, Carolyn. I can't." Miller thought it over as quickly as she could. What if she did let her out the door, would she promise never to do it again? What if she let her slip out the ER with no one knowing, faking being asleep, and her cuff keys on her side key ring? She couldn't do it. No, she couldn't ... she was right the first time.

"I love that you thought about it. But, don't get me wrong. I didn't expect it. I just had to ask ... you know, just in case I was wrong. It's okay. I wanted you to stop me. I didn't like doing it. And, I won't stop until you kill me. I won't let ..." she leaned up, grunting as she did, toward Miller, as close as she could get, "I won't let one more girl suffer what we did, Jennifer. Not one. I can't. I killed my father and blamed my mother and it was the best feeling I had ever experienced. It took me six years of studying, miserable sot of a person, always begging to be loved, always manipulating, always defective in really caring about anyone ... just like you. I won't let it happen." She took Jen's hand and held it. "We're kindred. I knew you could think like me, because you are me."

As gently as she could, Miller laid her back down as she spoke, letting go of her hand, "We are not kindred. I took the law and protect it; you break it. You killed men who could have been rehabilitated and destroyed the lives of the whole family ..."

"Don't go getting all patriotic on me. Your family is just as destroyed as mine is, only mine got what they deserved and don't for one moment think that I don't know you thought of it a million times, slicing his throat while he was on top of you grunting and sweating, telling you how wonderful you were and making you feel like a total piece of shit. He ruined your life and he deserves to die as well and ... I'll make a bet with you. I bet I get out of here and I bet you can't stop me before I kill your father ... I bet ..." Miller was too close to her. Carolyn had tightly grabbed and swung it at Miller in one movement and caught her by the throat, wrapping it around her neck. "You won't catch me, will you?" Carolyn watched Miller choke out, barely a sound coming from her. "Don't worry, I'm not going to kill you. Just hurry and come save daddy if you want him saved."

Miller was out, but not before Carolyn had her cuff keys off her key ring and was undoing the cuff from her own arm and placing Miller's wrist in it. From there Carolyn ripped off the bandages, even the soft cast on her arm and exchanged clothes quickly with Miller.

She dressed her in the gown, put Miller in the bed and cuffed her to it; Carolyn walked out the door. Veritably not a limp or clue that she was just in a near fatal car accident. She literally walked out the door of the ER, free again.

Chapter 42

Carolyn walked out the door of the ER at the side, where no one was paying attention. The ease with which hospital staff lost observation was uncanny. When she hit the outside, the pain increased. Her adrenalin was pumping and with every heartbeat her body screamed at her, but she could see the end of the race. A car sped into the ER parking lot and a man rushed out to take his wife, clearly in labor, out the passenger door. Carolyn walked up to him and helped.

"I'm Detective Jennifer Miller, let's get you inside and I'll park your car and leave the keys at the front desk." She could barely stand, but she helped him get his wife out of the car and rope her arm over his shoulder as she screamed with the next contraction. A Nurse came to their aid with a wheelchair and Carolyn slid behind the wheel of the 2010 Mustang and drove carefully out of the parking lot.

Once she hit the street, she began to think ahead. Miller would be awake within minutes, she couldn't choke her out to a point of danger and they would be after her. Hopefully the man whose car she just stole would be too busy dealing with the birth of the child to realize that his car was gone; she was going to bank on that and keep driving. Until she knew she could exchange, she had no alternative means of transportation. She had mailed her money to her next destination, Austin, Texas and that is where she would head. She had studied maps and had legends in her mind of back roads and stopping points. Without equipment, with Miller knowing her identity and without the means to make a new ID, for the first time in her escapade, she was really on her own.

For a fleeting moment, she thought of calling Janine. She needed money and stealing money was the best way to get caught. The hardest crime to commit was stealing money. People loved their money and she couldn't chance it. Miller would be on her tail within minutes. If someone saw her leave in the mustang, she was toast.

"Think fast, Karma ... think fast." she whispered.

Chapter 43

The nurse walked into the room and noticed something wrong as Miller woke up and started belting out orders.

"GET MY PARNTERS!!!! They are in the break room, page them and get me out of this bed. I need security. We have an escape!!!" She was literally raging inside. How could she let this happen? Did she secretly want it to happen? It was so fast, Karma had her in the choke hold and there was nothing she could do. How was she going to explain this to Reynolds without losing her job? "SHIT!!!!!!!!" she screamed as Wiler and Reynolds ran into the room.

Wiler quickly boosted her from the cuffs and helped her off the bed where she was already kneeling.

Reynolds was rattling off orders into her phone. "Get the Interstate closed and call the train, bus and air patrol. Code MERICUS-- alert stage 3, FBI status. I'll call and get the authorization number and call you back. Description? I'm sending it to you as we speak. I need two minutes." She paused and then answered, "Yes, Sir. Exactly."

She hung up the phone and turned her full attention to Miller who was being checked by a nurse. Her neck was burning where the oxygen hose burnt into her flesh in the struggle. She was so embarrassed. She couldn't look Reynolds in the eye.

Reynolds caught it immediately. "Did you let her go?"

"Hell No!" She was now standing at the edge of the bed, on the floor and pushing the nurse away. "I'm fine. Please." To Reynolds, she addressed the issue. "She asked me to let her go, but there was no way. I told her that. She's very smart. She set me up and I just …"

"You were talking to her without notifying me?" Reynolds was now steaming.

"I did. I was getting ready to call you when she wrapped the oxygen cord around my neck and the next thing I knew, I was waking up to the nurse and she was gone. I saw the clock at 6:58. It's just a few minutes. She can't be far and she's on foot. She has my ID, my badge and my gun." Even as she said it, she knew she was going to get blasted for it.

"I won't say a thing, but Detective, you know protocol … "Reynolds was out of the room in a flash.

Wiler had not said a word and when he started to, Miller blew him off. "Not now!"

She flew out of the room to follow Reynolds with Wiler on her heels. They met up with her in the faux office, she was deep in a phone conversation and it wasn't one that Miller or Wiler were about to interrupt.

When she was done, she turned to the two and said, "I will take complete charge from here and don't think for one moment that I am willing to hear anything that either of you has to say. This is critical time and if we don't catch her now, there is a good chance she will beat us for good." She started pacing before she turned back around. "I don't need anything from you except to know what she said to you." She dared Miller not to tell her everything. "What did she say? Did she watch you as she choked you out?"

Miller nodded.

"What did she say to you? She told you exactly what she's going to do, didn't she?"

Miller nodded again, "She's going to kill my father."

"Oh, Shit!" Reynolds sighed and then she began making a game plan.

"Where? When? How? Those are the questions you need to answer for me. She's counting on you to lead her, isn't she?"

"She said I can't stop her from killing my father. She meant that …"

Reynolds cut her off, "That she knows you will let her kill him for what he did to you. It's what you two have in common. She's toying with you and she knows it. She wants to see if you will protect him or let him die at her hand and that you will let her walk away. Which is it Miller? What decision will you make?"

Miller was furious at the world right now, but more furious with Reynolds than anyone else. She was mocking her, baiting her to make a decision that wasn't a decision. She was ready to do battle when Wiler stepped in with his answer. "Of course, she won't let her kill her father no matter what happened. That's why she picked Jennifer. Right, Jennifer? Right?" He waited for her to answer.

"She picked me, because she knew I would feel something about what she's doing. Reynolds is right. She thinks it will be a dilemma for me as to whether to let her kill him. But, she doesn't know me well enough. I want him to live through and suffer. Killing him would be too easy. So, she misjudged me, just like I misjudged her. We are dealing with a real psychopath. She has no recourse for what she's done. Brad Glassman is dead, but she said she didn't know if she killed him. She said she lost time ... disassociate disorder. That means we don't know who all we are dealing with. His ashes are buried in his barn behind his shack or something. She said she had him cremated. Now, are we just going to stand here or are we headed to find out where she can be? We need to stall out all exits. Where is she right now?"

With that, a security officer entered the room. "We know what she's driving? A guy brought his wife in to have a baby and she told him she was Detective Miller and she would park his car after she helped him get his wife out. She's in a white Mustang, 2010, tag KS GJI 894. We have an APB out on it and sent her pic across the wire. She's all over the country already."

"Thank you." Reynolds was walking toward the door with all her things before Wiler and Miller even realized what was going on. They ran behind her.

Miller felt inadequate and essentially at a loss. She was not a burden on the team, because she still had most of the answers. She could not let her feelings factor in to how she played out this investigation. They were hot on her trail and they had the advantage of numbers. They would have her back in custody before night fell.

Chapter 44

I was now traveling in a 1982 Cordova. I felt like the trade to the gang members was the easiest thing I could do. They would melt that car down in twenty minutes and it would never appear on the street again. The chop shop was something I came upon one night at the Owl's Nest. I had one stop and then I would be headed for Austin, but not alone.

At the Owl's Nest, I pulled up and headed in the back door. Judy should have just gotten to work. Hopefully she would be glad to see me. We were kin and I had to ask for the help I needed to survive this ordeal. One thing no one knew about while I was in Topeka was Judy. The Cordova would not make it to Austin, but Judy's car would. I needed the help and needed a secure ID to travel. That Judy could get me …

There she was, I saw her stocking the bar, pouring ice into the bin. She was more beautiful than I had remembered. Missing people wasn't an option, but just that tinge of a hint of the sadness in leaving her belted me in the stomach. My body hurt so badly. Judy saw me ...

"Can I help you?"

"It's me, Judy ... Randi." I barely could stand. My legs felt like jelly and the pain was incredible.

"What?" She dropped the ice bucket on the floor and moved forward.

As she approached me, she weighed the situation. "You don't look the same ... why would you say that?" She wasn't sure what to believe.

"I promise. Just ask me anything. I'm going to ask you something really hard." There were no customers yet, except two men who were always there at that time and she had no co-workers until nine. This was a bar that started hopping at ten. "Come away with me. That's the first question and while you're freaking out on that one, I'm going to tell you what the truth is ..."

"The truth?" Judy was ready to fall to the floor. She hadn't wanted to get attached to Randi, but she was so intriguing. It was a great relationship, no bullshit, no games. It was real and she had tried so hard to just forget her and move on, but she hadn't.

She was in love with me and when I started talking, Judy listened. I easily led her to a bar stool and we both sat down. With more trouble than I liked, all banged up, I spilled my guts. "Look, I have to make this short, because the law is after me and by that, I mean death row kind of after me. I undertook a mission a few years back. The reason I was here is that my job is to find men who are fucking their daughters and I kill them, blame it on the wives and they get convicted. I then move on to the next one. I am really sick and I know it. I could put you at risk, aiding and abetting charges, but I can't get out of this state without your help. I promise, I'll answer anything you wanna know, but I have to get out of here before Detective Jennifer Miller catches me again." I looked Judy in the eye the whole time she spoke.

"Your eyes are the same. What happened to the rest of you?" She reached out and stroked one set of stitches on her face.

"I was in a car accident this afternoon. Three people were killed, but I survived somehow and they had me at the hospital. I used to cover my hands and feet with gel-tex and, well, they figured out I wasn't a guy ... I had been posing as one since my last job got botched up by the wife."

"Wait ... I can't hear anymore. I'm overwhelmed. Just tell me what you need me to do and we will do it." She kissed me softly on the lips, closing her eyes. "I love you, Randi ..."

"Carolyn Riley ... that's my real name. My friends used to call me Karma."

"I love you, Karma. What do we need to do?"

"Take all the money out of the register and the safe and let's hit the road. We don't have time to pack or plan. We just have to get out of town, back roads only. I need you to put me in the trunk or something, I can't be seen. They are looking for me. Can you do that?"

"There's over $7,000 in the safe and a couple hundred in the till. If I just take what's in the safe and write Mohamad a note, he will let me pay it back. If not, we have something worse than the po-po to worry about. I'll be right back." She rushed away to the office and was back less than five minutes later with a bag full of things and her bag. "Let's go. Put your arm over my shoulder."

I could barely reach to her shoulder, but I leaned on her the whole way to the car where she dumped me and climbed in. We sped away.

Chapter 45

Miller and Wiler were in the squad room with the other officers listening to the briefing Reynolds was just finishing up. Never had Miller seen such a change in someone as she had seen in Reynolds. Now she understood why she was such a good gambler. That woman had the straightest game face she'd ever seen. No one could read a thing with her unless she wanted them to.

The FBI was now in charge of the whole operation. No doubt about that. We were misfits and civilian cops. She was in charge and had four of the top officials backing her up from Kansas City. They had flown in just to brief the team. The window of time was gone and we had let her slip through their fingers. Unless she was sitting pretty again, they had let her slip through the road blocks and the blocked transit areas.

Miller had gotten her ass chewed three times by Reynolds, enough to know not to say a thing, just 'Yes, Ma'am' and 'No, Ma'am.' She was

to leave that evening with Reynolds to travel to her hometown of

Tacoma, Washington. Miller was going home and she hadn't even

called her mom to tell her. The challenge of this was going to be the

fact that her father was in prison, still serving his sentence after Miller

had prosecuted him when she was seventeen. Her father had been

sentenced to 100 years in prison for sexual assault, extended sexual

assault, rape, felony incest, and several counts of sexual misconduct

with a minor. He was found to not be available for parole until after

fifty years had been served. Millers' father would not be able to parole

out until he was 87 years old. This was not something she wished to

deal with, but Karma made a grand statement when she challenged

Miller to not protect her father and to let the murder happen. THAT she

could not do.

Judy was now prepared to leave. The truck she traded her brand-

new Ford Explorer for was truly not a fair trade, but it had something

they needed, a tool box with a secret compartment big enough for me

to fit in. I was bedded down with a canteen and pain killers so that I could sleep and hopefully heal on the trip to Austin. Judy pulled out of Topeka on Independence Day, just after midnight. Every time she saw a cop, and it seemed like they were swarming the highway and back roads, her heart skipped a beat and then pounded for a couple of minutes. She could talk to me from the cab if nothing was causing interference, but it was rare. Every chance she got, Judy pulled over and checked on me. I slept most of the way to OKC. The back roads bounced and rolled and banged me around, but the pain killers made it easier to handle and I slept a restless, fitful sleep until we hit the half way point.

From OKC on, I rode in the cab. It was past the point that any cop would be on the lookout for two women. We had stopped early on and I had changed into a wig that Judy had in her apartment and dressed in some of her clothing after shaving. I looked like a girl again, didn't quite sound like one, but at least I looked like one. Makeup helped and we covered the stitches in the side of my face and head as much as possible. The rest and pain pills were helping and I made sure I ate and drank plenty of juice so that I could recover. I wasn't afraid of pain or injury. My body never betrayed me. And this time would be no different.

We stopped and got something to eat in OKC. It was just near five o'clock in the morning. We ate in the car, an all-night fast food restaurant with greasy food and stale hash browns, but it fed us and we continued the journey, this time taking the Interstate. Judy had lifted a driver's license from the club, someone had left it and it was a close enough match, because I was forty pounds lighter. We had discussed my dieting and how exciting it was to feel like a new person. Hair color, height and eye color matched and we felt like I could get away with it. I was Barbara Strong. What a great name.

Chapter 46

Wiler pulled up at the hotel and headed to the lobby where he was to meet Miller. She had agreed to spend the day with him before she went back home, to Washington state. It was a task, because Reynolds all but ignored Miller now that the case had gone haywire. Any good cop knew that it was accidental; the last thing you wanted to do was let a collared criminal get one past you. Lives were at stake. Miller's fumble was going to haunt her for months, if not longer.

Ten minutes to two and there she was. Miller was dressed in shorts and a tank top, a nice casual outfit, and ready to head out. The day promised to be eventful and exciting and in good company, she would be just fine. It was a great way to end the disastrous time she had in this city.

"Well, on time is your specialty." Wiler greeted her with a huge smile. He really liked Miller and wanted her to reciprocate, but he didn't feel the slightest chance. She didn't seem the kind to get involved on the job and he respected that. They would have a good time and he would have a beautiful date. "You ready to go?"

"I sure am. Are you sure you don't want me to bring anything?" She hesitated.

"What? You gonna whip something up in the hotel kitchen?" He laughed at the thought. "Look, it's my family. There'll be so much food you won't know what to try next. We have a large family and the fourth of July picnic is our way of just letting go. There's a pig on the spit, tons of potato salad, salads, pies, cakes, desserts, green bean salads, corn on the cob, I can't even begin to tell you how many tables will be laid out in the back yard. And then, tonight, we will watch the fireworks at Lake Shawnee. It's small, but they have a helluva show, let me tell ya." He took her hand and guided her out the door.

"If you're sure?"

"I'm positive. Let's get out of here. The fun has already started. Much of a horseshoe player?"

She laughed. "No. And, I'm not playing."

"Okay, but it's YOU who is missing out."

They continued the banter to the car and for most of the ten-minute ride before Miller asked a serious question, "Do you think she's still here?"

He thought about it for a minute. "No. I think she was headed out, just had to change plans. She never contacted Johnson like she said, she didn't have plans of letting you catch her. I think she was just baiting you. If you want my honest opinion ..."

She nodded.

"I wouldn't be surprised if she wasn't in Austin, going through your personal things. She is obsessed with you. She told you to go protect your dad ... that leaves you wide open personally. How about you give it a whirl and let's talk about real police investigation."

"I think you might be right. This feeling just won't leave me. She's too interested in me and she said one thing that stuck in my mind through all this ... makes me think she has watched me before. I'm going to go to Austin. Reynolds has my dad in protective custody already. For all we know, she could have accomplices. I won't ever put anything past her again. What I had via empathy flew the coop when she nearly killed me."

"Oh, c'mon, Jennifer. IF she had wanted you dead; you'd be dead. She wants you to follow her. It's part of the game. You ever read up on the Colvert case in Utah? It was very similar ... female killer, destined to be caught by male detective ... she had him made. Used to go spy on him. Even in trial, all she wanted to do was get close to the cop. I think it's a trait with female serial-ers. They have more interest in getting caught. The more rational sex; they know the chances of getting off are not good. So, they choose their captor. She railed you, ya know?"

"I know. Don't remind me. She played me like a fiddle. A car accident and she had the strength to pull me close before I knew what was going on. She could have killed me. And she had time to redress and leave, as me ... steal a car and head right off the lot without alerting a single person. I got played so hard. She pissed me off. No mercy now."

"That's right. No mercy. She looked you in the eye and had you deciding. When you were in that mode, she walked all over you."

Jennifer punched him in the arm. "Enough with the damage blurt. I KNOW!!!" She laughed.

They pulled in to his parent's home, a lavish estate just on the outskirts of town.

"Wow ..." Miller breathed.

"I know, huh? I should have gone into the family business."

"What's that?" Jennifer was intrigued.

"Mortician ..." He got a big kick out of that. "I just want to stop them from getting there ... my dad always says that I am trying to put him out of work."

"By the looks of it, business is gooood."

Jennifer met all Wiler's family. One at a time they were introduced. She wouldn't be able to remember a single name if she tried. They welcomed her with open arms and had her playing horseshoes within the hour. She ate so much she thought she would bust. "This is the best food I have ever eaten."

Wiler laughed at her again. "I know, huh? Told ya ... they know how to throw a party. Just wait til tonight when we watch the works. It's amazing. The lake is just over there ..." He pointed to the east. "Right over that ridge. The fireworks blow right above our heads. It's my favorite holiday."

"Better than Christmas or your birthday?"

"Yeah ... put together. And with you here," he was close enough to kiss her and she wouldn't have stopped him if he tried, "it will be the best." With that, he walked away, leaving her with two of his cousins and his uncle Bill.

She watched him walk away ... if only she had the capacity for a real relationship. But, she didn't. Work was her life and that was how it was to remain.

Chapter 47

On the road again, I slept for three more hours. At that point we took back roads and added another four hours to the trip. What would have been about six-and-a-half hours turned in to over ten. Judy was exhausted and I was sore, stiff and irritable. The back roads wound us around and in Killeen we stopped and ate again, trying to stay away from the military base for safe-keeping. At around four that afternoon, we pulled in to Georgetown, Texas and grabbed a hotel room.

Inside, we fell into bed and slept for nearly 24 hours, on-and-off. When I woke up, I knew I was in dire trouble. My body was on fire and my head was roaring with pain. I could barely open my eyes.

"Judy ... Judy ..." I prodded her in my weakened state. Barely able to reach over to her. Finally, she stirred.

"What, baby?" She opened her eyes and moved toward me to snuggle when she felt my skin. "Oh No. You have a fever." She climbed on her knees in the bed and felt my forehead. "You must have an infection. I need to get you to a doctor." She jumped from the bed and began dressing.

"No. No doctor. Here's what I want you to do." I rolled over and made a list for her on motel paper, very plain, very simple.

She read. "Okay, I got it. Let me find an address. Here or do you want me to drive away from the city? Either way. I don't want to risk anything."

She understood I wanted her to take a sample of my urine in a baggie and use it in the sample cup at the minor emergency clinic. I told her to tell them she had pain in her head and abdomen. If they wanted to do X-rays or other tests, she was to leave and try another clinic, saving urine, just in case. Then tell them to call the script in to the local mom-and-pop pharmacy

"Baby ... why? Why a mom-n-pop pharmacy?" She looked up from the phonebook where she was writing down the address.

"Because they don't keep computerized records. Most are local and serve local clients that they have known for years. The clinic here will be fine. No one would suspect we were this far out of Austin; it's a needle in a haystack trying to find us." I could barely keep my head up.

"Okay, I've got it. Will you be okay? We don't have a cell phone or anything. Why is that again?" She was trying hard to understand.

I was getting bored with the game, but I knew she meant well. "Because cell phones have tracking devices, GPS and I don't want anyone knowing where we are. And, most retail stores have cameras now, so when you buy a cell phone, they have your face on file. There are pay phones, but who do we need to contact, baby? We have no family or friends to give a crap. Go. I don't know how long I can last without being hospitalized if you don't get me some antibiotics."

"Let me get your pee. Can you get to the bathroom?" She helped me and it was laborious, but we had urine in a plastic cup covered with a lid of sorts and she headed out the door. I fell asleep before she was out the door and didn't wake back up until she returned almost three hours later.

"Cari … baby." Judy smelled the smell of death when she walked back into the room and had to stand back and watch Carolyn's chest to see if she was breathing. She whispered, "I'm back. Look what I've got." Judy held up a script for penicillin. She could not see any sign of life. She poked her, "Oh, God, wake up, Sugar. Don 't leave me here alone."

Finally, I stirred, but was so weak that I couldn't take the medicine.

"Shit. This isn't going to work." Judy was rifling through options. "Carolyn ... wake up." I had passed out again. "Wake up ... please, wake up. Don't die on me." She was shaking me, but I was unresponsive. "I know you won't like it, but dead or in jail, what's the difference? I'm too selfish to let you die. Please forgive me ..." Judy dialed 911. She was hoping the ID that she had given to Carolyn, Barbara Strong, would work for her and she was going to tell them that Carolyn was Judy McCallister. Little did Miss Carolyn Riley know, but Judy was from less than an hour away from where they were now. Need to know basis was all they had ever functioned by and it had never come up, even when they were traveling, because she was so sick they hadn't really spoken much other than to fill each other in on the headway to Austin. Judy's insurance would cover the ER visit and hospitalization if need be. Risky, yes. Necessary, double yes.

Judy waited for dispatch to answer, "Yes. I just found this lady in our motel, Motel Heaven on Elm and 14th street, room 5. She seems pretty sick. You might wanna send someone out."

Judy hung up the phone before they could ask her any questions, carefully changing her voice enough that a tape recording wouldn't directly associate them.

With all my strength, I held my head up long enough to beg her not to do what she was doing, but it didn't matter. I passed out again, swallowed by a black abyss. This was not part of the plan ...

Jennifer sat her groceries down on the table as she put her keys in her pocket and checked her gun again. She could feel Karma in Texas. Wiler was right. They had a great night of fireworks and fun, but in the back of her mind there was always a distant and remote memory of Carolyn Riley and a thought of where she might be.

The day had spun out of control with the investigation, so much information, so close and so grounded by the escape. She checked in with Mellie and informed her of the plan. It was amazing, but Mellie had said that she was under the same impression. Although she chose to stay at home base and have Jennifer's father moved to another facility under FBI care only; it did serve their purpose to continue in the investigation. They had relayed by phone and E-mail all day looking for answers.

The team had checked every interstate camera out of Kansas in a four-state area to find nothing. As the videos came in, Jennifer watched them all. She couldn't find anyone even resembling Carolyn. After hours of checking bus stations, airports and public transportation, they came up with nothing. They had found the Mustang abandoned and Carolyn's prints all over it. She was getting sloppy or she didn't care. They ran her criminal record through with the prints to find nothing. She had classified INTERPOL clearance which was a challenge Reynolds would face. Why had they given her clearance when she only dated an agent?

Miller's challenge was to figure out where Karma was going and how she was going to get there. With 48 hours passing, Miller felt compelled to go a different route. Karma had won that round and she would have gloated, given the chance. Something was wrong and Miller was going to figure out what it was. She picked up her phone and dialed 411.

"Stormont Vail Regional Hospital, Topeka, Ks. Please." She waited for the number, wrote it down and then dialed. She started to prepare a salad while she waited for an answer.

"Yes. Is Dr. Timmons working in the ER this evening?" She licked the dressing off her hand as she finished mixing it, fresh.

"I'll check. One moment please." The voice on the other end was gone.

She cut her salad, watching her windows, feeling as if she were being watched. The hair on the back of her neck stood straight up.

The woman came back on the line. "I'll transfer you now."

The next voice was that of Dr. Timmons. "Hello. Dr. Timmons."

"Timmons, this is Detective Jennifer Miller, Austin Homicide. I was in the ER ..."

He cut her off. "I know who you are. Is there anything I can help you with?" He sounded sincere.

"Yes. With the extent of injuries that Carolyn Riley had leaving the ER when she did, what do you think she's going through at this point?" She waited, baited breath. Still compelled to watch out her windows, she took her salad to the table and got pen and paper to write.

She took notes as Timmons spoke. "Well, she was banged up pretty good. With the pain, she's going to need something to reduce it or be completely paralyzed by it. If she really is mentally deficient, she might fare better, but still. She was badly bruised. I'd say she's laid up somewhere, healing. There is the problem of infection. She had over 200 stitches and with that kind of trauma, the worst part is that she might get a bacterial or Staph infection. I would say that she is not in a good place."

"What about traveling? Do you think it would make it worse?"

"Definitely. The vehicle will bounce her around no matter how near or far. I'd say she was pretty much in a position that travel would be a mistake."

"Do you think she could compensate on her own?"

He thought about it a minute, "Not likely, Detective. No matter how depraved she is, there is a point that her body will override her mind. At that point, you would have a hospital visit or death ... depending on the severity of the trauma. I am more worried about that fact that she might have injuries we had not yet discovered ..."

Chapter 48

The hospital was nearby and Judy had followed the ambulance by sitting outside the hotel and watching where they went, tailing, driving near enough to see, but far enough to go unnoticed.

She sat in the car for almost an hour before she saw the ambulance leave for the hospital, and then made her way inside to the reception desk in the ER.

A nurse in pink scrubs with Mickey Mouse on them asked Judy, "May I help you?"

Judy was so nervous, her hands were sweating, and her heart was pounding and for a second the thought, 'well, if I have a heart attack, at least I'm in the right place ...' before she spoke. "Yes. My friend, Judy McCallister might have been brought in by ambulance from the Motel Heaven?" She bit back a sob, so emotional and so afraid.

"Let me check ..." She got on the phone and called back to the ER itself. "Is there a Judy McCallister back with you? Came in by ambulance?" she listened. "Okay, thank you." She hung up and turned back to Judy. "Room 15. I'll just buzz you down through those doors."

It was that simple. She was headed down the hallway through two large doors and could see room 15 just ahead, when two police officers walked out of the room. Quickly Judy dodged into room 11, where she was met with a young lady puking over the side of the bed, who was, at best, very surprised.

Judy excused herself, "Sorry, I think I have the wrong room. I'm so lost." She played it up the best she could while trying to keep tabs on the cops that had left Carolyn's room. She made small talk until she saw the cops leave and she darted out the door. Afraid she was going to be arrested, or better yet, jailed for life in aiding and abetting a felon or whatever it was she was doing ... She walked down the hall. No matter what, she was going to check on Carolyn, because she loved her and no one had loved her like Carolyn since she was a young girl.

Inside room 15, she was mortified at the number of machines that Carolyn was hooked up to. She looked terrible, but she was awake.

I saw Judy walk in and spoke to her as soon as I saw her. "Play it cool. No one knows. I'm Judy and you are Barbara?"

Judy nodded.

"Say nothing in here ..." I pointed to the audio and the camera above. I covered what I could of my face.

"Are you okay?" She was genuinely concerned.

"Yes. They put me on an IV. I was really dehydrated. Do you have a purse or bag with you?"

Judy grabbed her bag from over her shoulder. "This one."

"Give it to me. I'm going to unhook myself and I'm going to have you grab as many fluid bags as you can out of the cabinet there ... it's not locked, I saw her leave it open. Put them in your bag." I pulled the IV out right after I shut off the machine. It would take them a few seconds before they would notice if we were lucky. "Okay, got them? Put this one in." I stood up and grabbed the IV stand and started pulling it beside me as I leaned on Judy's shoulder. "Walk with me. This will work."

I grabbed the nurses call button and pushed it. Within a minute a nurse came on and asked if she could help me. "Is it okay if my friend walks me to the restroom? I really have to go?"

"Sure. I'll have someone come right down and get you."

"No. I'm an EMT and I already have the stand and we can do it, if you don't mind."

"That's fine. The doctor will be back within thirty minutes."

"Thanks." I said into the intercom as we jetted out the door.

In the restroom, I changed back into my clothing. They had taken off my shirt and hooked me up to an EKG machine. I ripped off the electrodes and stuck them on the cold tile wall. I hung the gown on the back of the door and kissed Judy. "I'm okay. Got some good drugs in me. You have that penicillin still?"

She nodded.

"Good, because I have a big, bad ass infection on the side of my head and that, with the dehydration, is what 's kicking my ass. Let's get out of here." I jammed the IV saline bag in her bag after blocking it off and took everything I needed to use it when we left.

Once again, I walked right out of the ER on my own.

The truck was just outside and we headed to it as quickly as possible without drawing attention to ourselves. Once inside, she took off. This time I was in more control.

"Okay, Judy ... we have to make up for a couple of things. First, the parking lot has cameras everywhere. They saw you and they saw me. If alerted in any way, they know what we are driving now. Second, they have all your information ... which makes you a definite accessory and this is what I'd like to do ..."

She was driving fast, but in control as she listened to me talk. I loved watching her, graceful and carefree. She spoke, "I have a better plan."

I was taken aback. A better plan? Who left her in charge? I was sure I was still alive. I started to object when she spoke.

"I have a place for us to go." She glanced over to see my anger. "Don't throw an attitude with me, Bonnie ... If I am Clyde, then let me use things that I can to help us. My family lives an hour from here. Where I grew up. We need a vehicle. I can make a call and trade out. It might get us on the road and lost in Austin. I think that's what you want, isn't it?"

"I do." I shut up and listened. Having no idea, it was a shock.

"Okay. Well, since I sort of 'checked in' to the hospital, I think we should play it out. I'll hide you in an old family cabin on the property and get you well, while I visit my family. I already called them and told them I was a little sick and needed to just hang out a while. They are used to me quitting my life and just showing up." She laughed. "They hate that about me. Nothing out of the ordinary."

"Well, I hate to admit it. But that's a great plan. And I'll leave when I can and let you get out from underneath this wrath." I was impressed, once again. "Good plan, Judy. Good plan."

"Yeah? I was thinking about cutting myself in the places that you have cuts and letting you stitch me up, but that seems a little harsh. I'm allergic to pain."

"Not a bad idea. We need to stop at a pharmacy or store and buy some superglue and some butterfly stitching. I'll superglue some stitches on you. If your family asks, what would you tell them?"

"Bar fight ... won't be the first. The only thing is, what if someone puts us together and I get arrested. What should I say? It's hard to say I'm not a part of you. Can we work out a good lie? I don't really wanna go to jail, Randi ... I mean Carolyn. God, that's so hard ..."

"I'm sorry. And, yes, we can work out something for you to stick to." I saw a store up ahead. "Stop at that store and let me keep thinking. Then we'll stop back by the hotel and from there head out."

"I already packed us. Everything is in the back of the truck. We're on our way now. Wouldn't 't it be bad for us to show back up, in case someone called the police or something since you went missing? I mean, they did pick you up at the hotel?"

"No. You're right. Okay ... cool."

Chapter 49

After peeking at the clock, Jennifer realized she had been up all night long. Her kitchen table was littered with notes on possible options of escape for Karma. There were so many options, but there was only one reality. She kicked back in the chair, stretching and yawning. It would be time to check in with Mellie at nine and she was ready to hear about her father. It took some emotional restraint, but she felt as if this strange man needed to be safe and if she looked at it like that, she would be okay with being near her father again. Mellie had decided to move him to Texas, home turf would be a better venue. Her father would be delivered to the Federal Corrections Institution in Bastrop, TX, thirty miles south of Austin this afternoon. She was ready to live with him closer in proximity.

Promptly at nine o'clock the phone rang and Mellie filled her in on the move, how it was to play out and who would be involved. The only question she had was how could they let Karma know, bait her, so that she would head this way? They decided to wait for contact from Karma.

Miller went about her day and continued to play out the scenarios. At this point she was instructed to go back to work in Austin, business as usual. It would be difficult, but she could do it. She made the phone call to her Captain and was headed back in to work the next day. For the moment, her only worry should be resting up enough to start working tomorrow.

A day of nothing to do ... that left her with a dilemma. She wasn't used to having time for anything other than work. It was a true desire to go for a hike or something outside, but the heat was grueling and she didn't feel like being zapped of energy. She needed to be on her toes, but the level of insanity with this case was eating her alive. Through her head, she continued to locate things to do to keep her busy, while she showered. One of the seemingly impossible things for Jennifer to do was have idle time. She didn't have a pet, she had few friends and work was her constant drive. Once she decided, she felt secure and positive about it. She decided to sleep and then go out for lunch at a great diner she loved about fifteen minutes outside the city. It was just the ticket for her. A nice drive; a quiet calm with great food.

As she tucked herself in to her sheets, and looked to fall asleep, she went over the menu in her head. It was an easy choice, she would have the hot beef sandwich smothered in brown gravy with mashed potatoes and corn. It lulled her to sleep, a soft and steady slumber. She was exhausted.

Chapter 50

Judy snuck out of the house and headed out to the back forty with a pocket stuffed full of food. They had stopped and purchased the groceries and things so that Carolyn could fake her stitches, but she wanted Carolyn to have a home cooked meal if possible. She brought biscuits, bacon and cheese to make her a small sandwich. She couldn't wait to see her, worry overcame her in the night.

After they had gotten to the cabin, Carolyn hooked her IV back up and Judy had stayed until she got through one more bag. The difference in Carolyn was immense. Her color came back and her attitude was great. They kissed for a little bit and then Judy broke away to go see her family.

The table had been set with the fine china, food prepared, stories ready to be told and Judy's welcome was magnificent. Why she didn't come home more often, she didn't know. They made her feel so welcome. Her mother's concern for her face was a little over the top, but if the wounds had been real, it might have made a difference to Judy. She kept everything covered as much as possible and told the whopping lie of the bar fight that made her leave her job. They had agreed that she would stick to the story, even though the story could be uncovered at the Owl's Nest.

Judy snuck up the porch stairs and carefully lifted the old iron knob on the door and let herself in. Carolyn was sleeping soundly, so she crept to the bed and laid down with her. Little memory of the food in her pocket. She softly kissed Carolyn's cheek as she snored softly beside Judy. For twenty minutes, she stayed in the same place, just soaking it all in. The long trip down, the horrible news of Carolyn's real life and the accident were more than unsettling. It was the first time that Judy really thought about what was going on. This woman was a murderer and yet, the softness, the time spent with her told Judy anything but that. She was intelligent, charming, caring and compassionate. How could she be a serial killer? A sociopath as she had told Judy she was? How could Carolyn Riley be anything but the sweet woman she met at the Owl's Nest?

Through minutes of letting this all sink in, Judy started to wonder if she had made a mistake. For the first time, she really felt the breadth of her relationship to Carolyn. Could this all be a lie? Most people told a lie to look better. This must be the truth. What would it mean for Judy? Aiding and Abetting was a crime. Could Judy let her walk out the door and never expect to see her again? Would her family be in as much trouble? What if they all got caught and the family suffered as well?

Panic hit her like a tidal wave washing over her. She had to sit up to take any kind of breath. She was hyperventilating, but it wasn't something she could control. One time, when she was twenty-one, she had had a massive attack like this and she passed out. The fear increased and she started to feel her fingers and toes curl up. She couldn't breathe!!! Her life was over! What if she had to go to jail? What if Carolyn killed her and her family???

I awoke to feeling Judy next to me, but it wasn't a pleasant feeling. When I opened my eyes, I found her unable to breath. Her eyes were huge as if she had just experienced a huge torment. I grabbed her by the shoulders and pulled her closer so I could look in her eyes.

"Are you panicking?" I asked.

She nodded her head, fast and furious. She was gasping for air.

"Here …" I moved to the table as quickly as I could and poured all the bread out of the bag and ran back to the bed and held the bag for her. "Breath in this … you're hyperventilating. It's okay. I have you." I cooed to her as I held the bag and she got a couple of breaths in. "That's right. Just slow it all down. Just concentrate on my voice, feel how it soothes you … I'm right here. It's okay. Are we okay? Someone come to the house?" I was starting to wonder what her panic was about. "Are we safe?"

Judy nodded her head, grabbing the bag on her own and getting some good air. She took the bag away for a minute, "I'm okay. Everything's fine …"

I moved behind her and rubbed her shoulders. Trying to calm her as much as possible, I just rubbed softly and steadily. "I used to get these all the time. Awful little buggers, huh?" I tried to laugh a little.

She smiled a half-assed attempt at a smile, nodding her head.

"Okay … let's take it away and give it a go." I moved the bag where she could see it. She seemed a little calmer.

Deep breaths, she took a couple and then got up from the bed and stretched out her arms and legs. "Whew!" She said. "That was crazy. Sorry."

"Are you okay?" I asked.

"I am. Just got a little excited about the fact that I could go to jail." She smiled crookedly. "Not my favorite thought. But, it passed, see, I can say it now and not panic."

I felt horribly guilty. Never had I intended for anyone to run with me. My plans had always been to roll solo to prevent this. Relationships ended before I contacted the family, because I didn't want anyone caught up in my crap.

"I'm so sorry, baby." I rolled my eyes, trying to find a way to express myself. "I never meant to get you caught up in it all."

She nodded again. "I know. I think it's best if you go as soon as you can though. My family doesn't need to suffer this. I feel bad bringing them down if I fall."

"I understand." My head was spinning. She was really kicking me out as soon as I could go? How long would it be until it was safe for me to make a move? My money was in Austin and I could get to it, buy everything I needed off the street, and head back down the path of destruction, but I didn't want to.

She looked into my eyes as if I had died. It was cold, not the warm, safe place I always went. "I'm really sorry, Judy. I will go this afternoon."

"Thank you. I just can't be caught up in it. I'm claustrophobic, wouldn't do well in jail, Carolyn."

It hit me like a brick. I could save her. "I have it. You have to turn me in. Okay? You must call the police and tell them I am here right after I leave. Tell them that I must have stowed away, you know me. Tell them that I came in for a drink that night and must have stolen the key to your tool box or something, but that you think I might be in trouble or something. Just call the local police. That will alert Miller that I am here and that's all I need. I can get a couple hours' head start and I'll be fine." I watched for her reaction. There wasn't one. "That will work, right? You won't be in trouble then."

"There is so much room for a mistake, Carolyn. I'm sure that there will be more to it than that, but I can handle it. I won't go to jail for you

..." She was pacing now. "I'm glad I could help and it's almost been fun. But, the stress is too much for me. I just want to be with my family."

"How about telling them that I had you at gun point?"

She thought about it a minute. "That works better, because then when we are seen together, I would have been coerced. Believe me, Carolyn, I can lie. Don't worry. I can lie, was a pro as a child. You just get ready and go and I'll call it in ... but you will have to tie me up here first. My family will find me. Take the truck and get rid of it where I can find it in one piece, okay?"

I found her adoringly beautiful ... "Okay. I'll tie you to a chair so that you won't get hurt."

"If you don't hurt me, it won't look real ... knock me out so I don't have to watch you go, please ..."

She didn't have to say another word. I couldn't take the look in her eyes. I cold-cocked her right in the jaw and out she went. I caught her the best I could, but she hit her head and shoulder on the side stand. If I cleaned up the blood I would leave a trail. Everything was going wrong. I never thought it would be this difficult to recover from one mistake ...

having that accident was starting to piss me off. I didn't really want to kill Miller's dad, living was a lot more hellish. Now I had to decide what to do.

Before I made any other decisions, I had to get the hell out of Dodge. I gathered up what I needed and left everything else. The wig and the clothing, the food and I had what I needed. I was hoping that the keys to the truck were still in it where we left them. I kissed her cheek and was out the door. I felt a thousand times better, but my body still didn't react with the agility that it did prior to the accident. Running down the rough path, I found the truck, started it up and honked as loudly as I could, making it look like an accident, to alert the family that she was at the cabin and I was out the door. I hoped I had time to beat them …

Back in the cabin, ten minutes later, Shylo, Judy's younger brother rushed in the door to find her unconscious and bleeding. He undid the binding and carried her out the door, screaming the whole way. His two other brothers met him and his parents ran to phone the police. Carolyn Riley was now on the radar …

Chapter 51

Miller's phone rang and woke her from her deep sleep. Groggily, she said into the receiver, "Miller ... what?"

She popped up out of the bed, slipping on her clothes as she listened to Reynolds tell her that Karma was headed for her at this very moment. She had a twenty-minute head start and was thirty miles outside of Austin. Miller's heart was beating so fast that she didn't know what to do. Reynolds kept saying, over and over, "How did she know that we were moving him to Bastrop? She must have FBI insider information ... someone is leaking information. He's not even here yet, Jennifer. How could she have been there waiting for him?"

Miller had no idea, but she knew that the people that had been used as a place to stay would have more information and she was headed to them.

Down the stairs and into her car, she sped the entire way with lights and sirens. This was the thrill of the chase and she felt the tides had changed. For some reason, she knew that Karma didn't plan this one out and that Miller was now in charge of this game. It was going to all come down to who played the fastest and Miller knew her strength was thinking on her feet.

Less than a half hour later, Jennifer was pulling in to the ranch in Bastrop that had been used by Carolyn as a getaway. She slammed the car door shut and headed for the house as two young men greeted her at the door.

"She tied my sister up and beat her. Had her at gunpoint …" They escorted Miller into the house and to the kitchen where their sister was sipping coffee.

A deep breath and steady stream release, Miller introduced herself, "Hi, I'm Detective Jennifer Miller, Austin Homicide … this is a Federal case, with FBI involvement. I'd like to ask you some questions, please …"

Judy was freaking out. The lie must go down smoothly. She let out a little sob … "I don't know if I can help, but I'll try." She was in drama

344

her whole life. This was the easy part, faking the emotions. The hard part was telling just enough to get herself out of trouble, enough that could be proven and leave the rest out. She had been going over it in her mind and would do the best she could.

"Okay, so we believe that Carolyn Riley, aka Miranda Blanche and several other aliases' was here with you?"

Judy shook her head ... "Miranda ... that's her name. She goes by Randi ... met her in a bar in Topeka, Kansas a couple nights ago. She came in the back door and grabbed me from behind." Judy sobbed so hard it hurt her face where Carolyn had punched her. Thank you very much ... not a bad hit.

"Okay, so you were in the bar? She came up behind you ... abducted you?" Miller was writing everything down on a small notepad she pulled from her pocket. "Then what happened?"

"I dunno ..." She sobbed again, but regained with a sip of coffee, holding her face. Perfect opportunity ... "Look what she did to my face!!!!"

Miller noted that the scars and dressing were like those that Karma had suffered in the accident. "She cut you?"

"NO!!! They are FAKE!!! LOOK!!!" Judy ripped off the bandages to reveal no wounds, only black Sharpie marks. "She made me go to the hospital for her and get some stuff, she had an infection. She had a gun!!!" Judy was now crying like a baby, sobbing into her own hands. Her mother patting her shoulder.

"Officer, is this necessary?" Her mother was truly concerned.

"I'm sorry, Ma'am. I have to get the information as quickly as possible. I'll make it as easy as I can ..." Miller turned to Judy, "Can you work with me ... please. I have to catch her ..."

"I know who you are. You are all she ever talked about. She's going to kill your father!!!" Judy grabbed at her mother's hands and stood up. "I can't do this. She said if I told she would kill all of you!!!" Judy went into hysterics, ran to the window and looked out. She hid behind the curtains for affect. This was crazy, but she didn't want to make a mistake.

Miller had the feeling this woman was unstable or had seen one too many movies. There was something wrong with her story. She would get to the bottom of it. Addressing the mother, "Ms. McAllister, I'm sorry. I'm going to have to take your daughter in to the Austin station for questioning. Would you like to go with her?" Miller watched for a reaction from Judy McAllister and she got just what she wanted ...

Judy needed a better performance. She came back, "I know where she is going. I heard her say it on the phone." They had planned to let Miller know what was up, leading her astray would be bad. If Judy was point on target, that would give her story credibility and that would keep Miller from nosing around back in Topeka. Carolyn was headed for Miller's house ... "She is going to find you. You live on Henderson, just off west 6th Street ... near a dirt bike park or something?"

Miller's blood chilled in her veins. "Is there anything else you can tell me? Something about what she's driving, how much gas was in it, anything that might lead me to find a stopping point?"

"The truck was almost full of gas--the truck she stole in Topeka. She wanted me to tell my family it was mine and come here, because she knew I lived close to you. She made me drive her through road blocks and things so that we could get here. She is crazy, lady ... crazy!!! You should see her when she talks about you and how angry she is at you for messing this whole thing up."

"Did she say anything about killing my father?" Miller let her professionalism slide right out the door. Karma was engaging her, not her father. How did she know that her father was being transferred? Miller was so hell-bent on getting out of here that she had to be careful to fully question this woman, whom she did not trust. "Say anything about Tacoma, Washington or the FBI or anything else? Did she make phone calls, use a computer anywhere, anything like that?"

Two Detectives knocked on the door as she finished up her sentence. They were FBI agents, Miller could tell when the boys let them in. They dismissed her and took over with Judy before Miller got a chance to hear the answer, but she had enough information. Karma was headed for her and that was okay. Austin was her home turf and there was no way someone from New Hampshire could deal with Texas like Miller could deal with Texas. She knew exactly where she was going from here and it wasn't to work. If there was a leak, she needed to stay on her own or there was a chance Karma would have information and that jeopardized Miller's life. She watched as Judy played off the investigators, batting her eyes, no tears now and Miller knew that something wasn't right. Miller was always intuitive and for some reason there was more to this woman's story than they were going to get.

She excused herself and headed out the door, phone in hand, she dialed Wiler's number and filled him in as she drove back to the city. He would find out who Judy McAllister was and what had happened. "Be quick, Wiler. I'm in real trouble here. She's out for me, not my father ..."

"You know I will, Jennifer. Be careful. You heading stealth?" he asked, after she told him that there was a leak.

"Yeah ... I'll see ya around, Wiler. Thanks for the other night. I had a good time." She had that strange feeling that it would be the last time she spoke to him and she didn't want to let that spook her. She'd had that feeling before and she was wrong. After she hung up, she called the station and had them put out and APB on the truck, hoping they would pick it up before she had to face Karma. At this point, that encounter was something she was not prepared for.

All the way back to the city, Miller made calls to inform everyone of what was

happening. Her last call was to Grant. "Wyatt ... I need your help."

Grant was good at determining what was going on with Miller and knew that using his first name was an alert to her fear. "What's wrong, Jennifer?"

"She's coming after me. Not my father, she's after me. She kidnapped some woman whose story doesn't sit well with me, with some cock-a-mamie story of how they got here … there is a leak somewhere and I'm more afraid of the leak than most anything. I don't have any cash and I want to go in hiding. She knows my address and is headed for my house. The Captain is putting together a stake-out. It's time to stay safe."

"Wait a damned minute, Jennifer. Ain't no half-wit criminal threat ever sent you in hiding. What's different here?" He waited for the answer, half knew it, but needed to make sure she knew it.

"She knows too much about me—it's personal for her. The chess game is unfair. I am at a disadvantage." She hated admitting defeat, but if she was right and went home, this woman could have already set the bomb, had the letter coming with poison on it, set up the neighbors, etc. She had no way of knowing the extent of Karma's brilliance, but laying her life on the line for it was going to take a better plan of action.

"I need a game plan and it's going to take some real thought to get one."

"How much do you need? I've got about five grand in savings." He was all in.

"That should work. I'll give it back to you as soon as I get back. I can cover it easily. I need you to do me a favor. I emailed you all the information I could get from the witness. Get on it for me?"

"I'm on it."

"Meet me at the old diner on Highway 4. Half-hour enough time?"

"I'll be there." He was already headed to the bank.

Miller drove to the diner and waited in her car. She had already made calls to a couple of thugs she kept on payroll for information and got set up for a new car, trading her nice car for one that was 'less than perfect'. It was reasonable and not traceable. If Karma was getting information from someone, there had to be no way of leaking her actions. Her plan on staying someplace was to pick up with a gang member she had rescued from a domestic violence situation. 'Pippin', her street name, had offered any help, any time for getting her old man convicted of murder when Pippin turned state's evidence on him. She lived in another world now and Miller would beach out on her sofa for the next few days. This woman knew the meaning of trust and loyalty.

Grant showed up right on time with cash in hand. He gave her a hug and promised to keep her in his prayers. This was one serious situation. They had been threatened before, but nothing like this. The intelligence of Karma could not be taken lightly. This was the war; the battles had been waged.

Chapter 52

I waited for the pawn shop owner to get back from lunch. I had

been to the store before, assured by my contact in Washington that I

needed only to show up and say the word 'antiquated' and I would be

given special attention. Never had I paid someone to help me, but

when I came up with the idea to contact Miller months ago, because I

needed a way and a way to not get caught. It had gone great, but now I

was close to getting caught in so many ways, it was time to get the tools

to really get away.

Joel Wishman, a former FBI computer crimes consultant, had

turned bad. With my Interpol connections, I knew who was where and

what they were doing. Since my classification had never lapsed, a

reasonable amount of time was spent attaining information and then

delivering it to whom might need to help me. Blackmail was quite a

joyous weapon. I had only used him once before; Joel had plugged me in to over a million website mirrors so that I could email without hesitation, but I needed him again. His security clearance was still intact as well, and when I called him to get the information on a new bank account, new ID and how I might slide in to someone's life, I was reasonably disappointed to hear of his unwillingness to cooperate.

"Joel, need I remind you of those two beautiful children and Macy … your pregnant wife? Isn't she due, wow, in less than a month, August 16th? A little over a month … baby boy to those two little girls? Hate to see her in an accident, Joel. I've kept her safe so far." I knew that I needed all the energy I could use with him. "Let's just get this straight … you help me and they live. You don't, or if you turn me in, then they die. This is easy. A no-brainer."

"What do you want?" he said with mutant anger. He knew I was dangerous.

"Here is my list …" I rattled off the necessary equipment and the information I needed. When we were done, we arranged a meeting place to have it all delivered. Vested in his life, he would deliver.

Chapter 53

I stood by the new car in the diner parking lot waiting for the trucker to move through. It was another ten minutes of standing in my weakened state before he showed up. Joel Wishman, a scrawny wannabe, showed up ten minutes late, something that made me irate.

"Where the hell have you been?" I was losing my cool.

"Look, Lady ... I'm here now and have everything you need." He was not happy with me, but who would be in this situation?

"My money?"

He was unloading his list into my new car. I was only test driving it and had such a short window of time before I could go back and pay the $1500 bartered price. "Hurry up, Joel. I don't have time and I sure don't want to be seen with you. Didn't you even think of disguising yourself?"

"They aren't interested in me anymore. My time with them was up and I'm on my own. I keep my shit straight, Lady … Get yourself up to date." He slammed the trunk.

"Nice doing business with you." I said, cheerily.

"Don't call me again. I paid the price. You can't blackmail me anymore. I'll tell them everything I've done for you and let them have you if you don't leave me alone." He opened his shirt enough that I could see the colt revolver tucked in his pants.

I stood erect and leaned in close enough for him to effectively hear me. "I'll call whenever I like and if you do roll on me, your family will be dead within the month. I have friends and they have friends and they will protect me. You know who my 'friends' are," I leaned back, "remember?"

Joel visibly shuddered with fear.

"I thought so. Pull your gun and shoot me now …" I turned and went to the driver's door. "Oh, wait. That would be hard time in Federal Prison. I don't think so." I slid into the car and started it up, heading straight back to the place I got it from.

The five-minute drive gave me time to settle down. That bastard better not have taken any of my money, I thought. It would behoove him to never cross me.

Back at the house of the guy selling the car, I paid cash, careful not to let him see the money in the trunk as I took it out. "She's a real beauty. My grandmother, she will just be happy as a clam to have this new car. Thank 'ya, Sir."

He was such a country hick, "Let me get you a bill of sale." He hustled off into the house for a pad of paper while I stood in the drive. On his return, he had pen in hand, leaned on the hood and started to write.

"Will you just make it out to Latisha Hargrave?" I used my kindest voice. "Granma-ma will take it off her taxes. Her address is 111 S. New Haven Road, Lot 5. I'll just love the look on her face." What a moron. He didn't ask for ID, didn't need any verification. These people made crime easy. Non-suspecting individuals were the easiest to fool and the least observant. He would remember grandmother and find it hard to believe that I was even in his presence when the police questioned him. I made sure I dressed down, didn't leave anything blatant for him to remember, just a fondness for my grandmother. Within a couple of minutes, he ripped the sheet from the notebook and handed it to me. The sap did not make a copy for himself, nor did he ever ask my name.

I waved my best Texas goodbye as I headed out of the drive and hit the highway.

I wasn't going toward Austin, I was heading towards home. The drive to the East Coast would take a couple of days, so I had opted to fly. "Houston, here I come …" From Houston, I would take another highway, as if to lead them in the wrong direction. It should take at least 24 hours before Miller knew that I had left the city and bought the car. Anything less than that and my plan would backfire, but chances are, Judy had informed her and she would be afraid. Not afraid to die, but afraid I was always going to win. That dilemma would drive Miller nuts and keep her centered. It would keep her out of my hair until I got home and dealt with Max.

Chapter 54

Miller pulled up to Pippin's house. The word house was a little optimistic, really it was a trailer, complete with wheels, in one of the hardest sections of town. She pulled her car up and was immediately met with eyes from several neighboring trailer windows. Pulled curtains with peepers were checking the situation.

Pippin was quick to exit and take control. "Get cha eyes back in your own buz'ness. She's with me!" She nearly screamed throughout the neighborhood, throwing her hands up in the air, dramatically, as was traditional Pippin Style. The one thing that was good was that this was not a gang-infested neighborhood, more of a domestic violence, ghetto of trashy families, neighborhood. This was the area of town that abused and neglected children, children of domestic situations, and children left to their own were left to join gangs, but the gangs were not interested in recruiting from here. The reason they had placed Pippin in this situation was that she fit in, didn't stick out, but the gangs had no reason to come into a neighborhood devoid of income.

Pippin turned to Miller, "So, Mama ... how's you been?" She seemed very genuinely glad to see her and the big hug that she gave Jennifer was quite welcome.

"I'm good. So, this is what testifying gets you?" They both laughed.

"Yeah, better 'un three squares, a cot and an orange jumpsuit." She led Miller into the house and plopped on a dirty couch. "It's not the tam-hamaul, but its home."

Miller chose a broken arm chair that nearly tossed her on her ass when she sat down, but she felt safe and secure. They talked about Pippin and the changes she had made, her job at the restaurant and her two children in foster care. She was so young but had the life of someone much older. As they finished up the conversation about Pippin, Pippin asked, "So, why you gotta hide out, Mama?"

"Oh, the million-dollar question, huh?"

"Yeah, Mama ... I gots to know, if I'm gonna protect you." She was sincere.

"You, protecting me ... never thought I'd see this day."

"You 'mbarrassed about it? Cuz I can make some calls and you know, let some peeps know ware ya at." She laughed.

"No, I want you to protect me. I want to know that no one knows where I am, including the police department. The truth is that we have a leak somewhere and I don't know where. A serial killer is after me and I needed to disappear."

"Sumpin serious. I'm just sayin'." She contemplated before she spoke again. "You puttin' me in danger?"

"No, not if no one knows where I'm at. If the killer finds out, word is, she's out to find me, then yes, you are in danger."

"Damn! A female! That's not cool." She blew off the fear potential.

It was embarrassing; my only explanation was, "I left no trail. Cash only, quit using my phone, I left it at a diner where I met my partner and got money. I even traded cars, but this car needs to be ditched. Can you do that for me?"

"Sho' can, Mama. I's love a joy ride that didn't end me up in the pen." She was up and ready to go. "Where da keys? I'ma take it for a spin then I'll hitch a ride back. I got this. Want it at a chop shop? They's the best place, cuz they don't care about you. I can use the cash and they'a laugh at it a cop car."

"Sure ... just try not to lead anyone back to me, Sister."

Miller tossed her the keys and Pippin headed for the door. Before she left, she tossed out, "You can clean the place up if ya's like. I know your house is prolly a lot nice-a than mine. I don't mind."

Miller laughed at that one. "I can do that. Thanks, Pip ... thanks a lot."

"I know. I know ... you owe me one. Don' worry. I gots needs all da time. I'm outtie ..." She left Miller to fend for herself.

Finding cleaning supplies was nearly impossible, so she settled with some baking soda, stuffed in the back of an empty fridge, and some rags she found in a drawer. First things first, she headed for the kitchen and did dishes. At least there was plenty of dish soap and only a few dishes. While she worked, she got used to the noises of the neighborhood. It was totally different than here serene middle-class environment. Doors slammed a lot, people yelled at each other and no one seemed to mind, even if it did send Miller to the window on several occasions. Finally, she finished the dishes and moved to counters where she emptied food from fast food containers and scrubbed stains off the counter with the baking soda.

"Damn, my grandma would have died in here." She thought aloud. As she cleaned, she noticed that the place wasn't that bad. Once the kitchen floors were swept with a tiny broom and the dust pan emptied, the floors scrubbed with the same rags and dish soap, the place started to even smell differently. Next, she went to the dining area and pretty much swept the contents off into trash bags. Three bags later, there was a table that she cleaned with soap and water. The floor was carpeted, so she searched and found an antiquated vacuum that spit out more than it sucked up.

Frustrated with the equipment, she found a screwdriver in a drawer and took it apart, emptied out all the gunk and goo in the tube that caused the suction to be blocked, and put it back together. She vacuumed the floor and moved to the living room where she wiped the dust off the window ledges, and the television and rickety entertainment center scattered with trash, which got thrown away as well. She kept the bags of trash instead of throwing them in the gigantic barrel a couple of houses down more for the fact that she felt threatened, but knew she could use the premise that Pippin might need something and must look through. Papers went in one and food items and true trash in the others.

Less than three hours later, the entire trailer was clean except the bathroom and she felt invasive cleaning it, so she left it for Pippin. She was going to pay for her stay, so she didn't feel as though it were too demanding to ask Pippin to clean the restroom. Now, it was just too disgusting to even use. Going out back in the weeds would be better and Miller was sure safer from germs. She kicked back in the newly swept and doused with baking soda chair, and turned on the television to get a scratchy gray screen. No cable.

The DVD player on the side proved useful, and the collection of discs promising for her stay at the dwelling. She plopped in a movie and popped back over to the chair. Missing her phone was a fact at this point; she was jones-ing and had trouble focusing on the movie. A romantic comedy that took an hour before she became engrossed in kept her busy and she was almost to doze off when Pippin returned.

It was just after midnight when Pippin opened the door with a quick knock of notice. Miller jumped, but quickly recovered as Pippin sprawled out on the couch as if she took the car apart herself. She laid out six hundred dollar bills. "You gotsa nice car, Miller. They loved that car. I stuck around to make sure it got tore down, sometimes they will jerk you and drive it out the back and then it's still on da streets. You is safe. It's in pieces and headed out to underground auction. I'm sho."

"Good. Load off my mind." Miller tried to just relax and accept her environment. All her years of Alanon taught her to take control of what she could, accept what she couldn't control and decide the difference. She was okay with what she was doing. It was almost comical at this point though.

Pippin came up off that couch as quickly as she had dropped down on it. "What the fuck? What did you do to my house?"

Miller rose, defensively. "I'm sorry. I thought you would be happy

..."

Pippin walked from room to room, leaving Miller to her own anxiety. Great, she was going to get kicked out and then where would she be. For that five minutes Pippin was gone, she felt horrible about what she had done. She was contemplating her apology when Pippin returned.

"Girl, you is hired!!! This place looks great. I never knew it was this nice." She was truly amazed.

"What? It's okay?" Miller sighed in relief. Tired was a thing of the past, she was now truly exhausted.

"Hell ya's it's okay. I never knew it could look like this."

Miller took her usual attitude of self-sufficiency, "It might help if you had bought cleaning supplies."

Pippin ruffled up, big and tall, "Mama, I knows you isn't banging on the girl. I can barely eat, can't afford no Pine sol. Shit!"

"Whatever. I saw all the take-out boxes. That's expensive. If we are going to be roommates, you are gonna let me show you how to cook, how to clean your house and how to budget your money ... how's that for me being a control freak?"

"You would do that for me?" Pippin had a tear in her eye. Miller knew Pip's story and she had raised herself with a drug addicted, alcoholic mother. The life Pip knew was nothing compared to a normal childhood. She had helped her when the gang had said the release was okay and she would help her now. It was a true opportunity for her to thrive and the gang was not interested in making her stay, her husband had killed one of their own. She got her ticket out. On occasion Miller had visited, but never come through the door. She knew Pippin was embarrassed, so she had never wandered past it.

"I know how to survive, they said in group. But I don't really know how to 'live', ya know?" The street slang gone, Pip showed Miller a true moment of honesty.

"I do. And, for all your kindness, letting me stay here, I can pay you back that way. Plus, I'm going to pay rent. I'm going to give you $200 per week to stay here. Deal?"

"Hell, no! I don't pay but $250 all month." She put her hands on her supple hips in defiance.

"Then $200 is very fair. You have electric, gas, water, cable, whatever ... and then there is food. I'm not gonna starve here and I can't go anywhere. I'm in hiding. So, paying for your errands and the hospitality ... $200 a week." Miller stood and put her hands on her thin hips, a good three or four inches shorter than Pippin.

"White girl! Shit!" She laughed, taking her hands from her own hips. "I know you think you are big and tough ... but that gun stays in its hoe-ster. Shit!" She laughed again as she plopped back on the couch. "I sleep out here. You can sleep in that chair or take the bedroom ... but be careful what you wish fo." With that came a guttural laughter that Miller only understood when she headed to the back bedroom, which had a closed door and she had not entered it.

Upon opening the door Miller saw what she was talking about and had she not been so horrified and overwhelmed by the clutter, she would have laughed too. The room must have had a bed in it, because something was holding up a mountain of clothing, most with price tags still attached. She shook her head. A life of crime was hard to get rid of. The smell was not what you would think, seeing the clutter. It was a new smell, like a department store.

From down the hallway, Miller heard, "I tode you!!!" And the laughter began all over.

Miller headed back down the hallway to the chair across from the couch and grabbed the throw blanket Pippin had tossed on it, probably straight from goodwill.

"Sorry ... old habits is hard to break. I'm the best lifter I know ... most a them are from a street corner vendor anyways ... don't arrest me, officer!" she teased.

Miller shook her head and settled in to the chair. She watched Pippin watch her until they both laughed and Pippin threw herself over and faced the couch. Miller watched until Pippin fell asleep, steady breathing, before she felt the relief of sleep.

Chapter 55

The highway spread out before me and insanely enough, I was glad to be headed home. It had done me good to take this drive instead of flying. I had changed my mind, like I typically did when moving forward, because if I thought it, someone else would think it too. The cops might figure out that I was leaving and I didn't need to be stopped in an airport. Too many cameras, too many people. It seemed I had more time to deliberate my entrance back into the state of New Hampshire, even if for that brief moment it would take to do my necessary work. This one last thing had to be done before I was ready to decide if my crime spree was over, or if I was going to challenge this situation again. If I were right, and I was really a sociopath or psychopath, I would not be able to stop. This clarity would come now that I did not have a plan in mind for any deviant behavior. Seeing my brother would challenge the situation and walking in to the institution that Max was housed in would be incredibly difficult. I felt the brunt of this challenge.

Pulling in to Atlanta was familiar to me, because I had spent a year of my life with my family in the city. My father's job held a lot of traveling and at one point mother decided to take it upon herself to move the entire family, board up the mansion, all but the help's quarters and leave the house empty. Society life in Atlanta had been okay, but for a fifteen-year-old girl, it made my life hell. If mother would have let my father go alone, I would not have been a target. That is where my resentment started and my illness became apparent to me.

I stopped only long enough to eat on Peach Tree Plaza and to purchase a cell phone in my new identity-Tina Marie Rogers. Tina had been deceased for a little over a week, per the obituary in the paper.

My nickname chosen, "T-bird", I had the new fingerprints in place with the geltex covering, had purchased another fat suit, like the one I wore as 'Ruth' and had bought the used car off the street, testing my new ID by registering it in Texas. I had a Texas Driver's License, Texas address and a work log that took me all over the United States as a Pharmaceutical sales woman. The only problem with this ID is that I had never been a dead person. There wasn't time for me to research like I needed. My age was a problem, so the 'look' had to be very convincing.

I had the film crew special effects guy I hired make my face look very young. I paid the guy a very nice price to keep quiet and went to the DMV before I headed out and took the Texas Driver's test with the paperwork I created. That had put me behind almost six hours and I had not been to sleep in almost two days. I was a speed demon, planning and implementing it immediately. The fat suit took three hours, but the guy was as brilliant as his ad on Craigslist said he was. The less I was seen, the less I made an appearance, the less anyone had contact with me, the better. It was time to take my last resort at staying awake and alert.

I drove to a not-so-nice part of town and started looking for what I needed. These people didn't tell cops squat, so it was okay to be seen. From across the street, I parked and watched as some thugs sold drugs on the street. One kept looking around, seemed to be on the look-out for cops, so I thought I had a good target. I approached him.

In my young-fat suit, I probably looked ridiculous, but I took the chance. "You got any cocaine?"

"Go away, biotch!" He wasn't willing to listen.

"Look, I'm not a cop. Just ask me. Did you know if you ask a cop if they are a cop, by law they have to tell you?" I looked him square in the eye. "Ask me, mother fucker. I need some coke or I'm gonna be all up in your shit with the piece I have in my hand."

He looked at my hand on my Glock.

"Bitch … I said get out. I ain't got nothing. I'm just waiting fo my grandmother. Step off." He backed away from me.

"I don't think you understand." I grabbed him and shoved him up against the brick wall he was using as his shield so no one would see him. "This gun isn't registered and I need some coke. Give me what you have and we are done. Period." I pulled the Glock and put it against his throat. "Hand it over. NOW!" I hissed through my teeth.

"Okay … okay … but you don't know who you are messing with." He stared me down as he reached in his pocket and pulled out six little baggies of cocaine and a dozen or more baggies of pot. I took two and handed the rest back to him, putting my gun back inside my waistband.

"I only need these." I handed him two hundred dollars. "For your trouble. Forget you ever saw me, capish?" I loved saying the word 'capish', it just sounded cool, like I was a gangster too.

"Capish ..." He nodded his head in respect.

That was that, I was out of Atlanta within the hour and on the road again. This time I was working really hard to stay awake long enough to use the coke in the most beneficial way. Coke and I had a love-hate relationship. It could keep me awake, but it made me ultra-sensitive to my thoughts. I would become over analytical, almost rational and that was a problem for me. But, I was on an adventure. It was time.

I pulled over to the next rest area I found and headed for the restroom, a small piece of plastic stashed with my drugs. Once inside, I straddled the toilet backwards, remembering from my old days of addiction how this went ... and laid out my lines with my driver's license. I then rolled a bill and snorted three swift lines. ONE ... for relaxation and to not remember. TWO ... for the thrill of the chase. THREE ... to keep me awake another twelve hours until I could get to Briana's house ... Wilmington, DE.

Chapter 56

Pippin quietly opened the door and entered the house. She had woken up about ten thirty and saw that Miller was totally out of it. Even after she showered, she didn't feel like waking the lady up. This woman had really helped her out and she knew that it had to be pretty bad for her to call on this favor. Everything Miller had done for her was done with no expectation of return. Pippin was loyal and she would help as much as she could. She tiptoed back in with the groceries she had bought. With only eleven dollars they weren't luxurious, but she tried to think like a 'normal' person and had shopped the best she knew how. Miller could really teach her something and these were the things she wanted to know. Without an education, without a real up-bringing, she knew she was at a disadvantage and her dream of owning her own clothing store would go nowhere if she didn't learn simple, basic task responsibilities. No one would teach her, and she felt her motives were selfish, but she was going to use Miller just as Miller was using her. It was just a thought, no bad context.

In the kitchen, she worked quietly to put things away, but made the mistake of trying to open the fridge with the same hand she held the gallon of milk in and dropped the milk. With a thud, it hit the floor and Pippin watched the cop fly out of the chair, unaware of her surroundings for a moment until it all sunk in.

"Whoops!" She giggled.

Miller was awake, fully and her senses were keen ... jump-started she had to calm herself down after the misfire of adrenalin. "Gee ... no good morning?"

Pippin picked up the unscathed milk and put it away. "I thought I should give you the hood alarm ... you know, bounce the milk off the floor."

"Yeah, well ... it worked. Took me a second to realize where I was."

"At least you didn't pull that gun."

"Yeah ... okay, I'm good now. So, milk? Did you go out?"

"I went to da store. Spent some money so you could teach me how to cook. I'ms hungry, bitch. Teach me how to cook something good." Pippin baited her.

"Oh ... well, I knew there would be a catch. Okay ..." She headed for the kitchen. "What did you buy?" She looked through the bag as Pippin opened the cabinet.

Miller laughed. "How am I supposed to teach you how to cook, you bought six boxes of Pop tarts?" There really wasn't much but milk, Pop tarts and flour.

She opened the fridge to point out hot dogs and canned biscuits.

"I need to teach you how to shop. First-things-first, right now, there's only one thing I see that we can make ... pigs in the blankets. Grab the biscuits and the hot dogs.   "You got any ketchup?"

She pulled out all three.

"Okay," Jennifer was enjoying herself. "Pop the biscuits and I'll heat up the stove." She moved to the antiquated stove, cleared off everything Pippin had put on it and preheated it. "Now, we have to fold the hot dogs in the biscuit and then bake them. You want big pigs or little pigs?"

"Little pigs, please." She was like a child.

Miller wondered how a woman that carried a machine gun as second nature, could stand before her as childlike as she was, asking for little pigs instead of big. This was something she would make work. While the pigs were cooking, she took out paper and pen and made a list for Pippin to take back to the store later that afternoon. She also gave her a list of things she needed her to buy: laptop computer, Wi-Fi connection, prepaid cell phone with a month of unlimited time and three books of crossword puzzles to keep her busy. After they finished lunch and Pippin got the lists together, she stopped Miller as she washed the dishes.

"Um ... can I ask you questions, or do you wanna do dis all alone?" Pippin sat down at the table.

Miller pulled up a chair and sat with her. "You can ask. I'm just not sure you will like the answers."

"I'm aight." She smiled and Miller noticed she was a beautiful child. Her weight made it hard to see the beauty and she did not enhance any features. Used to being on the street and beauty for a girl-child a hassle, one Miller understood, she looked closely at Pippin's features, soft and naturally beautiful. "What choo looking at, Miller?"

"Call me Jen, please. I'm going to be here a few weeks or so, until I catch a clue or this fades to a point it's safe. Jen ... okay?"

"Nope."

"What do you mean, nope?" Miller was aghast.

"I said, no. I won't call you 'Jen' ... you always been Rider to me ... dat okay? It's my nick fo you. Rider, cuz you ride up and save da day on more than one situation." She smiled, endearing Jen to hear what she said.

"I can live with Rider ... makes me sound cool, huh?" She liked it.

"It is cool and, Rider, we needs to make you safe. What choo runnin' from, Mama?"

"A serial killer. Female, serial killer." She waited to see how it sunk in.

"HuH? You were serious? You skert of a female?" She thought about it. "Damn, she must be a seriously crazy shit to run you out choo house."

"She is. And she fixated on me. She's killed at least six men and set up their wives to take the fall. She's smart and she's focused and she's a step ahead of me. Now she says she's coming after me and my family."

"What? You let me get at her ... I'll take care of her murderin' ass. I ain't skert of her. Where is she?"

"That's the problem. I don't know. I don't know where she is headed or what she is after right now. My father is safe, and I don't think she would hurt the rest of my family, but she likes to stalk me. I found out she's been to my house before and she was headed there. The unit is staking it out, FBI is on it, but I don't want to be there. If I am there, she has the chance to follow me. So, I'm here. There is no way anyone would know to look for me here."

She went to the window ... "You don't fink the FBI would come here? Do ya?"

"No. They aren't worried about me. And, when you get me these items, I will have you communicate for me, look for information if I need to. I screwed up catching Karma and let her get ahead of me. I had her in my hand and she slipped away, could have killed me if she wanted to."

"Karma?"

"The woman after me." Miller watched her reaction of sadness and how helpless it seemed she felt.

"What can I do?"

Miller thought about it a minute. "You can teach me about the streets. You are much more a survivor than I am and you know the ways to get around the cops. I need your help with that. She can outwit us every step of the way and I can't let her win …"

"I got choo. Okay, what do you want to know?"

For the next hour, they sat and Pippin explained to Miller things she never knew. How to get around the cops was to put yourself right up in front of them. To a certain extent, Miller knew that, but to hear how easy it was to outthink the cops, was really a blow to her ego.

"Okay, so let me try …" Miller took a chance. "If I wanted to get close to someone and I knew they would be under surveillance, I would find a way to know the surveillance, so I would stake out the stake out?"

"We watch you. Gangs got dis down. Ya see, if we know what you are doing, then we know where not to be. So, this Karma chica, she smarter than you. So, what if this … what if she said she was going to get you, cuz that would put you on the defense and she headed somewhere else? Dats what I would do. I would send you on a goose chase of your own. Or, steer you away from where I thought I wanted to be. Say we hittin a big score, we always find a way to get you somewhere else. Like, say, we set up some poor nigga down five blocks away. Far enough away you cain't see us … close enough we can hear you and we can watch you."

"Okay … so gangs are big enough to do that. She's one person, Pip. One person can outwit me like this?"

"She know you well. You said she been in ya house? She watchin' you. She know you well enough to know what put you on offense and defense. She needs you on defense so she can get out. She gonna hide. We know when to hide. So, what she doin, if fakin you out, cuz she too smart to let somebody tell you 'zactly where she's going. You know enuff to figga it out? She thinks you a fool." She raised her eyebrows.

Miller thought long and hard.

Pippin watched her thinking, giving her time to really determine what the route could be. "You know how she thinks? You got sta know how she thinks. She got you figga'd out, Mama. You nottin' but a pawn in her game wit choo." She sat back, proud she could lead Miller.

"You're right. I'll make contact and see if they have any new information. I just have to do it like she would. I can't leave a trace at all that I'm even alive right now. She's like a shark in the water. And, I do believe she would try and get out—the smart thing to do would be leave, not be on the offense, unless she wants to get caught. She said that if she was going to stop, I would have to stop her ... The lady she kidnapped to come down to Texas ... there are answers there. But even though I knew that she was lying, I couldn't get her to break. She sent me straight home with fear. You think she was lying?"

"What 'bout?" Pippin squared off. She needed to know all this.

For all the education, she did not have, evading the police she knew like the back of her hand. This was familiar to her.

"I went to question her …" Miller explained the whole situation.

"Bitch waddant telling' you no truth. She said she called ahead the day before to talk to her parents and tell her she was coming?" She leaned forward, contemplating her words. "She set yo ass up, Mama. I bet you got no idea where Karma at and what she doin'. She set you up. Who was this chica to Karma?" Pip waited for the answer.

"I don't know. She said Karma came into the bar and abducted her out the back door."

Pip was already shaking her head. "Un, uh … Sounds like shit to me. What if they had a relationship of some kind or something? She sounds like she wasn't skert enough to have been kidnapped. That's some real shit. You know? It's all about how they holt themselves. I know it, cuz I got kidnapped. No fear like that. Being held against your will, never knowing if you gonna live through it, get raped, get stabbed, you know … nothing makes sense. She seem that skert? Cuz you need to let me talk to her. Where she at? Let me talk to her. No body gotta know nothun'. Nothun'."

"She's in Bastrop."

"Wait a damned minute. You stupid, Rider? Seriously, are you stupid?"

"What?"

"How she go and kidnap somebody in Kansas that got family living in Bastrop? HUH? Bitch just," She got up from the table and started walking around like she was a white girl, "falls into some random bar and snags some hootch, who juz happens to live in the city where bouts your daddy is gonna be and you live thirty miles away. Yeah. This girl had some serious insight into this. Wadn't no good luck charm. They know each other."

Miller thought about it. It was time to let things stand as they may and she really thought about Pippin questioning Judy, from two different worlds. What if she got information out of her no one else could use? It was worth a try and she wasn't about to play fair anymore. Would she be a bad cop if she let Pippin at Judy? Would she lose her job?

"Look, Mama ... is there a reward for Karma?"

Miller nodded. "Yeah, the FBI put out a reward for information that leads to an arrest. Like maybe a hundred thousand, I think."

"JOY! Let me do this. I need the money and you can use the information."

"No. You would have to turn it over to the FBI and let them at her. I mean, you can if you want, but they would know I told you, could be a real bad thing. Sorry. I'll do what I can if you help out, you know I will."

"No worries. Ain't nobody got sta know nothing. I disguise in and disguise out. I got me some friends can help. That woman won't have no choice but tell the truth. You let me at her and tonight we know where Karma at ... at least know whether she after you or not." She nodded her head slowly, biting her lip, gangster-like.

"Okay. But no one knows anything. And, when you find out, I can't use it against Judy. She will have been intimidated, so her information is worth nothing."

"Catch you a killer, Mama. Ain't nothing wrong with that. If you cops would just learn that, and leave 'law' out of it, you would stop a lot more crime. Mama, learn the lesson, crime about cheating. You gotsta cheat to get ahead."

"I'm trying to teach you not to cheat, Pip." Miller pleaded with her that law and justice were the way.

"You gotsta know when to say when and now ... you say when."

"Here's the address. Don't tell me anything about how, when, with whom you go ... just find out where Karma is and what happened to bring her to Texas."

Pippin grabbed the paper and was out the door.

"Did I just make the biggest mistake of my life?" Miller mumbled.

White lighting flared across the sky as the early morning sun peeked over the horizon. I had been driving all night long, wrestling with my thoughts. Twice I had to stop and wake back up with more coke. That made it impossible for me to ignore my thought process. It did help that my brother was just around the corner and any bit of conscience I had was more for his sake.

Max was institutionalized for severe mental retardation. I had horrible guilt for leaving him without parents, but they caused his problem anyway. My father was just as abusive to Max as he was to me, but in a different way. Max was the product of Shaken Baby Syndrome. He was just now thirteen-years-old, but when he was just a little baby, mom had left me and dad home alone. I was nearing the end of my abuse from my father, I had had enough, but that day, when Maxie wouldn't stop crying and I couldn't get him to settle down, my father's hand had come cracking down on my skull. Because he hit me from the top of my head, I lost consciousness for a bit. Long enough to only see him shaking the shit out of my little baby brother when I came to. Maxie was my hope; I worried more about getting him out of the situation than myself. From that moment on, Max's development was stunted. Father, in his own friendly way—with his pants down, teaching me a lesson by grunting on top of me, sweat pouring on to my face, hard to tell the difference between the taste of his sweat and my tears—taught me that if I told, he would not kill me, oh, no, that would make my life better—He had other plans. My father changed his tune of killing my mother to killing my baby brother. Maxie became my reason to live; my reason to thrive; my reason to kill. But that glaring guilt kept coming back. I had to go home and get Max out of the institution and I had made up my mind. I hadn't seen him since the killing. At that point, Max couldn't do anything for himself and he had a lot of seizures. I would play Las Vegas craps—If Max knew who I was, I would stop killing; I would find a place for us both to live and I would care for Max from now on. If not, another victim would be sought and I would make sure I got caught on that one, just as I pulled the trigger ... or I would pull the trigger myself.

That's what I could thank cocaine for. Before the drugs, I just felt like seeing Max, but, with conviction, I now had to decide. When I left him, I signed papers to put him in this place, because I knew there would be a day I had to come get him. I also knew that no one else needed to be around him. The grandparents couldn't possibly care for us, their social calendar was extensively overwrought. I had one aunt, Delores, who was crazier than me—she wouldn't do. Max and I were on our own and at the trial I knew that we were going to be that way forever. When my mom didn't even know that she didn't kill my father, it was amazing. The power, the control, the feeling of being super-human ... she thought she did it. That's when I knew that I could go out and vindicate this crime.

The miles flew underneath me, luckily, I didn't speed or do

anything wrong and I showed up in Wilmington in time for dinner. Briana Flarety was my best friend in college. She had married a man from a very prestigious family and had done quite well for herself. My goal was to have a place to stay, they owed me. In college, I had caught them in a predicament and my family bailed them out. They had embezzled hundreds of thousands of dollars from the alumni foundation, Ben Flarety, Bri's husband to be, was working for them. I bailed them out by paying the money back, kept good records of the crime in a safe deposit box in Wilmington and all I had to do was stop and pick that up before I showed up at their house. Blackmail always got me what I needed.

The bank closed at 5:30 and I was barely going to make it. "Oh, Crap!" I slowed the car down and pulled over at the curb. My mind was racing. What was I thinking? I couldn't waltz in to the bank and ask for my OWN box. I had no ID of my own and I was on the FBI radar, any movement in my name at all would cause an immediate pin-down. "SHIT!" I banged on the steering wheel.

What could I do? Why did I need to see them? To get some sleep? I was not thinking clearly. The exhaustion, the expense of energy to heal my wounds, the total and complete sleep deprivation ... I was not thinking clearly. Reroute. That was the answer. Nowhere near Wilmington was safe. How could I get Max out of the institution? Or, should I just leave him there? My conscience began to gnaw at me. Sleep ... I needed sleep.

Epiphany! The beauty of the idea that works. I would rent a home. Apartment hunting 101. No one needed ID to rent a house in a bad neighborhood and that is where I was headed with a sob story of losing my job. I could pay cash, have a temporary place to sleep and have no one in my business. Cash talked a talk I could use. My eyes blurred as I entered traffic again, but I drove to the desired destination.

Chapter 57

Pippin sat in the front seat of the car that Carlos was careening down the abandoned lane to Judy's house. Miller had described it perfectly and given an address. They saw the house come into sight and drove on past, parking less than a mile away. It was time that chores had started and they could sneak right into the room Judy was in, given they could figure out which one it was. It was still dark, so they drove with the lights off and the constant purr of the engine was the only threat to their anonymity.

"I got a betta idea." Carlos said to Trey. The four of them together were a gruesome crowd to face. "You got that phone kit still?"

Trey knew exactly what he meant. "Yeah. It's in the trunk with the rest of the stuff. You want me to call her out?"

Carlos just nodded as he parked the car. "Yeah, T gonna call her out, we gotta watch for everyone leaving. Copper said there was three boys, a dad, mom and our biotch?"

"Yeah." Pippin quietly answered. She knew her place with this group. Former gang members stuck together, but they had no intent upon ending up in jail now. They had to call out the white girl so that they could question her, or they went with the original idea. Two of them would take mom and two would take the daughter.

"Wait ... we can't call her out, cuz she gonna buzz on us. I don't wanna do no time. Let me go in and get her if we gonna do that, then I's the only one at risk. Muvver Fucker won't mess wit me." Trey was all up on it.

"Why don't we wait and see who leaves? Let's ditch off the car and see if we can just get the looksie and see what's up." Skee said. He was the fourth member and the most volatile. Tattooed from head to toe, he had done his time in prison and was not about to make mistakes. Pippin knew he was tough, that's why she asked him. Even cops feared him, but he was her brother.

"Bro ... we got to get in and get out." Pippin said.

"We got to get out, period. Let me pull the cop-n-gun show. We got the riff in the back and we can get in."

That meant that he wanted to pose as a police officer and snatch her up for questioning. Pippin was all for piping her out of the house. All they had to do was tap into the phone line and make her answer. None of this would work. She was starting to stress, because she really wanted to do this right. Rider had always been kind to her. She had to be successful.

She started to make another suggestion to Skee, Carlos and Trey, when Judy walked out the door and headed for her truck.

They all looked at each other.

"Shit ... that her?" Carlos asked.

"Dunno. Looks young enough. Trucks right. I say yeah." Pippin was ready. This made it objectively easier if they could just grab her in her vehicle and make the interrogation right there. This was a much better prospect. "Patience is a virtue."

"Girl," Skee said, "I know you don't think you got any virtue." They all laughed, even when she punched him. "Wait for her to get far enough down that no one will think to look out again."

They waited. When the time was right, Carlos headed back out the road they came, and once out of hearing range of the house, he stepped on the gas to catch up with and pass the truck Judy was driving.

Inside the cab, Judy drove serenely down the road. Waiting for the sun to come up was her favorite part of the day. The music softly led her down the road, headed to the grocery store and to find a Starbucks. She was having coffee withdrawal. If she had to drink one more cup of her father's stiff and stale brew, she would puke.

In the rearview mirror, Judy saw the approaching car. Unusual for that time of the day and that road, which ended up at a lake down the lane, she pulled to the far right so that they could pass. When they drove by, she saw four people in the car, but only one of them looked at her, a female.

"Cut her off now!" Trey pointed out the opposite lane and Carlos drilled the car in front of Judy. The car swung around, blocking the road completely with a slam of the brakes. Dirt flew everywhere

When Judy came to a stop, slamming on her brakes, she instantly realized that they were stopping her from going anywhere. Judy sat in total unawareness taking in the breadth of the situation. It did not, however, provide her with insight enough to dodge the ensuing bombardment.

They were on her in a moment. In their planning, they were at the advantage.

Trey grabbed the door handle, black mask in place, along with gloves and clothing that covered every inch of his body except for his eyes and mouth. "Get out!" He screamed in her face as he grabbed her. "Get out! Now!!!" He nearly drug her from the vehicle.

"What's going on?" Judy was terrified. The tears started before she knew what was going on.

Carlos crawled behind the wheel of the truck and drove it off with Judy clearly unable to comprehend. She screamed just as Skee put his hand over her mouth, assuming responsibility for her and dragging her, kicking and screaming, with Trey, to the awaiting car and Pippin.

Inside the car, Pippin remained calm, never moved a muscle with exception of placing the hood over her face and a voice box on her throat to alter her pitch. She had gloves on and if she stayed in her seat and remained calm, there would be no way of describing her to the authorities. They had stolen the car that morning from Trey's girlfriend's boss, managing a joyride if they could get the car back before one o'clock in the afternoon. The plan was in motion.

Judy was thrown into the car, followed by Skee, and Trevor got in on the other side as Pippin slid into the driver's seat and began to follow behind Carlos. They had found a meeting place and were headed in that direction.

Pippin spoke through the voice altering device. "Shut up. Keep calm and you live ... if not, we do without you and I'll slit your throat. Understand?"

Trey let go of his hand over Judy's mouth. She nodded her head.

"You got yourself into a bit of a mess with your friend. We know's you helped that woman get here and you lied to the cops. Problem is, you gonna tell the truth now or you gonna die." She pulled the car over to where Carlos had stopped the truck.

He got out and entered the car as Pippin slid back to her seat, now facing Judy.

Judy was terrified but if they were going to kill her, she had no choice but to tell the truth. "Who are you? Who are you working for?"

They all laughed. Skee commented, "Oh, we try real hard NOT to work. This is just fun."

"Hush." Pippin fired at Skee. "You don't need to worry about anything right now other than filling me in. Where you first meet 'Karma'?"

Judy got it now ... this was no game. Carolyn had said she was in deep, but putting Judy in jeopardy was starting to really annoy her. Basically, her emotions were out of control, because Carolyn hadn't even called to check in with her. Judy's anger had started to bubble in the pit of her stomach. "We met in Topeka, Ks."

Pippin was starting to get into her role. "You betta start spilling your guts or I'm gonna get pissed, Miss Thang. WHERE???"

Judy commenced to fill them in on the entire story and only needed prompted twice. Once she lipped off to Pippin and Skee literally punched her in the side of the head with his balled fist. The second time he belted her was when she really didn't know the answer.

Pippin asked her again, "Where is she headed?"

"I swear. I don't know." Judy's head was pounding. Skee hit her with enough power to make her brain feel like jelly. "I don't know …" She whined.

Pippin was getting frustrated, "What did she tell you?"

"She said she wanted everyone to think she was going after Detective Miller, but she really just needed an escape route. If they focused on something else, she had a chance of getting out. I gave her a beat-up truck that we got along the way and she left that morning. I swear, I don't know where she is going."

"She contacted you?" Pippin asked very nicely. At least the woman was cooperating and they were getting somewhere.

"No … I haven't heard a word from her." Judy took a chance. "Who are you working for? Is she in more trouble?" The genuine concern came forth and Pippin caught it immediately.

"Look, Bitch!" She reached into the back seat and grabbed Judy's shirt, ripping her forward, directly in her face. "You better spill everything you know or," the gun came out of nowhere; slammed against Judy's forehead, "I will blow you away."

Judy gasped, but she knew that look. Pippin was fighting no demons. She could pull the trigger and not have a problem doing it.

Pippin had seen it done, she had come close before and she had no problem with it. Her life of crime was so innate, it was just a way of life for her and she would never have a problem doing whatever it took, when it came to protecting her own and Miller was hers.

Judy was crying now, sobbing uncontrollably. Trey and Skee pulled her back. Skee took charge, "Don't do it. Let her calm down so she can talk." He pushed the gun away gently. His sister was easy to anger and out of control at a point. She was getting frustrated.

Pippin heard Skee and calmed herself some. Careful that the voice alteration box was in place. "Okay," she put the gun back on the seat. "Start over. What do you know that will help me know this woman? I have to know where she is going."

Judy tried so hard to stop the emotion that was welling up inside her. She would not live to see another day. If she told them everything, she would tell them nothing. If she made something up and they took her with them to check it out, they would know she lied. Either way, she was screwed.

Pippin became frustrated again. Judy was taking too much time and Pippin knew from getting information from others that Judy was contemplating what to say. She had had enough. The gun came back out and she fired.

BLAM!!! The car shook with the echoing of the shot.

Chapter 58

I rolled up to the dilapidated house fifteen minutes early to get a good look at it and survey the neighborhood. People walked around, eyeing me resolutely as I sat in the car in front of the FOR RENT sign in the yard. I had been driving for hours, trying to find the best situation and this was it. Everyone was suspicious of me, and that meant they would be suspicious of others and that worked. Calling the number on the sign earlier and making an appointment, I still had fifteen minutes to wait.

There was a guy across the street, typical drug dealer, dressed in bling from head to toe, rolling in dough, but living in the ghetto. He kept watching me. I gave him a short head nod and looked the other way. On the porch, next door were three black women, all looked to be in their early twenties. I got out of the car and headed to the porch to peek in a window, truly a bother to them.

One of them yelled from the porch, "They rented that out yesterday." They all laughed until they nearly peed themselves.

The 'landlord' showed up, a sixty-year-old white man with no teeth and rented me the place without so much as asking my name. First and last month's rent, and a promise to show up on the first to get my next month's rent. If I was gone, I was gone. If I didn't pay, he would call his two sons and they would beat my ass until I was out. The clarity was striking. If more landlords represented like he did, rent would get paid. I paid the man and with a handshake asked for the keys to have him laugh in my face.

"You want locks, put 'em on the doors. I got so tired of trying to get keys from people, spend less money to bust out the damned window. It's boarded up in the back if you wanna reach through and open the back door." He walked away laughing.

Left standing in my own foolishness, I looked around one more time. The little drug-thug was still perched on the corner and the three black girls still sitting with nothing better to do. I was so incredibly tired, it pissed me off that I had to take control of the situation. I went to the car and opened the trunk, when I caught the thug's attention, I motioned for him to come over. Reluctantly, he did.

"Sup?" he swayed to the side like a good thug with a gangster walk.

Oh, Lord, what would I do with these people? "I could use some help carrying these things into the house."

He thought that was funny, put a hand to his mouth and laughed, swaying more to the side.

"Aren't you a regular Sammy the gun?" I said, rather dulled by the display.

"Huh?" He didn't even get the reference.

"Never mind ..." I said, "see this gun?" I showed him the gun in my waistband, my trusted Glock. "I'm going to blow you away if you don't carry my fucking bags in the house. I'm too damned tired to do this right now. Get it?" I waited for him to nod up before I asked, "You got a gun?" I put my hand on mine.

He nodded.

"Give it to me." I was really done playing any games. "How old are you?"

He was all business now, "Eleven. But I'll be twelve in a monf.?"

"Not if you fuck with me." I was not alert enough to do this and I knew it. But, he gave me his gun and took some of the bags. When he got close enough for me to get a good look at him; he was so young it amazed me. "Why are you on the street there? You don't run colors?" I knew enough about gangs to know that solo sales were dangerous.

"Na. My mom won't let me."

Now I laughed.

He took great offense to that.

"I'm sorry," I said. "You just seem so tough and your mom won't let you. I don't wanna mess with you or anything, I just need some sleep and in order to get some--I'm running from the law myself ... I gotta use you. So," we walked now, toward the house, "you are going to be kidnapped by me. You'll make the papers someday, when they catch me or if they find out, or when you squeal on me, like a little narc-pig ... anyway, it'll make you famous. So, get in the house."

We dropped the bags on the floor. "What a fucking hell hole." I said as I saw the inside of the filthy place.

"I wouldn't even live here." He grunted a little as he put the bags down and turned to me for direction.

"Your mother has raised you right. Even though you're a shit, selling on the street and gonna get yourself killed and hurt her … she's raising you right. Over there." I pointed. "Sit down and wait for me." He did and I opened one of the cases Joel brought me to pull out the equipment to make my sleep a little sounder.

Thirty-seven minutes later and I was ready to take care of the girls next door. 'Tigger', his nickname, was all 'tied up' for the moment. Down the porch stairs I went.

If looks could kill, the three of these girls would have done the job. As I walked up, the middle girl looked to the right, "Shameeka, is that bitch really coming up on our yard?"

Shameeka laughed, "She shore is. She the Welcome Wagon."

The other woman entered in the contest, "An lookin' how she dressed." They all got a real big laugh out of that.

For a minute, I forgot I was in the fat suit and that I was a homely girl about their age. Downing bottle after bottle of water and Gatorade, the sweating was just second nature. I didn't fit in here with this look. What they saw was bait. They would rob me blind, kill me in my sleep, make my life hell and I wouldn't get the sleep I so desperately needed, the healing time to recover fully. What the hell would I do? I walked with conviction and when I got in front of them I had already decided how I would handle this.

"Hey ..." I let it roll softly off my tongue.

"You lost?" The middle one asked.

The one on the left said, "She aint got no sense, Tamika. No sense at all."

"Actually, I have great sense and if I tell you who I am, I will have to kill you. BUT ... I can make you some money. Up for two grand?"

"Two G's?" Tamika was interested. "I ain't dealing no drugs. I got four strikes now and my parole officer said no mo'." She looked at the other two before grinding her eyes into mine as she leaned forward. "What choo need, bitch?"

Shameeka was right behind her, as they all three huddled in closer. I leaned in with them. "I need a place to sleep. I'm sure you would turn me in just as soon as look at me, so I figure two G's to start with right now, forty G's when I wake up alive and the cops ain't nowhere near me …" It was truly difficult to decide whether they would call and turn me in or not. The reward offered for me was $100,000 for any information leading to my arrest. I wasn't stupid; I checked when I could. It wasn't safe to check more than once, because if the FBI pulled the IP address they might know where I was headed. Maybe I could fool these girls long enough to get through all this.

"What'd ya do?" The one without a name asked.

Shameeka chimed in, "You rob a bank or something, Whitebread?" They laughed again.

There was only one way to handle this … "Look, you low-life rat-ass bitches wouldn't understand." I pulled the fat suit zipper out enough for them to see. "I'm fully covered, from head to toe. You can turn me in for $25G's, but then when I get out, I find you … and I will kill you. I won't get caught again." I stared them down. "You don't know shit about nothing. Got that?" I let them wrestle with it. The one thing you could do to people like this was intimidate them. If they would have been in a place to resist even the slightest intimidation, they never would have listened to me. There would be too much involved.

Tamika asked, "So you want us to do what for a lousy 2G's ... not rat you out?"

"No." I stated it clearly, "I have Tigger tied up and a bomb is hooked to him. If anyone touches my house, it will blow. Not just my house, but yours, and the rest of the block into the second block." Their eyes were as big as pumpkins, a dumb look on each one of their faces. I finished, "Sorry, but I gotta get some sleep and then get the hell out of here."

"Whatever, bitch." Shameeka got up and started to come near me, but before she could walk another inch, I was on the porch and in her face.

Very calmly, but with confidence, I said between my teeth, "Bitch, I don't have time for you. Sit the fuck down and don't move until I come back out of that house. You hear me?"

She sat right back down, but Tamika got up and got so close to me that she bumped me. "Shut up, Shameeka, sit your ass down.' She turned to me, "YOU look, mother fuuuucker … I help you out, but you let go of the attitude. We ain't like the other shit you think you know. We help you cuz we want to and Tigger is my brother. Ain't nothing gonna happen to anybody … got that? Do what you need to do."

"Good. We have an understanding?"

She looked at me with rage, but controlled rage. I had her brother and she knew it. "I got cho back, bitch. How long you need? If you let my brother go, I'll go in with you and I'll make sure no one does nothing. They will listen to me. But if my sib don't show up for dinner, my momma gonna come looking. She don't mess with nobody. You need to let him go and take me. She don't spect me home no time."

I thought about it. "That makes perfect sense. Will he keep quiet?"

"Iffin I tell him to he will." She started to walk off the porch, looking back, over her shoulder she said, "Cova fo me with Momma. Tell her I went with Darnelle."

They agreed as we left the porch and headed next door.

I let Tigger go, laughed because he peed his pants, and told him to never steal, cheat or lie again. His sister actually seemed impressed by it as she kissed him goodbye, and said, "You don't know noffin. Go home, eat dinner and I'll be fine. This lady just in trouble. She ain't out for us. She just protectin. Got it?" She turned to me. "Tell him."

"I won't hurt her if I can just get some sleep. Promise." I was genuinely making a pledge.

He left as though this was just an everyday part of life. I shook my head.

"I dunno why, but you seem okay, Miss."

"Now, how do you go turning into someone who is polite and has manners from the pig I saw on the porch?" I was confused.

"That's a show. My family growed up in this neighborhood and it ain't safe. You gotta really put things in perspective with life, ya know?"

"I do know … Okay, so here is what I am going to do. This bomb is set to go off when triggered. What I'm going to do is just hold the igniter while I sleep and hope I don't push it accidentally. I shouldn't, but I do sleep hard." I saw the look on her face, "Okay, I'll just lay it to the side of me."

"Okay." She swallowed hard.

"I'm going to tie you to the chair and then strap the bomb on you. Sorry, Tamika, but I have to get some sleep."

"It's aight. At least Tig got to go home. I'll be okay." She manned up and sat down in the chair Tigger was in initially. It was as if she were convincing herself.

"I respect you for this. I'll make it worth your while, Tamika. And, if you call the cops after I leave, you can be famous. But you gotta wait til I go." I finished tying her up and twisting the bomb in place and picked up one of the duffle bags and smashed it enough that I could lay my head on it. This place was disgusting, but it was all I had now. I laid the detonator on the table in front of the ratty-dirty-nasty sofa. I was so tired I didn't care if I laid on the smelly filth.

I wrestled with being so tired that I couldn't relax to go to sleep. Tossing and turning, trying to get comfortable, I was just wasting time. Facing Tamika, I wondered what it would be like to be in her shoes. She eyed me, probably wondering the same.

I spoke to her calmly, "What is your life like?"

"What's that gotta do wit anything?" She squirmed in the seat.

"I know I'm an asshole. I have to be in my position. I've killed nine people in 19 years."

Her eyes flew open wide.

I kept talking. "I'm not kidding. I'm too tired to kid," I sighed. "My father molested me every night, like I was his wife. So, when I was old enough, I killed him, blamed it on my mom and she went to prison. Bet that she never says I'm lying again, huh?" I tried to laugh. Truth was, I missed having a family, hated being on the run and Max suffered at the hand of all of us.

"Why you gotta go and do dat? Really?"

"Really ... then I found another man molesting his daughter, a girl I knew from school. So, I hunted him down and did the same thing. It was so easy, I just kept doing it."

"It was easy? Don' sound easy."

"It was. I planned my father so well that no one would ever know I

413

did it and my mom got the blame. It worked. Not one person looked for another suspect; it's like they completely believed it and didn't need to look any further."

"Smoking gun shit?"

"Yeah. Something like that. You're pretty smart, aren't you?" I asked her.

"I'm real smart. I don't talk it, cuz then someone would just be jealous and try to beat me down. I can handle my own. Like right now, you ain't gonna kill me, are you?" She watched me for the answer.

I didn't flinch. "No, sweetie. I have no intention of killing you. If you get in my way of freedom, I'm not sure. Mental illness must come in to play at some point. I am wondering if I can stop. Right now, my plan is to never kill again. But, I never really know." I got more comfortable on the couch, lying back with my hands behind my head, I closed my eyes and listened to her.

"You got a lotta shit going on. You gotta name?" When I didn't answer, she questioned me more. "How long you been on the run? How do you do that? Gotta be hardcore."

"Hmmmm … I'm not sure I know anymore. For as long as I can remember. I was always running from my dad, so it's second nature. Sleepovers at people's house I hated. Never wanting to be home, always wondering what he was doing to my baby brother, Max. It's hard to tell, Tamika. Hard to tell …" My voice got softer and softer.

"I won't narc on you. You let me be and I won't narc on you. I know you can't trust anyone if that mother fucker did that to you … my uncle did it to me every time he was around, fucking pig. I got chore back. You try and get some sleep." She kept on talking …

Her voice lulled me to sleep, a good sleep, a deep slumber, restful and relaxed.

Chapter 59

Pippin got back into the car. Everything had come to a head when she fired the gun, but it did the trick. Judy started yapping her ass off. It was about getting everything she knew, and they did. Too bad it wasn't worth anything, but Judy's information was coming right back to Miller. After Pippin bought her soda, they had just dumped the stolen car and were back in Trey's car, she climbed back in.

Trey was still mad at her for scaring the crap out of him, but Carlos and Skee were not phased at all.

"C'mon, Trey. I said I was sorry. It worked, didn't it?" They all started laughing at Pippin even talking to him.

Trey was so angry. "You say one more thing about my shitting myself and I swear, I will knock yo ass out, bitch."

They all laughed again. How could they help it? They ribbed him the entire ride until he dropped Pippin off two blocks from her house. They had thrown out the gloves and clothing they had worn and were fairly certain no one was the wiser. Judy was safely back in her vehicle, knocked out and shot up with Depakote, which would make her feel funny, fuzz up her memory and make her wonder if she even really went through anything. They parked her truck just where they found her, dead center, in the middle of the road. Worst thing about things like this, and they had all four been through it, was you really didn't know if it was real or not. In their world, they didn't tell anyone, because they were so below the line with the cops it would surely lead to an arrest. Hopefully no one did anything that would pinpoint them, and if they did, the boys would not pin Pippin with anything. They had been paid two hundred dollars and they were happy.

Pippin walked the two blocks in the blazing heat, something she hated more than anything. She mumbled the entire time, cursing the heat, her shoes and overall anything that moved in front of her. In one respect, she was glorified at having gotten to the lady, but in another she felt that the information was not consistent and would not be of help. The expectations that would be held for the interrogation by

Miller were more her source of anger. What would she do if Miller

didn't get the information she needed? Failure was not an option.

When she got home, she was sweating profusely. Miller was

cleaning again. "You don't got nothing better to do?" Her accent was

even thicker now that she was tired, hot and hungry.

Miller stopped what she was doing immediately. "I am not used to

letting someone else do my work. Did you find her?"

"Oh, yeah." Pippin was filling a glass with water at the kitchen sink.

"We put her in the car and we got everything she knew. At gunpoint,

for real."

"You used a gun?" Miller started sweating. The heat outside was

like a Barbeque, but even in the room with the window A/C, she was

sweating profusely. "Lay it on the line, what did she say?"

"Nodda dayumed thing. She don't know shit. But that's cuz Karma

didn't tell her anything. They were girlfriends before and so Karma

went to her and asked her to get her out of Kansas. She brought her

home. Karma didn't even know she lived down here. Bastrop was a

secret until Judy decided that she wanted out. Reason Karma left was cuz she didn't want Judy to get in trouble."

"Damn it!" Miller wanted to kick something, smack the crap out of the world. "I let her get away too."

"She ain't no criminal, Rider. Let her be. She told us everything she knew." Pip started laughing.

"How do you know?"

"Cuz I shot the window out da back of the car and she thought I was gonna kill her. She started babbling all kinda shit." Pip was so proud of herself. "She blew it all, but she don' know nothing."

"Okay ..." Miller was now deep in thought.

Pip drank all the water and put the cup back on the sink very slowly. "Hey, Rider ... she did say something about Karma being delirious on the way down. Who is Max?"

"Max?"

"Yeah. Judy said she was mumbling about a Max ... what do you know? Maybe it's a piece. Maybe Max is a daddy or boyfriend or brother or someone helping her?"

Miller was on it in two seconds. "Shit!" She fumbled for a thought. Who could she call? How could she make a call? Was anyone safe?

"What?" Pip was at the table now, trying to get Miller to sit down.

"I think I remember the name Max …" It hit Miller like a ton of bricks. "She has a brother named Max."

"There it is …" Pip was all kinds of proud of herself. "What about him?"

"He's younger, in an institution in …" she couldn't get the place in her head. "Damn … I know it was someplace weird." She paced.

Pip just watched her.

Around the room, hands on hips and then down to her side, she looked up and then down, moving all around trying to jiggle the memory. Miller thought back to the paperwork they got when the files were in her hand. Reynolds read most of them to her … should she call Reynolds and let her in on it?

"What, Mama? What cha thinking?" Pip wanted to have her win this one.

"I have to decide what to do. I don't know what's safe." It then hit Miller. "Wilmington, Delaware." She nearly jumped for joy.

"We headin to Wilmington?" Pippin was excited.

"You wanna go with me?" Miller hadn't thought about it, but she could use the help and the mind behind the crime. Would she put her in danger? What was the chance that was where Karma was going? Should she just call the Wilmington police department and give them an anonymous head's up? She had to decide what to do.

"I do. I wanna see this bitch."

"I don't think I have time. I can't decide what to do." Miller was perplexed. She needed to calm down.

Chapter 60

I awoke to an unfamiliar place, pitch black, afraid for the first time in a long time. My dreams had been filled with my father molesting me and Max screaming for me to help him. Sweating profusely, still in the fat suit, I felt completely dehydrated and out of energy. To wake feeling no more rested than when I fell asleep, shook me back to reality. Tamika was sitting in the chair, wide awake, a look of terror on her face.

"You okay?" I asked her.

"Just need to pee really bad. You been asleep for a long time. I didn't think about needing to pee."

"You held it this long?" I worked to get her undone so she could go to the bathroom. My gun in my waistband again, I led her to the facility. "Sorry, Tamika."

She peed in front of me, no shame. "It's aight. I just didn't want to go in my pants. Thought I might set off the bomb."

"Damn. I'd be pissed." I really didn't understand why this girl was so compliant.

"I got no problem with you. I just wanna go home soon. You done sleeping?" She looked around for toilet paper before she got up without it and pulled up her shorts.

"Yeah. Not sure it helped." I led her back into the other room and undid the detonator that I had set on the door that led out back. "Before you go, I need to gather up my stuff and get on the road. I don't want to tie you up, but it all has to look real. You understand?"

"Yeah. I guess." She cast her eyes down and headed back into the living room without being asked and sat down in the chair. "You gonna set the things on the door again?"

"No ... I'll even disarm it fully, so that you don't have to worry. I need the C-2 with me. I won't leave it. You will just be tied up. Okay?" I worked furiously to get the bomb disassembled and back in my case and to get her tied up so that I could hit the road again. Once the fuzz wore off, I felt completely rested, much better than I had before. My body wasn't up to par, but it was a far cry better. I needed fluids. "There ya go."

I was done and ready to leave. "I will call the police myself and make sure they pick you up …" It was hard, but I didn't want her to sit around and be afraid. I liked her.

"Here, you got a phone?" She asked.

"Yeah …"

"Put Shameeka's number in it and just call her. I don't need to tell the cops nothing unless they ask. Just call her and tell her to come and get me."

"Okay … I can do that." I felt like waving as I left, but it was inappropriate so I just walked out of Tamika's life like I walked in to it, a stranger.

In the car and out on the road again, I felt like crying for being mean to her and her family. Hopefully I didn't scar her for life. It was probably because she told me her uncle did the same thing to her. What people didn't know is how often girls were molested and raped by people they knew. If I could, I would blow them all away.

I had to ditch the car and get another, just in case she was a liar like everyone else in my life. It was time to take public transportation. I drove to Briana's house and parked in front. It was almost four-thirty in the morning. With a brief note of regret, I walked away and headed to the corner three blocks away, where I could catch a bus.

The bus stop was isolated and lonely, but I sat there until the next bus came around, nearly six o'clock. I thought about how I could get to Max with the security that would be in place. The fat suit offered me some luxury, but I had no idea what ID badges were used, how things were set up or even what he looked like now. It had been years since I had seen him. He was just a baby. Now he was a boy, almost a man. How could he possibly recognize me? I was overwhelmed with emotion.

For the first time in years, tears of sadness at the loss of my family and the guilt of what I had done hit me with power, baffled me to a point I was completely overwhelmed. The bus pulled up just as the tears hit me and I had to push it all away. I brushed the back of my hand over my eyes, wiped away the tears and entered the doorway to the bus. "I don't have tokens, I have dollars ..."

He let me buy tokens from him and I scooted to the back of the bus where the other three people sat sparsely amid the empty seats. One backpack, my things safely stashed, I sat down to finish coming up with a plan. My options were to watch from afar, but I didn't even know if he was still in the same spot … "Holy hell …" I whispered. My lawyer was the one person who could not tell where I was. If I called him and had him set up a release for Max, I could have him placed in another situation so that I could see him. That was it! I could succeed! All I had to do was wait another two hours and see Patrick Delaney, ESQ.

I knew where his office was and would get off the bus somewhere downtown. Looking forward to a good brewed coffee with some food of some sort, I let myself think ahead to what it would do for me to see my Max. Joy and peace were instantaneous. I enjoyed the ride through the now waking city as I headed downtown.

At the sixth street stop, I exited the now full bus and walked down the street until I found a coffee shop. Café Espresso was my next stop.

Inside the shop, filled with half-awake morning drones, I found a coffee blend I enjoyed and picked up a newspaper to enjoy my three scones. Front page was barely enticing at all. More war from Iraq, when we should have been out of that country years ago. The upcoming election ... blah, blah, blah ... Nothing caught my eye at all until I turned to the fourth page. There was a gallery opening that night for Briana. Apparently, she had acquired a show and was presenting that night. I wondered what would happen if I showed up at the gallery and let her know I was there. Loving the look on people's faces when I intimidated them was something I would surely have to give up if I were going to give up my life of vengeance. Wait? Was I giving it up? What was I planning? Did I really think that I could steal Max out of the institution and live happily ever after? Maybe I was delusional enough to think that I could reopen the mansion and go back home ... home to my princess comforter with pink and purple stars all over the walls, the childish white desk that I remember writing death threats and stories about how I would kill my father as I smoked out the window at twelve. Did I really think I was going to get away with this? Now, after eating my scones and feeling the brunt of the accident, the infection, the dehydration from the fat suit ... feeling like complete shit, did I really think I would get away with this?

I folded up the newspaper calmly, placed it on the table and watched the people walking in and out of the shop. Smiles on their faces for the most part, people were happily engaging in their morning addiction. Those that were in a bad mood could be spotted immediately.

I needed a passport, transportation, a new country of origin and a way out. No one in Wilmington was available to me to use without research. If not the last part of my plan was in place and it would have to work. Years of planning, perhaps it was just time to let things lie. There was no way I could go to see Max, but I did have another option. I needed to check, but it was time for me to go see Patrick Delaney and figure out what the best plan of action would be for Max ... for all I knew, he was dead.

Down the street, I walked, lighter in step than I had been in days, the coffee finally coursing through my veins. It was about four blocks to the building that Delaney worked in. Once there, I waited in the parking garage. Luckily it was only one floor and from the courtesy gate I could see who came and went. I had no real way to get in the garage, but I could see the cars as they entered. The automated system annoyed me because there was a camera system and I ducked it best I could. Delaney had not necessarily done work for me, but I considered him as an attorney, because I dated him when I was in London. We both went pre-med to change our minds. That short period of dating, he was so nice to me, brought me to Wilmington a few times a year while I was at Dartmouth ... And then there was Briana.

I saw him through the window of the black Mercedes ... waving frantically, I approached. He saw me and rolled down the window about two inches.

He was very hesitant, "Can I help you?"

I kept forgetting about the damned fat suit. "It's me, Pattie ... Carolyn Riley."

Immediately he focused. "Get in and get in fast ... they are looking for you."

Crap! He knew everything probably. I climbed in the car quickly and he pulled farther into the garage. He couldn't get in trouble for seeing me or having contact, but it didn't do me any good for anyone to know he saw me in town. The threat became real. I felt really trapped.

"You okay?" He asked the minute I got in.

"No. Do I look okay?"

"You don't look anything ... what happened?"

"Oh, I didn't gain weight. I have on a fat suit, disguise ... you know. Serial killer needs to keep on the low-down."

"Did you do it?"

"Everything they say and more ... I'm sure." I could be honest with him. We were to the end of it all. Feelings were always on target and I was starting to feel remorse. "Max? Where is Max?"

"You didn't know?" Patrick turned off the car and turned to me.

"Know what, Pattie?"

I knew it before he said it, but it was not clear even when I heard him.

"Car, he passed away three years ago. I never had a way of contacting you but the house. I sent multiple messages ... I'm sorry." He placed his hand atop mine.

Anger welled from deep inside the pit of my stomach. I felt like throwing up ... my scones doing a dance in my stomach. "What?" I watched his eyes.

"His situation was never right, Sweetie. He just passed in his sleep one night. They thought his brain forgot to tell him to breathe. Multiple problems arose through the years. I did visit him once a week. We had a pretty good relationship ... it's been almost thirteen years since I've seen you, since you sat in my office and we decided what was best for him ... thirteen long years, Car."

"I know." I was numb to anything.

"Look, you are in deep shit. How can I help you? They have to be watching me if they know anything about our past dealing. They will link me to Max, right away." He was concerned.

"Have they contacted you?" My voice even sounded dead.

"They did weeks ago ... told them the truth. I had no dealings with you since you found out your brother passed away."

Something came alive in me, if only for a moment. "What?"

"I knew you were in some real bad stuff in Europe and just figured you never contacted me because you knew ... it wasn't until I called to the house to find the service staff answer, that I found out the letters had never been opened. The west wing is still open. Your mother runs it from prison." He laughed.

"She still thinks I'm coming home?"

"She must. I've spoken to her a couple of times in relation to Max. It must still be incredibly hard to deal with what you had to deal with ... all coming out at the trial and all ..." He was remorseful. "They came and questioned me, as if they thought I would tell them anything. You know me, made it look like I gave them everything I knew ... and told them nothing. I honestly can't believe it ... murder?"

"Nine ..." I was tired of lying.

"Your dad?"

I did nothing but nod.

"I'm estate and civil litigation, but I know some good attorneys. What would you like me to do? You are putting yourself at risk being here ... unless you want to turn yourself in. I don't think a plea bargain will help you out, Car ..."

"It won't … lethal injection in two of the states … problem with federal crime. I laid out a plan, but one slip and it's the needle for me. Without Max, I don't care … what defense options do I have, Pattie?" I stared out the window.

"You can go with mental incapacity. That will land you in an institution for life. From what I understand, you are pretty fucked, sister. I wish I had better news." He paused before he added, "A couple of countries will not allow extradition …"

"Yeah, I already knew that … pretty much my only option other than suicide." I got out of the car, bent back down to say goodbye, "Thanks, Pattie … thanks for visiting him. At least he doesn't have to deal with this shit anymore … and I won't have to either."

"Don't do that, Car … I would miss you."

As I walked away, I said, "You will be the only one …"

I picked my phone up out of the back pack and dialed the number to Austin homicide … I asked for Detective Miller.

"What the fuck do you mean she's not there? Patch me in to her cell."

The female voice on the other side said, "She isn't available ... I can give you to her partner, Wyatt Grant?"

"That will work ..."

Chapter 61

Miller and Pippin sat in the car watching Patrick Delaney and the woman who got in his car with him. They sat and talked for a little bit. It seemed quite intimate.

Pippin did her best to keep quiet, but she just couldn't stand it anymore when the girl got out of the car. "Whadya think?"

"It's her …"

Again, complete silence ensued. Miller could tell by the way she walked, head held down, avoiding anyone looking at her, but the weight was miraculous. How did she do it? Just her demeanor when she bent back in the car to say the last bit of what she had to say to the attorney, Miller knew it was Carolyn Riley. Now what?

Pippin was freaking out. "It's her?" She whispered almost as if

Carolyn might hear them.

"Yeah ... and for some reason, she's let her guard down. She doesn't even look around to see if anyone is watching. Look at the way she is walking ..."

Carolyn walked slowly back down to the exit of the garage. Miller followed as far back as she felt necessary. Taking the phone out of her pack, Carolyn made a call, punching in the numbers on the phone.

They watched as she got angry, talked in to the phone and then waited.

Miller said, "She must be on hold. I wonder who she's calling."

It wasn't but a couple of minutes later when Carolyn started talking again, this time she was angrier, at one point, slamming the phone shut.

Pippin watched her walk. "That there is a woman with the weight of the world on her shoulders."

Miller was caught in a horrible situation. Her very morality was on the line ... her job, her life, her everything. She was thinking about letting her walk away.

Pippin caught the thought as if Miller said it out loud. "Why don't you talk to her first? Collar her and put her in the car ... just talk to her."

"Huh ...?" Miller was confused. Did she say anything out loud? She kept focus on Carolyn walking, now headed down the street.

"You wanna let her go? She got reason to kill those people?"

"No, no one has the right to take a life. She had reason to be upset, but she had no right to kill those people, make their families suffer and there's the chance she'll never quit. It doesn't matter what I think, she needs stopped and I can stop her right now."

"What if she got a gun and she shoots at us? I don't got no gun, Rider." Pippin started to think she was out of her league. This woman was different than street fighters. "She gonna kill us?"

"She will try. I'm sure." Miller kept crawling behind her.

Carolyn kept walking, meandering, not looking up or down, fixated on the street in front of her as if in a fog.

Miller had no idea what to do. She fought herself. When she had notified the police that Carolyn might be coming to see her brother, they hooked in to high security. But, within the hour, Miller had the information that Carolyn's brother had passed away. She interviewed the institution administrator to find out that the boy had only had one visitor the entire time he had been with them, Patrick Delaney. Why she kept that information to herself, she did not know, but she did. The next best thing was to tail Delaney and here is where it brought them.

Miller and Pippin had flown out immediately. She had notified the Captain and Reynolds, and they had developed a plan of action for the area. Surprised that she had not seen any agents, Miller wondered where they were, because if she knew about Delaney, so did they. It was her responsibility to take Karma in ... that was her wish.

As she thought, Miller's phone rang and she reached to answer it, as Carolyn answered her phone ...

Chapter 62

Not that it ever really did, but the world did not make sense to me right now. It eluded me that I was truly alone in this life. Max was my everything. The tears streamed down my face. My phone finally rang. Grant Wyatt had taken the call, but I refused to talk to him. I gave him my number and told him to patch Miller in immediately to me, Officer Debra Pattingsly, FBI. What a dip-shit. Maybe he knew it was me.

I answered the phone. "Pattingsly, what can I do for you?" She hoped it was Miller and this was all over and done with.

Miller watched as she answered her phone and Wyatt told her he was patching her in to the FBI through Austin, just in case. Within a few seconds, Carolyn's phone rang. Could it be? What if it were?

"Hello ... Pattingsly." Carolyn started to feel that old uneasy feeling.

"Hello, this is Detective Miller ..." Miller watched Carolyn answer her as she heard her voice.

"This is Karma ... I'm all yours."

"How do I know that?" Miller was baiting her. If she was right, she was less than a hundred yards right behind her. Something about the chase came in to play and the old Miller took over. There was no way she would let her get away from justice now. How dare she make a call right to her when she was so close to having found her anyway? No. Karma would not take this away from her.

"I'm done. I can't do this anymore. No more running, no more hiding, no more lying ... I can tell you where I am."

Miller hung up the phone. She looked at Pippin who was absorbing it all. "Could you hear?"

She nodded. "Take her down, Rider. Take her down."

They both watched as Carolyn slammed the phone shut. Her anger was now rage. She stopped and turned, looking around, making Miller and Pip duck in the car. Dialing the phone again, she listened to the operator and then asked for Grant Wyatt again. "The bitch hung up on me. Get her back on the phone."

Wyatt was confused, "Who is this?"

"This is Karma and I had Miller on the phone ... get her back on the phone so I can tell her where I am so she can come and get me. I want her to do it."

Miller walked slowly toward Karma, adjusting her stance with every step, trying to make sure she was balanced. Pippin just a few steps to the side. Arguing with her was not going to happen and Miller might need the help. Karma would have a gun, but when she saw Miller the focus would be there, Pippin could handle herself.

"Get her on the fucking phone!" Carolyn was now yelling. Standing in the middle of the sidewalk, her back to Miller and Pippin, screaming into the phone. "Right now ... please!" She pled.

Miller was less than ten feet away when she spoke, gun pulled, aimed at Carolyn's chest. "Karma ... I'm right here." Miller's heart was racing, but her hand was steady and her mind relaxed. She was ready for the reaction.

Carolyn looked up, dropped the phone and held her wrists out to be cuffed. "Take me in, please."

Miller couldn't believe there was no fuss over any of this. Pippin was right on time, cuffing her in an instant, scaring her from the side.

Miller apologized, "Sorry, I have help."

Pippin's grin was as big as Texas.

Miller approached. "Do you have a gun, any weapons, anything that will stick me?" She then spoke to Pippin. "Hold her hands out in front of her and don't let her go, not for anything."

Pippin nodded. "Gotcha."

"Is this your new partner? I haven't seen any paperwork on her. FBI?" She was stunned, she had done her research and this woman didn't look like Austin PD. "Are you from here?"

Pippin didn't know what to do now that Carolyn was speaking to her. "Shut yo mouth. She gotta do her thang."

Karma laughed. "Who is she, Jennifer?" She turned a little so she could see Miller as Miller undid the pack and dropped it to the ground, found her gun, found the zipper to the fat suit, found it all. No resistance from Carolyn at all. "Can you legally arrest me here?"

Miller started to anger until she saw Karma's expression. It was relaxed. "She's with me, that's all that matters."

From her phone, Miller called for back-up directly to dispatch. When done, she hung up and put her gun back in her holster. They headed back to the car. Once there, Miller took another pair of cuffs and cuffed Karma to the car interior.

"You don't wanna let me go, do you?" Karma chided her.

Miller laughed, this was too easy; she couldn't let her guard down. "We have about two minutes before the PD gets here … wanna talk?"

"I'd love nothing more." Carolyn said. "What would you like to know?"

"Why me?" Blunt and to the point, Miller laid it on the line. "In front of her?" She asked.

Miller nodded.

"You know what I went through. Maybe you can find it in your heart to be easy on me and not treat me like a common criminal?"

"You are anything but common, Carolyn." Miller smiled at her.

"I'm not going to do anything. I'm beat, done and you won without my help. I like that. You were definitely a worthy adversary, Miller, definitely worthy." Carolyn smiled at her. "Can you get me out of this suit?"

Miller wasn't about to chance it. "Nope ... down at the station. We can talk more there, but they will hear everything we say. If you got something to say, say it right now. Off the record ..."

"Off the record?" Carolyn asked.

Miller confirmed.

"I did it because he was a bastard and I thought you would understand. I know that they will put a needle in my arm, but I don't care. Nine men are dead and six women paid the price for not believing their children. All I ask of you is that somehow you start fighting for us ... my fight wasn't fair and I know that. I will die with honor and you can let the wives out. I'll give you all the details, take the guilty pleas, all of it ... but please go fight for the women that were once girls, just like we were ... the girls that were ruined, Jennifer. It's not like we ever have a chance at a real relationship."

Miller watched her as she spoke with genuine empathy. She said, "I promise, Carolyn" as the sirens from the Wilmington, DE Police Department swarmed in on them.

EPILOGUE

As the booking agent finished and delivered Carolyn to her cell, the call came to bring her in for questioning. The point had not come that Carolyn requested an attorney, so they escorted her to the interrogation room at the end of the hall. While she waited, she adjusted her light blue jumpsuit. The one-way mirror made her nervous, she wondered if Miller was outside. She waved, just to see if anything moved, but she really couldn't see through it. Her hands were chained and cuffed to her sides, but she could still lift them a bit. So far everyone had been pleasant to her, but Miller was the key. She wanted to talk to Jennifer Miller.

Within five minutes, the two duty officers escorted Jennifer down to the interrogation room where she waited outside, watching Carolyn walk around, wave at the window and then sit down to wait.

Miller said, "She doesn't seem like a killer, does she?"

The officers didn't comment, but walking up behind her was the staff psychologist, Daniel Casey. "It's very hard to determine a 'type' for a female serial killer. So few have been up for review." He offered his hand. "Dr. Daniel Casey, Criminal Psychologist. I'm here to do an initial analysis so that we properly place her in the facility."

"I see." Miller wondered if she were ever going to get to talk to Carolyn. Since the pick-up, she had not seen Carolyn. The Feds were in line for her, but before they decided where to transfer her, Carolyn's request to see Miller had been granted.

"Several of us would like for you to ask her pertinent questions. We need to determine her mental capacity. Would you be willing?"

"I think if you just go in and talk to her, she'll tell you anything. She seemed like she was done playing games. You can try it. I just want to talk to her."

Three men came down the hall, headed in their direction, all suits, and all business. She knew the Feds were making their presence known.

The first approached, a smaller man, he introduced them all, "I'm agent Ralph Vera, supervising interrogation, Baltimore. This is Agent Ross and Agent Phillips. We will be conducting the interviews to determine where we will send her first. A series of documents are being drawn up at the current time to be presented to the judge this afternoon. We want expedited intent to be a priority." They each shook Miller's hand.

Agent Ross, approached Miller, "I think that your ability to converse with her freely will allow us to have the best chance of a full confession. We've asked Dr. Casey to analyze the situation so that we might present that to the judge as well."

"I see." Miller needed to say as little as possible. She had promised Karma that she would do her best to help others, but she felt compelled to help her as well. She was facing so much now, but, then again, she had to be stopped and Miller had done just that … thanks to Pippin.

Miller pointed to the door. "Can I go in?"

They nodded in agreement and she opened the door so that she and Dr. Casey could enter. This was the first time she had actually faced

Carolyn Riley without bullshit between them. It was just the two of them, the moment Jennifer entered the room, and she knew that this was going to be the interview she would never forget.

Carolyn was glad to see her, moving forward in her chair. "I'd shake your hand, but it's a little difficult." She smiled.

"No problem." Jennifer reached across the table and touched her shoulder. "You doing okay?"

Carolyn nodded, "I'm in jail, but, hey … not too bad. They gave me a something to drink and I needed that. A little dehydration problem from the fat suit and the antibiotics, well, the cocaine didn't help, but … I'm a little dry." She puckered her lips and tried to make the best of this. For years she wondered what this very moment would be like, because in the back of her mind, she knew it would come. "What can I tell you?"

Miller wanted so badly to ask her to lawyer up, but she knew she could not do that, instead, she leaned forward, "You tell me whatever you would like me to know, Carolyn. I will listen to it all."

"I have questions for you, mostly. My confession will come when

I'm ready." She raised her voice and looked through the two-way mirror. "Who the hell are you?" She addressed Dr. Casey.

"I'm Dr. Daniel Casey, psychologist." He started to sit down when she got up abruptly.

"I won't talk with him in the room, Jennifer. Get rid of him." Carolyn became very distraught. Her nervousness was very apparent. She began to shake, paced, and moved around the room to get away from him. "I have a shrink. Call Dr. Elvira Mendez. She's in Thornton's Ferry, New Hampshire, where I'm from. She will tell you everything and then you can arrest her for not telling authorities that my father was fucking me for all those years that I told her about it. Oh, yeah, she's crippled ... add that to my list."

Jennifer was appalled. What all would she find out in this crazy case? "Carolyn, are you sure you want to talk about all of this?"

Carolyn looked at her. Judging for a moment the person in front of her, she figured it out. "I don't want a lawyer. No one can help me with any of this; there is no plea bargain; the only thing that will be difficult is determining where I will be tried first. I know what I'm in for ... I did my research. Now, Dr. Casey, was it?"

He nodded.

"I am mentally sound. If I am a sociopath, I will not let you know that. If I am a psychopath, it will not be discovered. Now, go tell them I am competent to stand trial and leave me with Jennifer. I will give only her my confession. Ask them, they have had several people in here trying, quite good law enforcement officers, but I am pre-meditated. I have waited for this moment forever. Leave me in peace, please."

"I just want to ask …" Dr. Casey spoke before she cut him off.

Standing in anger, "Look, mother fucker. What part of shut your trap do you not understand? Get out and let me do what I need to do. Good ole Elvira will keep you busy for days with my file. I used to tell her stuff just to see if she would rat me out. Not one time did she open her mouth when I told her exactly what I was going to do … you worry about her." She couldn't get to him and Miller had her under control, standing as well.

"Calm down, Carolyn. He's just trying to do his job." Miller looked closely in her eyes, much different than when she had the oxygen cord around Miller's neck. "Calm down."

"Just tell them to let us have this conversation. I've been waiting for it for years." She pleaded with Jennifer, who looked through the glass to get the knock at the door and Dr. Casey left the room.

"You know they are listening to what you say, right?" Jennifer asked.

"I do. It's okay. I have it rehearsed so that while you get my confession, you get the rest of what I want you to do." Carolyn sat down and relaxed.

"I don't think I can do anything for you. I put criminals away, Carolyn, and right now, you qualify. I believe you are a harm to others and possibly yourself. What could you possibly want me to do?"

"Okay, just listen before you make any decisions. I killed my father." She looked through the glass and then back at Miller, "SEE ..." she yelled so they could hear, apparently unaware that recording devices were in various parts of the room. "I will give you what you want too, just let me talk to her." She moved to get more comfortable, leaning in to Jennifer. "I killed my father and made it look like my mother did it. My ace in the hole was that I administered Proplanlol to each of my female victims so that they were fuzzy enough when I killed

452

their husbands that upon awakening, they probably thought they did it. I planted evidence on my mother that made it look as if she did the deed. But, she didn't. It was me. He was molesting me. He had sex with me almost every night for most of my life at home. From as young as six, he would come in to my bedroom, undress from the waist down or undo his pajama pants and get on top of me. I had several threats of harm to my pets, my mother, the staff that I had loved ... he would kill them if I told. But, he sent me to a shrink when I got to the age I defied him. I never told anyone until after he was dead. I was really afraid, Jennifer ... I really thought he would kill my mom or my nanny, Debra."

"I know, baby ..." Jennifer's heart bled for Carolyn. She did know; all too well, she did know.

"So, he kept on doing it. He would buy me presents, sent me on trips when it seemed like I was unwilling. I learned how to lay still, real still and not make a sound, not participate at all ... and that got me my first beating. He beat my ass. I had to stay home from school for three days, twelve years old, and my mom didn't get it. I purposely dressed so you could see the bruises he put on me and she ignored it. I swear, the bitch acted like it never happened, like I didn't have a mark on me.

So, I hated her. I started telling the shrink all kinds of things that were the truth and she called me a liar too … so I rigged up her office stairs for her to fall … all it did was screw up her leg forever. She fell, but it wasn't foolproof. That's when I started planning better. Let me tell you, that was the first time I got revenge and it felt good. It felt sooooo good." She took a breath, adjusted herself in the seat and then continued, "When we moved to Atlanta--I was fifteen, that's when it got bad. Mother decided that she needed to be involved in the community in more ways and had some late nights. I think she was having an affair, but he didn't care. He treated me like I was his wife. I had to sit at dinner with him, shop with him, he even took me to a party with him and sold me to a friend of his for $5000 saying I was a virgin." Carolyn laughed heartily at that one. "Let me tell you how I fucked that man. When I was done with him, he knew I was no virgin. I told him I was no virgin and he kicked my dad's ass and demanded that he get his money back. Well, I got mine too. I liked it when he beat me up, because that pain I could handle. The smell of him, no. Absolutely made me puke, but when he hit me … I imagined what I was going to do to him one day. Cutting off the penis was my favorite thing. Cutting off his balls and shoving them down his throat … sorry for my mom to look so insane, but it was the best. So, I know that my remorse is not there and they will look at me with contempt, but I have full mental faculty," She yelled again.

"Carolyn, you don't have to do this …." Jennifer was almost sick at having to hear all this.

"No. I want you to know."

"Why? I don't understand why …" Jennifer said.

"Because you can help others in a way that I cannot. That website you used to go on?"

Without noticing, Jennifer immediately glanced back at the window.

"I saw what you said to that little girl who was going to kill herself. I saw it. That's why I picked you. You understand and you made her feel better. Do you know what happened to that little girl, Jennifer?"

Jennifer shook her head. "No …"

"I made sure I knew. You see, born into wealth is an amazing thing. I never run out of money. Never do I have to worry about what I want to use or how I want to do it, because money is no object. I was sole heir to my father, because I forged his name on documents and then had him file them or I was going to tell. He must have known I was going to kill him. He didn't come near me for days, so I had mother do it ... they hadn't had sex in a couple years and I talked her in to working on their relationship. I dared the bastard not to have relations with her. When they went to the bedroom, I was hiding in the closet and I could hear it all. I knew when he was about done and that's when I jumped in and made it known exactly what happened. I know mom can't remember, but you should have seen her face when I shot him. Just like the others, no one cared that they died. It's such a relief for them to have me kill those fuckers."

She parted her shoulders trying to get more comfortable again. "So, I did what I wanted to do and came out if it not so afraid. As a matter of fact, I've been afraid of very little since that night. I did the same thing to everyone; set them up and went in for the kill. I made sure the girls were honest when they said they were being molested, every one of them. When you told Sarah Endive that she was going to be okay and that she had a way out ... when you gave her the number to the bus station and told her to borrow the money from her friend and go … she did."

Carolyn now whispered. "She left and went to a whole 'nother city … she had the guts to do what I could never do. She borrowed $300 and when I found her just after that … You can't imagine how rich I am. I found her and I opened an account for her with over $300,000. She has not had to struggle since. She put herself through school and opened her own business. She owns her own home, is married and she seems happy. I check on her every once in a while, just like I did you. I check on them all."

"What about you?" Jennifer couldn't resist. "How about your happiness. Why didn't you try to be happy?"

"I am broken. Once I pulled the trigger on him, I knew I would tell, so I just made the list. One person at a time, I went to the site and found little girls that I could help. Each one of them is rid of their loser parents and on their own. If you check, they all have gotten 'gifts'. I made sure I didn't give them too much; that's what ruined me. Never wanting for anything makes everything you want worthless. The one thing I ever wanted … I never got."

"What was that, Carolyn? What do you want?"

"I wanted my mother to protect me. She should have told me I was okay, that it would be okay and that she would make him stop. I hate her, Jennifer. I don't even want to apologize to her ... and I know I should. She's just another fuck up. Did she really deserve what I did to her?"

Jennifer said, "I don't know. I'm not her judge. Nor am I yours." She made sure the eye contact was inclusive.

"Yeah ... well, my judge is coming. More story ... I killed Ricardo Dillon because I found Sylvia online and he had gotten her pregnant and then taken her for an abortion. They ripped out her insides, Jen ... she will never have babies. Just like me, she will never have a baby because of the damage he had done to her. She was twelve years old. The clinic name is St. Joseph Day Clinic in St. Paul, Minnesota. The doctor was Dr. James Alagami. The second murder was Nathan Jones, well, my third if I count my father. I need a break for a second ..."

Jennifer was hesitant. She was filling in all details necessary to block out the evidence. There was no way she would ever get out of any of this. Nine murders, how many states? Jennifer's head was filled with so many questions. This was going to take forever and the worst part of it was that it sounded like Carolyn wanted to die. "I understand," is all she could say.

"Have you gotten the appeals started for the wives?" She asked Miller.

"I'm not sure how that works. I'm law enforcement, definitely not a lawyer."

"I think I would like to ask you to make sure each of these is dismissed and that they are released. It's only fair. What would I have to do?"

"I'll check on it for you. Maybe you could ask your lawyer?" Jen was trying not to lose her job over this, but this woman needed to shut her mouth and lawyer up.

"No. I'll call him after I'm done with you. You deserve to know the whole truth." She tried to itch her nose but couldn't. Struggling with it, she finally gave up and looked to Miller, "Can you help me out?"

She laughed. "Sure."

As she leaned in to scratch her nose, Carolyn started to whisper,

"Find each of the girls and tell them it's time to testify." Louder, she said, "right there … a little lower." And then to a whisper again, "No worries, they know what to do." She pulled back to her usual seat and said, "Thank you …"

Outside the room, the agents were watching, eating up every word, making documentation in note pads, especially Dr. Casey. When he saw Carolyn whispering, "What did she say just then?" He moved to get a different view, because Carolyn was between them and Miller at that point. "She whispered something …"

Agent Ross chimed in, "I didn't see anything. She was scratching her nose and let me tell you, you cannot reach your nose in arm shackles. I don't think it was anything."

Agent Phillips agreed, "I didn't see anything. We can hear everything she is saying …"

Dr. Casey resolved to be wrong. "Okay … Maybe it was nothing."

Carolyn continued for the next hour telling every intimate detail about the killings of the six men who molested their daughters, before she mentioned the two men who raped her.

Miller asked, "So there were six families … but you say you killed nine people."

"Yeah, well, about that … two guys raped me one night when I was twenty-six. I had just gotten off work and they jumped me in the parking lot. You'll never find them, nor will you find the other one. Those I won't admit to. First and foremost, the guys who raped me, at gunpoint, mind you, it was self-defense and not worth wasting tax payer's money and the other … I'm not sure I actually killed him. I'll take responsibility for the act if I've done it, but not sure on that one. I did dispose of him and I don't think you will ever find him, so I'm not worried about it. It was crazy, but I couldn't even tell if I did it."

"What happened?" Jennifer asked.

"Well, I needed an identity to escape and I met him at a bar. He was a great guy and said he was leaving for Europe, my favorite thing when I wanted to use an ID or something, you know … live in their house they closed, get hired as a house sitter, or whatever and then just use their ID. I never did anything bad with it, cash is all I use. No trace, no deviant behavior toward them … just borrowed their ID and got in places I needed to get in to. That night I went to a bar and I wanted to

461

use a guy's this time, just to see what it was like."

"That's why you were speaking deeper and had a little facial hair when you had your accident?" Jennifer was awed.

"Yeah."

"Where is his body?"

Carolyn didn't fall for it. "What body? Whose body, Jennifer?"

"Okay, we are not playing this game. Go back to the murders of the gents that were in incestuous relationships with their daughters." Jennifer steered the conversation back to the confession.

"No. I'm done." She was very matter-of-fact. "You have all you need to do what I want you to do."

Jennifer's mouth gaped open.

"Close your mouth. Did you really think that I would sit here without a lawyer and tell you everything? As a matter of fact, did I tell you all that I did cocaine right before you arrested me and I'm not sure I remember much? Isn't that a hallucinatory drug? I feel really weird … I want my lawyer. Please call Janine Johnson, Topeka, KS … I would like her to be the head of my legal team."

Jennifer couldn't speak. Had she just been used? What the hell?

As the door opened, Carolyn leaned down where no one could see and whispered again, "Get the girls, they know what to do ... please? I didn't kill any of them, I just set it up."

Jennifer's head exploded like a firecracker went off in her ear. "You didn't kill any of them?"

She smiled at Jennifer as Agent Ross helped her up to lead her outside to the awaiting officer.

"I'll be extradited soon. I'm sure New Hampshire wants me, first crime, first dibs ... call Janine ... I want my phone call. I won't say anything else until I have my lawyer.

They led her out of the room when Dr. Casey came in. "Are you okay?"

"She just recanted an entire confession and said she didn't kill anyone. What the hell???"

"She's not mentally sound, Detective Miller. She is playing a huge game with us. I'm not sure what the game is, but it is definitely a fact that this woman is disturbed. At the very least, she will be locked up the rest of her life."

Jennifer was not convinced. The list of charges was not significant now. They had only one sure thing and that was attempted murder on Miller in Topeka when she escaped. She needed to check that out, because they had originally listed only a few things. Miller had to check that list. Could Karma be smart enough to get off on all of this? Why did she want her to get the girls? How would they know what to do??? This was starting to overwhelm her in a significantly negative way. She was being mind-fucked and it was going to be a problem. 'Miller, get your head in the game.'

Hillsborough County Superior Court was called to order by Judge Paul D. Jones. Carolyn Riley sat at the defendant's table with her team of attorney's: Janine Johnson, Peter McGiven, Lance Stanley and Marshall Forbes. These attorneys were guarded, grave and impeccably dressed as everyone stood to honor the judges' entrance into the room.

Judge Jones called the trial to order. "Thank you. Be seated. Hillsborough Superior Court is now in session." He slammed the gavel, picked up the file and the clerk called the first case, Carolyn Riley.

At this arraignment hearing, Carolyn was read the charges of Aggravated Assault and Murder in the First Degree. She pled not guilty and her team of attorneys pushed for bail, but she was remanded without, and that was that.

Jennifer Miller sat in the back of the court with Pippin, her now tag-a-long friend. They worked well together and Miller liked having the company. Carolyn turned to her in the courtroom and asked, "Did you get a hold of each of them?"

Miller nodded. She now knew what Carolyn meant when she said they knew what to do. Each one of the young girls she spoke with had given her the same reaction. 'Okay. I'm ready.' She didn't know what they were ready for, but they each stated they were ready. Six girls, six states, all very pleasant when they heard from her as if they knew she was calling.

Carolyn's trial was set for November 17.

From the arraignment hearing Miller worked along-side the prosecuting team when asked for information. The FBI and Austin Homicide and Topeka PD all turned over the information that they had obtained and Miller, Wyatt and Wiler were all deposed. The discovery went smoothly. The day they were all deposed, in Merrimack, NH, the three amigos decided to have lunch.

September 10, 2012

Miller and Wyatt met Wiler at an old Victorian style restaurant that now served Italian food. A table spread with lasagna, bread, salad and anti-pasta fulfilled their physical hunger and their conversation steered to the case at hand.

Wiler was the first to bring it up. "You think they will get a conviction?"

Wyatt, mouth stuffed full of bread, talked between bites. "They should have everything they need. What do you think, Miller?"

She thought about it. What did she think? First and foremost, the evidence was dicey. With her confession, the appellate court had overturned her mother's conviction. At least they knew it was not her. The evidence supported the fact that an appeal was possible and they had won. Her release date was coming up in four days.

"I think there is a problem. She's too smart." Miller took a sip of her water.

"You think she'll get off?" Wiler stopped eating and stared at her in disbelief.

"I think there is a chance. I've been piecing it together. First, she had to talk to me when she was captured and then she asked me to get a hold of all the victim's daughters; the real victims. When I did, and told them what she wanted me to, they all reacted exactly the same. I'm telling you, she's got something up her sleeve. I just don't know what it could be."

Wyatt finished chewing and added, "I wondered about that. Let's take it down to size here ... first, she came to you to catch her. Right? Reasoning behind that? First, you think she's a lunatic, but that's not the case in anything I've seen, not in patterns of the crime, nothing. Second, she wants you to capture her and literally sets it all up. With that, you come to the interrogation and you are at a disadvantage, because it sounds like she really just wanted an ally on the outside. You fit that description to a tee. You have empathy for her that no one else will and you are always concerned with justice."

Wiler added, "She had used you from the beginning, but why? How?"

Miller coughed it all up. She could trust these men. "She used me to set up a defense. I'm sure of it. I just can't figure out how she is going to do it."

"And, if she does ... are you going to let her run with it?" Wiler stuffed another bite in his mouth awaiting the answer.

"What choice do I have?" Miller asked.

"You always have a choice, Jennifer." Wyatt wouldn't let her slide on that one.

Wiler said, "You have to be a step ahead of her. Why in the world would she want you to contact the victims? What did she want?"

They all three sat in silence trying to figure it out when it occurred to Miller, "She has them set to testify. How could she use them to her benefit? She took care of one of them, Sylvia, by admittance. She had contact. So, how is she going to use that?"

Wyatt was on top of it. "It's easy. What if she can use them to provide reasonable doubt? Has anyone checked her alibi? I think we need to do some more investigation. I have to go back home tomorrow afternoon, but I have until then."

Wiler chimed in, "I'm leaving then too. I can help."

Miller said, "I am here until the trial is over. They consider me a key witness because she talks to me. She wants me to come visit. I set up an office here and Pippin and I have been out trying to piece together her life as a child. I talked to her grandparents the other day. Both living, feisty and tight-lipped."

"They say anything?" Wiler asked.

"Not so much. But, they did say that the family had problems that shamed the name of all of them." Miller finished with, "And they said that Carolyn was always compliant. They could not believe that this innocent, intelligent, interesting child was to blame for any of this. They hate the mother … apparently, daddy married below their 'means' and it's a sore spot."

"I think we need to get to the bottom of this." Wyatt said. "She have any friends growing up? College buddies? Who can we talk to?"

Miller withdrew a list from her jacket pocket. "Here's what I could find. I go and visit her this afternoon … I can get more. However, when will they find me tampering if I don't turn everything over to the prosecution?"

Wiler asked, "Why would you even ask that?"

Wyatt agreed, "You planning to help her defense?"

Miller stammered, "No … I mean, well, I just want to know what went on. What if she didn't do it?"

Wyatt dropped his fork on the table with a clang, "Are you kidding me? What?" He looked at Wiler, "Does this woman have that much charm?"

"It's not like that. I mean, I just want to see justice and I'm not sure she did it. That's all I'm saying. I want to be sure."

"How the fuck much more sure can you be, Jennifer?" Wyatt was steaming. "She gave you a confession. She wrote to you and told you to stop her. She's a sociopath. You really are twisted in all of this. Maybe she picked the right person to collar her for all the right reasons." He was so angry he got up and left the table and headed out the door with a tossing of his cloth napkin on the table. "I'm out of here. This is bullshit." He stopped only long enough to turn back to Miller, "You better get your head out of your ass before they set that maniac back out on the streets to castrate more men."

Miller was furious. Those men had deserved castration ...

Wiler saw the reaction she had and placed his hand atop hers. "Jennifer ..."

Her full attention to him. "Yeah?"

"She's got you where she wants you. Is that really where you want to be?"

She shook her head in confusion. This was so difficult. Pippin and Miller had talked about this many times. Pippin thought the same, but they saw it from a different vantage point. Karma had a reason to seek revenge. "I dunno. I just want justice."

"That's how she has you by the balls ... so to speak. Think about it, Jen." He spoke softly and calmly. "You of all people will understand where she is coming from. She uses you, because she knows that when you see justice, you see her point of view. Now, morality and ethics come in to play. What is it that you really see?" He took another bite, back to normal sitting position as to not threaten her answer. "What do you think and feel? You know I won't judge you."

She did know that. As she nibbled on some lasagna she thought about it. Within a couple of minutes, she did have an answer. "I think she had every right to do it to her father and blame her mother. But, when she stepped into the arena with the others, it gets dicey for me, because then she sought revenge and a vigilante on the loose has never been a good thing."

"Okay, good start. Now, go deeper. She knows this is how you feel. How can you be of use to her? Think from her vantage point. BE KARMA for just a minute." He continued with his meal.

Questions formulated in her mind, but Miller couldn't make sense of it. How could she use someone to her advantage? "Holy shit ..."

"What?" Wiler sat down his utensil. "What?"

"I got it ... think about this. What if you got all these women convicted? We both, you and me, Wiler, we both know that the evidence to support that she committed these crimes is only based on her confession, which she recanted. IF she pulls the information that she sent me the letter, which NEVER said she did anything, just come and get me ... and you pull her confession, what the fuck is left?"

"Yeah. That's what I was thinking ... they have a friend who was next to the wife. If the wives do not testify as to the context of their relationship ... if they cannot pinpoint Carolyn Riley as the woman they were friends with ... what do we have?"

"Not a fucking thing, Wiler. Not a fucking thing. AND ... what if she set those girls up to lie for her?"

"What do you mean?"

"Every one of them, when I called, knew I would be calling and said, 'Okay. I'm ready.' They knew this was coming. How smart is she? Can we discredit these girls? Is their testimony going to help or hurt the prosecution? Will the defense call them? We are witnesses for the prosecution and in my deposition today, I realized they have nothing. They have what we saw, which was Karma leaving the scene at Janine and Peter Johnson's. They aren't even involved in this shit. I mean, my Gawwwwd; she's her lead attorney and not even a criminal attorney, has taken the helm of this case. How much has she told Janine? What is their plan?" Miller gulped. "What if they can provide reasonable doubt? What if all of them work together?"

"Shit ..." Wiler saw what she was talking about.

"She's had it all planned from the beginning. Hypothetically speaking, she taught the women a lesson and they know it. They are happy to be out, probably happy to have their miserable husbands gone and are now able to have a relationship with their daughters, make up for lost time. She set it up that way. Now she confesses, they overturn their convictions ... and somehow, I think she knows that. They are on her side, completely indebted to her. They testify that she is NOT the one who was their friend. I mean, for Christ's sake, she had a whole identity, mode of personality and none of them sound the same. I've interviewed each wife and the descriptions, the attitudes, the manner of talk all sound completely different. All they have to say is they do not know Carolyn Riley and the prosecution can't place her at the scene … double jeopardy says you can only try me once."

"Fuck me. I see it. She has them tried, now they are off. She gets tried, if she gets off, with their help, no one does time and they get away with … murder."

Carolyn Riley was found not guilty on every count of murder, aggravated assault, burglary, identity theft and the likes. Six cases, six states, three years and four months later, she sat in the last trial by jury in Cincinnati, OH. The Evan Gerard Case. When Carolyn was arrested, Julie Gerard had just begun her trial and with the evidence presented by her defense, she was acquitted of all charges in relation to her husband's death. At Carolyn's trial, Julie Gerard did just as the other wives, declined knowing Carolyn in any way, never having seen her before, nothing like her friend Charlene McCants ... and the jury realized that by not being able to place Carolyn at the scene of the crime, no less in the life of Julie and Evan Gerard, she was acquitted on every count.

Somehow Carolyn had found concrete alibi for every situation. Someone in every case had spent the evening in question with her in a public venue, had records, phone records and visual sightings by other attendees. Carolyn was more brilliant than we had even given her credit for. She walked away from the courtroom, filled with every wife from every case, every daughter from every case and Miller and Pippin.

As they adjourned and Pippin and Miller headed outside to wait for the other women, now all familiar with each other, Pippin said, "That bitch is my hero, Rider."

"Great ... now serial killer is on your list of things to do?" She laughed. There was some serenity in this outcome, but she knew that her job would never be the same. She could never go back into homicide, trying criminals or finding them again. Carolyn had made it impossible for Jennifer to conceptualize justice in the same way.

"Na, Mama ... she just smart and that's all. I wish I had her money." They both laughed. It had been disclosed that even when the estate was read that Carolyn and her mother having split the inheritance, were both well into the title of 'billionairess'.

Jennifer watched for the others.

"What choo gonna do now, Rider?" Pip and she had discussed how Jennifer felt about the law now.

"I dunno. I was thinking that something in the line of counseling or private investigative work or you know ... just taking a little time off. I've been paid and gave up my apartment long ago. The prosecution paid for all my expenses in each of the trials and now I have over a hundred grand in savings. I'm okay. At least I have time to think about it. I'm glad I resigned from Austin. I think it's time to move on."

Pippin was a little sad, "I will miss you."

"Come with me? I can always use a top-notch assistant." Miller didn't even know where she wanted to go, but Pippin had become her best friend, like a sister to her and she wasn't willing to let her go. Jennifer had gone home, faced her issues with her family and the ramifications were the same. Her mother did not believe her, and so it was uncomfortable. Maybe her mother would never come to terms with what her father did to her.

"I would go anywhere you go. That's kewl ..." She was all smiles.

That evening Monica Dillon, Roberta Jones, Stephanie Rios-De La Cruz, Elaine Stanley, Julie Gerard, Janine Johnson, Pippin and Jennifer sat down to dinner in the private dining area of Leon's Steak & Ale. Miller had invited them all, on her, to dine and discuss. That discussion showed the pretext, premise and plan that Carolyn Riley had put together. Miller was astounded at the truth.

Carolyn had set it up so that they took the fall, had discussed it with each one of them at gun point, but had gotten her point across and they went along with it. It wasn't perjury, because they really had no recollection of either situation. Proplanlol was a mind-eraser. They told the truth, they didn't know Carolyn Riley, their friends had come and gone but they were nothing like the woman sitting at the defense table in her diamonds and suits, perfect hair, perfect nails and a prisoner convicted of murder. Never was any DNA found, no evidence to put Carolyn in the room, but each woman she had portrayed testified. Each set of fingerprints for the convicted criminal was brought up by the defense and torn apart by the prosecution with alibis, mostly that they were already incarcerated on other crimes. The finger pointed everywhere but to Carolyn. She calmly sat through each trial. Carolyn had alibis that were airtight, never fought for a moment. Because all that was needed was reasonable doubt, putting the finger on a burglary, self-inflicted wounds, crimes of passion, most of the evidence pointed back to the wives, who had already had convictions turned due to Carolyn's confessions. They didn't time out right. The appeals were won before Carolyn went to trial for the conviction and with her acquittal, they were all subject to double-jeopardy. She had gotten every one of them off. I had but one question for Carolyn and it concerned my time in Topeka, Kansas.

Within a few days, Carolyn was released from the Cincinnati jail and Miller was there to meet her upon release. When Carolyn saw her, she was met with a huge smile. It was not the first time Miller saw Carolyn, but it was the first time she saw her outside the law. Carolyn was slim, fit and calm. Her black slacks and cream sweater with pearl necklace and matching earrings held such a class and distinction that Miller barely recognized her as the same woman she had known on the streets.

Carolyn greeted her, "Jennifer. I'm so glad you came to meet me." They walked through the back hallways, escorted by police officers to a car awaiting them. The press was vicious, but they had plans to deceive even them.

Once in the car and out of the range of other ears, Carolyn spoke again, "I know ... I have some explaining to do."

The car lulled them, a black limousine with a driver cut off from their words through a thick pane of glass.

"I would like that ... yes." Jennifer said.

"Okay … where to start? You know most of the story. How about you ask me questions and I'll just answer them." Carolyn turned in the seat, tucking her leg underneath her so she could be more comfortable.

"Why me?"

"Because you understood the ramifications of what he did to me and it would always take you where I needed you to go. I needed you to put me at the crime scene in Topeka in some way, but yet not really put me at the scene. That would leave me open to being at the other scenes and I had already set them up to show my alibi."

"Did you kill them?"

"Every single one of them." Carolyn said.

"Did you pay off your alibis?"

"You're pretty smart. I did. Grandly. Having enough money to do whatever you wanted worked for me and I used it. Yes, indeedy, I did." Carolyn waited for the next question, but it didn't come. "Are you offended by it?"

"I'm offended that you just got off for killing six men …"

"They deserved to be punished and no one would punish them without punishing those children. You and I both know that ... when does the suffering end for us, Jennifer? I've lived it my whole life. This is the first time I have experienced freedom of any kind."

"What if they could have convicted you?"

"I took my chances. It just so happens that they didn't. The great part was the fact that each of the women I portrayed, I had no experience doing their jobs. I loved it when the bosses came in and told what immaculate employees they had, all of them me ... and that there is no way that person could be one and the same with the woman sitting at the table, i.e. me!" She was proud of her win.

"It's just plain crazy."

"No. I'm just plain crazy. What really helped was that through most of it my emotions were so jumbled that it kept me grounded and away from anyone. The Topeka thing went south very quickly when Jannie decided to kill her own husband. I couldn't have planned it better. Honestly, I had no idea that she was going to go that route. My intention was to have her vindicate me and take me on as a client. We just needed to catch Pete in action and when I sat the trap, you were there too soon. I was very surprised at your ability to find me."

"I never caught you. Even when I caught you, you escaped. Nearly killed me, I might add."

Carolyn was completely serious. "I had no intention of killing you. You just got in the way and I thought you were going to get hurt. That accident blew my cover for everything and leaves a scar on my record. I still won't be safe from accusation."

"Did you kill Brad Glassman?"

"I don't think so ..." Carolyn was being honest. "But, no one will ever find him to give them a chance to blame me."

"You better hope they don't ..." Miller knew that the rest of her life she would always look for Bradley Glassman's body.

Carolyn knew the same, but she was still going to tempt Jennifer Miller to help her with phase two of her life ... using legal means to take care of incestuous relationships where fathers were fucking their daughters. They would make a great team and there was no way that Jennifer Miller would turn her down. The offer she was going to make her was one that could not be turned down, that she was sure of.

NOT EVEN CLOSE TO THE

END

ABOUT THE AUTHOR

Michelle LeFort is a Kansas-girl, born and bred. Her writing comes from a lifetime of creating stories and giving them to people to read. Educationally, she challenged a unique set of coursework and received undergraduate degrees in Bible Studies/Ethics and Management. From there, she obtained her MBA and started her Ph D in Organizational Behavior. As a foster parent for twelve years, she met with children that were abused and neglected, some of the rawest cases seen. The children all had a very special place in her heart and it is Michelle's goal to forcibly change the foster care system in the State of Kansas to one that plays by the rules. It is a travesty that the system of foster care is so broken in many states.

Michelle writes a variety of genre and dabbles in bringing to light issues of intent. She wishes to bring about change and creates thought-provoking stories that arouse interest in groups and organizations to incite change for the better. This story is definitely one with a flair for passion. It is fiction and no characters in the book are based on living individuals. As a writer, Michelle prefers to write movies and work in the film industry, but is always working on a book in the background.

www.ingramcontent.com/pod-product-compliance
Lightning Source LLC
Chambersburg PA
CBHW071216250626
47163CB00001B/8